CHAMELEONS
of TRUTH

TERRY CARLSON

OAKTARA

Waterford, Virginia

Chameleons of Truth

Published in the U.S. by:
OakTara Publishers
P.O. Box 8, Waterford, VA 20197
www.oaktara.com

Cover design by Yvonne Parks at www.pearcreative.ca
Cover images © shutterstock.com: crossroads in the forest, 6749395/Stanislav
Bokach; © thinkstockphotos.ca: old suitcase, 89707836
Author photo © Jaymi Lee

Scripture quotations are taken from the *New American Standard Bible®*,
copyright © 1960, 1962, 1963, 1968, 1971, 1972, 1973, 1975, 1977, 1995 by
The Lockman Foundation. Used by permission.

ISBN: 978-1-60290-301-2

Chameleons of Truth is a work of fiction. References to real people, events,
establishments, organizations, or locales are intended only to provide a sense
of authenticity and are used fictitiously. All other characters, incidents, and
dialogue are drawn from the author's imagination.

Printed in the U.S.A.

⌘⌘⌘

To all those who feel God is answering
their neighbor's prayers, their best friend's prayers,
their coworker's prayers, their hairstylist's prayers—
everyone's prayers but their own.

Anna & Tim —

Thank you for not only
catching that flub on Facebook
but for your friendship.
Have a merry christmas!!!!

[signature]

Acknowledgments

I would like to thank Steve Austin, for finding someone in Korea who was able to figure out how to retrieve my manuscript from hard-drive purgatory.

Thank you to Michael Carlson, for taking the time out of your busy schedule to proofread my manuscript.

Thank you to Jaymi Lee, for taking my picture and bringing a smile to my face every time you're with me.

Thank you, Katie Kelley, for our long-distance talks.

And last, but not least, a big thank you to my wife, Karen, who went the extra mile for me so I could write *Chameleons of Truth*.

Prologue

My name is Ryan. My last name isn't important, as many things don't seem important once death straps you in and takes you for a ride. I don't mean to sound morbid or melodramatic, but the plain truth is, I am—at least that's what my parents used to tell me, especially when I would write, which I still love to do. I'm pretty good at it, too.

At thirteen, I entered a writing contest, and my story came in first place. My mother and I were flown to New York to show my manuscript to a big-shot editor. The editor loved it and knew only a teenager could come up with the title I chose. *Even the Mummy Uses Toilet Paper* wasn't a #1 best seller, but it was fun meeting Oprah, and my royalties will go a long way toward paying for college.

At one time I had a free ride to the college of my choice locked up, but as my mummy friend found out, crap happens. You see, God gifted me with highly exceptional motor skills, a bloodthirsty desire for competition, and a forty-three-inch vertical leap. All this is packed into an awesome six-foot, six-inch body with a basketball attached to my right hand from birth...at least that's what my mother used to say.

Yeah, I could school you by nailing your Nikes to the floor with a wicked crossover dribble. Then with my left hand I'd take you to the hole and finish you off with a windmill, 360 two-handed jam. I received over 100 letters from NCAA Division 1 schools. Most would have traded half their richest alumni to an arch rival college just to have my signature on their letter of intent to play basketball for them. I had narrowed my choices to Gonzaga and Duke while planning to play out my senior year before making a decision.

I know what you're thinking. *This Ryan kid is full of himself. He's got an ego the size of a baseball player on steroids.*

Before you make any rash conclusions about me, though, you need to know I'm the son of a blue-collar, nondenominational pastor. I used to attend church every Sunday, unless it interfered with an AAU basketball game. I was a Youth For Christ leader mentoring junior high kids who all looked up to me like *I* was Jesus Christ. I never smoked, drank alcohol, or did drugs, because it could cost me millions on future endorsement deals. I also got good grades so I wouldn't waste two years of eligibility while playing basketball at a junior college to catch up academically.

Of course, your first instincts of me are correct. I am a prideful, arrogant, self-centered teenager, or at least I was. I suppose trying to convince you I'm no longer full of pride is prideful in itself. The best thing to do is to get right on with my story. That's right—I'm going to write another book. This one, though, won't teach personal hygiene using the bodily functions of all my favorite Hollywood monsters as role models. Several verses in Proverbs teach the principle that "pride comes before a fall." What happens when we fall has been thoroughly documented forever on syndicated television reruns by the wise and immortal words of Steve Urkel when he said, "I've fallen, and I can't get up."

Last year I fell and couldn't get up. To be perfectly honest, I had fallen many years earlier but only noticed my prone position when last year it caused me pain. Now if it pains you to think you will have to read hundreds of pages about me, written by me and my cocky, self-inflating writing style, don't worry. I know how to write to fit the tragic mood this story requires. This book will be about many people who have a hard time staying on their feet. I will be in the story, but the real star will be Joan. Her last name isn't important right now because, like me, trivial things mean nothing when death comes knocking.

I know my introduction probably seems a little too breezy, too casual for the topic I'll cover, but hey, I'm still a teenager. We all think we will live forever.

1

"So, have you swapped spit with Hank yet?"

Joan swung her long legs off the armrest of the sofa. The bowl of popcorn, nestled on her lap, exploded around her. "Shhhh!" Joan squeezed the phone receiver with both hands and whispered, "Sue, you can be a real spaz sometimes. What if your neighbor, Mrs. Eavesdropper, is listening in again?"

"Don't have a cow." Sue let out an exaggerated sigh. "She's been in bed a couple hours now, and besides, I'm just giving you a bad time. It's not every day you find out your best friend has the hots for a famous person she babysits for. The guy is a stud, but hello, Joan, he's married, and he's old enough to be your old man."

"And how old would my old man have been if he were still around?"

"I'm sorry, Joan, I wasn't thinking."

"Don't sweat it. Besides, a girl can dream, can't she?" Joan wrapped the telephone cord several times around her finger, and lazily plopped back onto the popcorn-covered sofa.

"That's your problem, Joan. You want to live in Camelot. You have King Arthur, but you long for what you can't have."

"Lancelot?" Joan asked.

Sue exhaled another long sigh. "Hank...you can't have him. There's plenty of Arthurs right here in Soundview High School."

"Okay," Joan said while picking stray popcorn off the couch, "lay it on me." She tossed a kernel into her mouth.

"What about Joe Erickson?" Sue asked. "He's captain of the football team, has a righteous bod, and has wanted to go steady with you since eighth grade."

"The only 'go' Joe knows is 'go' all the way. Besides, he isn't good enough to play college ball, so he'll end up bagging groceries for your parents down at the IGA for the rest of his life."

"What about Bob Foster?" Sue sounded hopeful. "He's cute, smart, funny, and has that cherry '57 Chevy. You said you two had a blast at the prom last year."

Joan yawned and looked at the clock—10:30. "Bob is about as funny as a wedgie."

"Well, I think both Bob's jokes and wedgies are funny."

"Who wants their underwear yanked up their crack, and who wants to be on the receiving end of one of Bob's stupid jokes?" Joan glanced at the clock again. "Besides, Bob's old man will give him the Phillips 66 station after he retires. Bob will be a Soundview lifer just like the rest of the boys I don't want you to mention."

"You really can't stand it here anymore, can you?" Sue asked.

"I'm leaving, Sue. I don't know how, I don't know where, but after graduation I'm leaving."

"You've been threatening to run away ever since..."

"Ever since the first time we watched *The Wizard of Oz* together. Do you remember how I couldn't stop crying after the movie ended?"

"Yeah, that was really weird." Sue said. "You never cry."

"I don't unless I watch the bummer ending to that movie."

"What's wrong with the ending? Oh, wait, let me guess. You wanted Dorothy to stay in her dream world. You get bummed out when Dorothy chooses to click those ruby slippers together, so she can go back to boring Kansas. It's really a drag she can't marry the scarecrow. She had a crush on him, you know. Hey, they could have lived in the wicked witch's castle; I hear there's a vacancy." Sue giggled. "The cowardly lion would've made such a cute pet. Now that he isn't cowardly anymore, he could even scare away all those pesky, flying monkeys. She wouldn't even have to worry about housework. I bet the tin man has every modern kitchen appliance known to man hidden in him somewhere." Sue was laughing.

Joan was laughing, too. "All I would need are some chrome and pipes to make that hot air balloon very cherry."

Sue stopped laughing. "You just said, 'all I would need.'"

Joan tried to stifle another giggle. "I meant, she—all *she* would need."

"No, you didn't. Why can't you find a neat guy from town, marry him, move next door to Billy and me, and have lots of kids? That's the American dream—not Lancelot, not Hank."

Joan grabbed a book hidden between her algebra and world history books and thumbed through the first chapter. "Remember that book I've been telling you about?"

"You mean that feminine mystery book?"

"For the umpteenth time, it's called *The Feminine Mystique.*" On the other end of the line she could hear the rhythmic, squishy cadence of Sue chewing bubble gum. "Let me read you the first paragraph of the book."

A loud *pop* burst from the receiver into Joan's ear. "Lay it on me," Sue said and blew another bubble.

"I know you're getting bored when you start chewing your cud. I want you to understand where I'm coming from, because I'm just beginning to understand myself."

Joan heard another loud *pop*. "I said, 'lay it on me,'" Sue repeated.

Joan put her finger on the page and read aloud:

The problem lay buried, unspoken, for many years in the minds of American women. It was a strange stirring, a sense of dissatisfaction, a yearning that women suffered in the middle of the twentieth century in the United States. Each suburban wife struggled with it alone. As she made the beds, shopped for groceries, matched slipcover material, ate peanut butter sandwiches with her children, chauffeured Cub Scouts and Brownies, lay beside her husband at night—she was afraid to ask even of herself the silent question, "Is this all?"

Pop!

Joan hurriedly flipped the pages. "Let me read the last sentence of the first chapter. This will really tie it all together."

Pop!

Joan read on:

We can no longer ignore that voice within women that says: "I want something more than my husband and my children and my home."

She glanced around Pastor Johnson's study. The large, alabaster globe of the world, perched on its marble base, dominated the room. In the ancient bookshelf, volumes of thick books neatly lined its rugged shelves. *Bartlett's Familiar Quotations, Webster's Dictionary of English Usage, Strong's Hebrew and Greek Dictionary,* and *Roget's Thesaurus* all looked worn with use.

Pop...pop!

Joan tapped the receiver on the oak coffee table three times. "Quit popping in my ear! Did you hear *anything* I read to you?"

"It's a good thing you read it *before* you broke my eardrums."

"That's me, Sue." Even though the house was always on the chilly side, Joan felt sweaty and hot. "Betty Friedan is writing about me."

Joan heard Sue spit out her gum. "It's not about you. You're not even married," Sue said.

"Then it's written to me as a warning." The air in the room became thick, and with every breath Joan had to gulp it down. She began to drown in the rich, nutty aroma of Pastor Johnson's Balkan Sobranie's, Original Blend pipe tobacco that seemed to permeate from every molecule of his den. "If I stay here, I'll become another statistic, married to false expectations and values I don't even share."

"That's heavy," Sue said. "Don't know what you're talking about, but it's deep."

Joan stood and three pieces of popcorn joined the other eighty-nine on the floor. She pulled the telephone as far as the cord would allow her into the next room alongside the piano, a few feet to the left of the study door. She shut the door, blocking the wave of exotic aromas from pouring into the living room.

"I can't stay here just to make Joe Erickson happy. I can't stay here to make you happy, or to make Grandma happy." She began to tap out "Chop Sticks" on the piano. "I don't want to live out my dreams through my husband or children. I want to go to college, to travel, to meet men who wear clothes other than a Soundview letterman's jacket."

"So what's with the thing you have toward Hank then?" Sue asked. "He may not wear a letterman's jacket, but he's as much a part of the Soundview landscape as Puget Sound."

Joan plunked on the keys a little harder. "He understands me, Sue. He challenges me to explore who God made me to be. He tells me I'm gifted, and he doesn't mean only to make babies and clean toilets but gifted from God to do incredible things." Joan heard footsteps upstairs; Johnny was awake.

"Don't get all religious on me," Sue said.

"He took my hand yesterday. After serving dinner at the shelter in Seattle, he dropped the other kids off from the youth group, and in my grandma's driveway he took my hand in both of his." Joan heard footsteps coming down the stairs. "He grabbed my hand with his Paul Bunyan hands, looked me straight in the eyes, and said..."

"I'm hungry!"

"What did you say?" Sue asked.

"Johnny's up." Joan patted the bottom of the five-year-old wearing Daniel Boone pajamas and a coonskin cap. "There's popcorn in the study, Mr. Boone; go help yourself." She opened the door, and the little boy scurried inside.

"Meanwhile, back at the ranch," Sue blurted out. "He looked you straight in the eyes and said—what?"

"He said, and I quote, 'Joan, I've seen you grow up from a fat little toddler in Mrs. Farms' Sunday school class, to a beautiful young lady.'"

Sue snickered. "That was romantic. He sure has a way with words."

"Shut up. I'm not finished." Joan was about to continue when Johnny darted out from the study, across the living room, and opened the front door. "Mr. Boone, you can't go outside; it's pouring down rain."

A huge, black lab bounded into the room, vigorously shaking his rain-drenched body, soaking everything within five feet, including Daniel Boone. "Johnny! Get Moses out! You know he's not supposed to be in the house!" Joan pointed toward the door.

The little boy climbed on top of his dog. "Come on, Moses." Johnny said. "Let's go hunt some bear." Moses galloped toward Joan. The dog's thick, powerful tail, while happily swinging side to side, knocked over a vase full of roses as easily as a horse swatting flies. Daniel Boone and his steed barged into the study leaving a trail of muddy paw prints on the newly refinished, Potomac cherry, hardwood floor.

"Listen, Sue, I've gotta split. There's a mess to clean up."

Sue raised her voice. "I'm putting the kibosh to that idea right now. I'm not hanging up 'til you finish the story. Can't you put the brat to bed?"

"Don't call him that. You know how much he means to me. He's like a little brother I never had. He even calls me 'sister Joan.'"

Sue let out an exasperated sigh. "I know you babysit for them a lot, but I didn't know they were adopting you."

Joan drew in a deep breath. "Grandma's house sold. She'll be moving into the nursing home in a month. Pastor Johnson said if he could work things out with Betty, he would like me to move in with them as a nanny."

Sue was silent for a moment. "You can live with me."

The study door flew open with a bang. Moses bolted into the room like a bucking bronco with Johnny clinging to his back with one hand and holding the empty bowl of popcorn over the poor dog's head with the other. Johnny flew off of Moses' back like a limp, rag doll and crashed into an end table headfirst, launching a glass bowl of M&M candies to the floor, where it shattered into a million pieces.

Joan heard the front door open.

"Babysitter, what's going on here?" Mrs. Johnson exclaimed.

Mr. Johnson's huge, wet frame clogged the doorway behind his wife, preventing the driving rain from entering the house. Moses stopped in front of his masters, lifted his leg, and peed. Daniel Boone began to cry, Moses continued to pee, and Mr. Johnson held a huge hand over his mouth trying to hide a smile as Mrs. Johnson screamed, "Babysitter!"

"Gotta go, Sue. Pastor Hank and his wife are home."

Joan stood in the entryway to the kitchen, a broom in one hand and a dust pan full of glass shards and M&Ms in the other. She leaned against the refrigerator admiring the large man in the chair by the fireplace. The mess was cleaned up, the living room was dark, and Hank's burly frame was silhouetted against the glow from the fire. Nestled in Hank's sturdy arms was Johnny. Hank's booming pastor's voice could now barely be heard over the gentle crackle and pop of the burning cedar logs as he finished another one of his tall tales about Daniel Boone and Davy Crockett.

Hank removed the hot water bottle filled with ice cubes from his son's forehead and silently rose from the chair. Johnny's limp arm dangled over his father's, but Mr. Boone still held a firm grip on his coonskin cap. As Hank turned and walked toward the stairs, Joan backpedaled deeper into the kitchen. The last thing she wanted was to be caught gawking at him. She dumped the contents of the dust pan into the garbage and hurried back into the living room. She then grabbed her coat and gathered up her books. Joan was about to leave when she heard Hank gently close the door to Johnny's bedroom and call down from the upstairs landing. She walked directly below him so he wouldn't have to talk too loud.

"When we arrived home, I noticed you had left the lights on to your car." The railing groaned under his weight, and Joan thought for sure it would give way if he leaned over any farther. "I loaned out my jumper cables, so there's no way to get your car started tonight." He cupped his hand to his mouth as if to yell but instead whispered while pointing with his other hand to a room at the other end of the hall. "I am going to tell Mrs. Johnson you need a ride home, so hold on to your horses for a few minutes and I'll be right down."

Mrs. Betty Johnson—the woman who would only call Joan "the babysitter," even though Joan was practically part of the family; the woman who drove herself to church whenever Hank gave Joan a ride; the woman who taught Sunday school and led the local Woman's Coffee Fellowship group by day and drank martinis and watched television until it signed off at night; the woman sporting the hourglass figure with sand pouring through her soul.

Joan opened the record player cabinet and began to sort through the albums. There was no Elvis, no Del Shannon, and no Neil Sedaka. There were clearly two different musical tastes represented in this cabinet: his and hers. His was country-western: Johnny Cash, Hank Williams, George Jones. Hers was, well, whatever was left: Bing Crosby's *White Christmas*, the Ray Conniff Singers, Beethoven, and Bach.

A piece of typing paper was taped to the inside lid of the cabinet with a message boldly written in black crayon: **BABYSITTER—DON'T TOUCH!!!** What a bummer. Actually, even though Joan hated classical music, she would sacrifice her eardrums to spite the old lady. She would listen to a few minutes of Mozart or Chopin, usually with Sue listening over the telephone. When they couldn't stand it anymore, Joan would *accidentally* bump the cabinet, making the needle skip, hoping to cause a minuscule scratch on Betty's precious record. Then Joan would carefully wipe the record of any fingerprints, put the vinyl back in the album, and put the album back exactly from where she had pulled it. Joan wouldn't have to go through this ridiculous routine, if only the old lady could forgive her for breaking a record when Joan first met the Johnsons ten years earlier.

Joan jumped at the sound of breaking glass and a scream from upstairs. She dropped her books and raced up the stairs. skipping every other step. Without hesitating, she pushed the door open to the Johnsons' bedroom. Light from the hallway illuminated Hank. He was slumped over, bracing himself on his bedroom dresser. Broken glass littered the floor from the shattered mirror behind him.

Hank slowly shook his head and peeked over toward Joan. "Johnny?" Drops of blood dripped from a gash in his forehead.

"It's me." She rushed into the dark bedroom. "Hank, you're hurt."

"So there's the little tramp." The words poured, thick and syrupy, from the darkness.

Joan's eyes quickly adjusted to the darker half of the bedroom. To her right was the bed. Betty knelt on the mattress wearing only a bra and underpants. While swaying against a nonexistent wind, she tried to pour herself a drink from a bottle of vodka but spilled half of it on herself.

Hank gently pushed Joan toward the door. "Go check on Johnny; make sure he stays in bed."

Joan lunged back into the room and grabbed Hank by the arm. "What's going on? What happened?"

"Let go of him, babysitter!" Betty screamed. "He's mine!" She awkwardly wound up and threw the half-full glass of vodka at Joan. The tumbler harmlessly bounced off the wall but splattered alcohol over Joan's blouse.

"For heaven's sake, Joan!" Hank shoved her more firmly. "Go to Johnny's room and stay there until I come and get you."

Betty pointed her bottle at Joan. "Leave my Johnny alone; he loves me more than you." Betty began to blubber. "He loves me more than you."

"Mrs. Johnson, I..." Before Joan could finish, she instinctively brought up her arms to protect her head from the oncoming bottle. It missed her head, instead striking the right side of her rib cage. She doubled over in pain. Hank scooped her up and carried her down the stairs, into the study, and onto the couch.

He snatched a handkerchief from his back pocket and dabbed at the blood dripping from his forehead. All he said before leaving to go back upstairs was, "Stay put!"

She was back in the study, but his time the walls weren't closing in on her from the suffocating smell of stale pipe tobacco. Rather, she felt safe, protected by the familiar surroundings. Joan grabbed a knitted afghan from the back of the sofa and wrapped it tightly around her. Gingerly pressing the right side of her ribs, she doubted any were broken.

Needing a distraction, she studied the familiar photographs and paintings hanging from every wall in the office. To her right, the wall contained the mementos of Hank's "former life," as he liked to call it. A purple and gold University of Washington banner stretched the length of one wall. Many of Hank's college accomplishments hung under the banner: his degree in business administration, his many football awards, team pictures and a plaque honoring him as Pacific Coast Conference "Player of the Year." Centered among all these was an enlarged, framed photograph of Hank. He was in full military uniform. A football helmet dangled from one hand, while he balanced a pretty brunette holding her pom-poms and a football above his head with the other hand. Written in black ink across the picture was, *To My Favorite Husky—Love Betty.*

On the wall to Joan's left hung things important to him after his "born again" conversion: a picture of his baptism as an adult in the frigid waters of Puget Sound, a crucifix his mother gave him, many photos of significant mentors, and one of Hank shaking hands with evangelist Billy Graham. Centered on this wall hung a framed painting by an eight-year-old girl. A crude rendition of Pastor Hank's church, Soundview Chapel, dominated the painting. The windows were painted too large, the front door too small, and the cross atop the steeple was crooked. None of that mattered to the artist. The only thing that truly mattered were the people standing hand-in-hand in front of the church: the pipe-smoking pastor with the kind smile, the pastor's pretty, dark-haired wife, and in between them the little blond girl who painted the picture.

This was the same little girl whose mother died while giving her life, the little girl whose father committed suicide on her third birthday, the little girl whose only family consisted of a cantankerous grandmother, who spent her

8

days playing bingo and nights getting blitzed at the American Legion Hall. This was the same little girl who wanted the nice pastor and his pretty wife to be her parents.

In reality, the pastor and his wife had a little baby boy four years after the little girl painted that picture. The wall behind her was covered with pictures of that little boy and his parents. It was true that the little girl was in a few photographs on this wall, but only as "the babysitter," as the mother would begin to call her.

Only one thing hung from the wall directly across from her—a huge painting of Jesus hanging from the cross. Jesus in pain. Blood dripping from the wounds in his brow, caused by the wreath of one-inch thorns pressed into his skull. The pain from having nails driven through his hands and feet would have been excruciating. From the many sermons Hank gave covering the crucifixion, she knew Jesus slowly asphyxiated. In the painting, below the cross, soldiers mock him and divide up his clothes. Despite all this, a glow radiates from Jesus' face, a face filled with so much sorrow, yet revealing peace. Jesus' words, "Father, forgive them; for they do not know what they are doing," are inscribed on a little silver plate attached to the oak frame below the painting. Also attached to the frame is the purple heart Hank was awarded for taking a bullet while saving the lives of four men during the D-Day invasion.

"Are you okay?" Joan jumped at Hank's voice. "Sorry, I didn't mean to startle you." Hank stood in the doorway, a blood-soaked handkerchief tied around his head, and the half-empty bottle, which had struck Joan, in his right hand. As he walked toward Joan, he placed the bottle in a metal garbage can next to his desk. "How is your side?" He asked, kneeling next to her. She smelled alcohol on his breath.

"Oh, I feel just b—" Joan winced as she sat up.

"Why, Joan, I don't believe I've ever heard my little dove say a swear word before."

"And I don't believe I've ever smelled alcohol on my pastor's breath before." She pulled off the afghan and walked to the trash can. "I think I deserve a drink as much as you do." She grabbed the bottle, unscrewed the cap, and took a big drink.

Once, at a slumber party in eighth grade, all the girls shared two bottles of beer Sue had ripped off from her parents' secret hiding place. The two things Joan remembered most was how disappointed she was for not feeling drunk, so she pretended she was loaded. The second thing was how raunchy the beer tasted. Besides being warm from hiding under Sue's bed for two days, it tasted like skunk water. The vodka was entirely different. The liquid fire burnt all the way down her throat to her belly where, like a rock landing in a pond, it sent ripples of heat spreading throughout her body. She set the bottle on Hank's desk and coughed violently.

Hank calmly walked over and patted her on the back.

"Why"—*cough, cough*—"didn't you"—*cough*—"try to stop me?"

"You have a free will to do what you want." Hank grabbed the bottle and took a big gulp. "Just remember, a consequence will always follow every decision you make."

She grabbed the bottle and took a much smaller drink. "You mean by having one drink could lead to another and another?" She coughed only once into her fist this time.

"That is possibly true, and if it is, the consequence would most likely be a hangover in the morning." He snatched the bottle back from her, took another drink, and twisted the cap firmly back on. "I'm sorry about what happened. Mrs. Johnson has had a rough night." He sat back on the sofa, placing the bottle between his legs. "She is sleeping like a log now." He shook his head. "Actually, she passed out, cold drunk in her own vomit."

Joan sat next to him. "It's my fault. The house was a zoo when you two walked in. I could tell something was wrong right away when she didn't go ape and yell at me but instead ran upstairs to her room."

"No, if blame has to be put on anybody's shoulders, it should rest squarely on mine. She never asked to be a pastor's wife; never wanted to be a pastor's wife; never would have married me if she knew she would someday become a pastor's wife."

"I don't understand," Joan said. "She didn't know you were going to be a pastor?"

Hank stood, uncapped the bottle, and offered Joan a drink. She took another little sip and handed it back to him. He took the bottle in both hands, studying what remained of its liquid contents as if studying the Holy Scriptures. His massive, square jaw relaxed, and his lip quivered. His eyes swell up with tears. Reluctantly he raised the bottle to his lips and drank, his Adam's apple methodically rising and falling with each swallow. After the last of the liquid fire disappeared down his throat, he turned the bottle upside down. Not one drop was left.

Satisfied, Hank bent over and picked up his pipe. He tapped the pipe against the top of his desk releasing a fine, white ash. "Holy smokes," Hank said while glancing at his wrist watch, "I think it's time to take you home."

She watched as Hank opened the pouch to his Balkan Sobrainie tobacco.

10

"Why didn't Betty know you were going to be a pastor?" Joan's words plowed through her thickening tongue.

Hank stuffed the woodsy-smelling black mixture into the bowl of his pipe and, after several attempts, succeeded in lighting it. After several quick puffs, he drew in deeply and exhaled. The study was consumed with a nutty aroma. "Grab your books and coat, and I'll meet you out in the station wagon." Hank held out his hand and helped Joan to her feet.

She took a step toward the door but stopped. She turned to face her pastor and gently placed her hand on his. "Why didn't Betty know?"

Tears again welled in his eyes, and he turned from her. "She couldn't have known, because I didn't even know until after I shot and killed a woman and her unborn child."

2

I knew something was weird the moment Mom opened the door. She stood in the entryway between the garage and kitchen staring wide-eyed into the room like Dad was the Grim Reaper and I was Dracula's son. She blinked a couple times while clutching an opened cardboard box that had been wrapped with at least a whole roll of duct tape.

Dad put down his bowl of vanilla ice cream. "Something wrong, Mary?"

As usual, Michael and Jordan scampered around my mother's feet begging her for attention. Instead of talking to them in her cute animal dialect, she carelessly stepped on the cat's bushy tail as she entered the kitchen. Jordan yowled and scampered to the most remote region of the house. Mom stood unattached from reality like a mindless zombie, her eyes swollen and black from her oozing mascara.

"You look shook up," Dad said. "That must have been an emotional funeral. For the life of me, Mary, I can't even remember which friend you said died. Did I know this friend?" He walked to her. "That box looks heavy. Can I take it from you?"

Mom pulled the box closer to her chest. "I thought you two had a meeting to go to tonight?" She sounded disappointed we were home.

"The varsity basketball meeting for parents and players was at seven. We've been home for over two hours."

Mom was acting spooky. I almost convinced myself the box contained an alien who was manipulating her with mind control. "Hey Mom, put down that package of duct tape and give your only son a hug." I attempted to take the box from her, but she yanked it back, ran to her room, and locked herself in.

I inherited my passion for melodrama from my mom. She loved soap operas; she loved church gossip; she loved weddings, but not as much as she loved Dad and me. It may seem strange, but I don't remember them fighting, and it wasn't because my mother didn't have a temper. Mom and I could scream at each other like a couple of back-alley cats, but then minutes later cuddle up on the couch together with a bowl of popcorn like nothing had happened. She could yell at Dad too, but he never yelled back. He had figured out how to turn down Mom's thermostat whenever she got too hot. He would tease her, he would tickle her, he would whisper magical words into her ear, and suddenly they would be laughing and kissing.

I inherited my sense of humor or sarcasm, depending on who you talked to, from my dad.

His church congregation nicknamed him the "merry minister" for his penchant of weaving humor into his sermons. Dad looked for the best in people and seemed to always find it. He said his compass was prayer, and the light to find his way into a person's heart was God's word.

Dad needed both that night as he and I tried for over an hour to get Mom to open the door. The only thing she said during those sixty frustrating minutes was that she would open up when she "figured it out." It was past midnight when I decided to let Dad go it alone. Tomorrow was the first basketball practice of my senior year, and Dad would smooth things out with Mom as soon as she would let him in.

⌘⌘⌘

The next morning when I opened my eyes, fatigue wasn't pulling my eyelids back shut like it usually does. This had the feeling of waking on a Saturday morning after twelve hours of sleep. The electric clock beside my bed glowed 10:51 a.m.in bright, big numbers. I had missed my first two morning classes and should have been in Mr. Carl's room taking a calculus test right now. I jumped out of bed and ran into the hall.

"Why didn't anybody wake me?" I pounded on my parents' door, and it swung open to an abandoned bedroom. On top of the bed were the remains of an empty cardboard box. Ripped strands of duct tape lay scattered on top of the comforter.

I ran into a deserted kitchen, but voices could be heard from the living room. My parents sat on the couch together wearing the same clothes they had on the previous night. Before them was Dad's brown suitcase full of different colored notebooks and diaries with the words **PRIVATE—PLEASE DON'T READ** written across the front of each with a black permanent marker. Mom zipped shut the lid to the suitcase as I approached.

"You two pull an all-nighter?" They both looked at me with that zombie, I-didn't-sleep-a-wink-last-night stare, and my first thought was that whatever alien had control of Mom now had Dad as well.

"I'm sure diaries make fascinating reading," I said, pointing to the suitcase, "but couldn't one of you have pulled yourself away long enough to wake me? Now you're going to have to write me a note, so I can go to school and basketball turnout."

"You're not going to school for a few days," Mom said.

My father frowned at her. "I think that's a decision Ryan should make for himself."

"What's going on? Why should I stay home from school? I'm not sick, and senior skip day isn't until June, so what gives? Must be 'Son of the Month' persecution day?"

Dad placed his hand gently on Mom's knee. "Mary, I don't think Ryan needs to be dragged into this."

"And what?" Mom knocked his hand off her knee. "Keep our family tradition of scandal and secrecy alive for Ryan to pass on down to future generations!"

"So this is something you really want him to know about?"

"For heaven's sake, Luke." Mom stood, glaring down at my father. "It's about time our so called 'holy' family starts practicing what it preaches regarding John 8:32."

"'Then you will know the truth, and the truth will set you free?'" Dad picked up the suitcase from the coffee table and threw it on the floor at her feet. "Is *this* truth setting *you* free, Mary?" My father brushed past me as he stormed out of the room.

"Mom, what's going on? I've never seen Dad like this."

"Go pack your suitcase, Ryan. We're heading west of the mountains for a few days."

West of the mountains. To me that meant the Tacoma Dome, the site of the 4A Washington State Basketball Tournament. My North Spokane Rattlers have been beaten by the Mt. Vernon Bulldogs the past two years in Tacoma. Now that I'd shattered almost every individual basketball record at North Spokane High, I knew I'd get my scholarship. The only accomplishment left for me was to bring my Rattlers a state basketball championship. Driving to who knows where, to achieve who knows what, was an irritating obstacle for me getting that trophy. I had to be there that first week of practice not necessarily for *my* benefit, but to provide senior leadership to my less talented teammates.

⌘⌘⌘

Mom and Dad fought from the moment we hit I-90 heading west out of Spokane. Normally at this point of a trip, I'd already have my iPod headphones glued to my ears and be chillin' to Good Charlette, but after an hour, my headphones still dangled around my neck. The conversation between my parents was similar to watching a good horror movie; I was disturbed by what I saw, but at the same time felt a sick desire to keep watching as the tension built. I expected Dad to do something to make Mom laugh, but it never happened.

Snow began to fall as we approached Ellensburg while my parents' heated discussion grew cold. Finally, time to listen to some music. I pulled the headphones over my ears and after a time, dozed off. Good Charlette's moody melodies haunted my dreams until I was thrown left and awoke to the pain of the shoulder harness digging into my neck.

"Slow down!" Mom screamed. "Are you trying to get us all killed?"

The back of my father's neck and ears turned bright red. "We're almost to the summit. I'll put the chains on there."

Mom rubbed her temples. "I can't believe the jerk didn't even tell me the truth at her funeral."

"And I still can't believe you didn't tell me the truth about whose funeral you actually went to." Dad's knuckles were white from clenching the steering wheel.

I couldn't believe my mom and dad were still fighting.

"Before last night, you felt differently about her, didn't you?" Mom said. "If I knew then what I know now, I would have told you she'd passed away."

"Are we there yet?" I asked sarcastically.

Mom pulled down the visor and squinted at me through the little mirror. "I didn't know you were awake."

"The suspense is killing me here. I can hear everything you two are arguing about, but everything is *he* this and *she* that or this *jerk* and that *son of a...*"

"Watch your mouth, Son," Dad warned while straining his eyes to see through the thick snow.

"What I'm saying Dad, is that you two dragged me away from school, and my first week of basketball, to risk our lives driving through a blizzard—for what? To unravel some dark and mysterious secret about our family tree? They're all dead, so who really gives a rip? Excuse me, Mom, I forgot about your famous aunt in California, who I've only seen once."

I could see my mother's dark brown eyes glaring at me through the visor mirror. "Well, now you'll get to see Cathy for the second time," she said and pushed the visor up. "That reminds me—I'd better call to tell her we might be running a little late because of the weather."

She took out her cell phone and dialed a number scribbled on a napkin. "She might be the only one willing to help us straighten out this mess."

"Dad, I deserve to know what's going on."

"Not right now, Ryan. I need to concentrate on the road. I've never seen it snow like this. It's almost white-out conditions."

"Hello, Aunt Cathy? I can hardly hear you. Yes, this is Mary."

"Dad, please—come on—this isn't tons of gold bricks locked away at Fort Knox. This is a suitcase full of some dead relatives diaries locked in the trunk of our car. Just pull over for a second, open the trunk, and let me look at one."

"Ryan, can you make out any road signs? I can't see two feet in front of me."

"Cathy"—Mom raised her voice over Dad's—"I'm not sure what time we'll be at your hotel. Wait, I'll ask him. Luke, are we at the summit yet?"

Dad was leaning over the steering wheel. "For all I know, we could have passed it."

"Promise me, Dad; when we get to the summit, you'll let me read one of those diaries."

"For heaven's sake, Ryan!" My father reached into his coat pocket and pulled out a green envelope. "Here, you can read this. It's a letter written to you from one of your dead relatives."

As Dad tried to hand the envelope to me, my mother tried to stop him. "Just a minute, Cathy—hold on." My parents played tug-of-war with the envelope.

"Luke, let go; you know there's a reason he hasn't seen any of those yet."

The envelope slipped from both of their fingers onto the floor, under the driver's seat. I unstrapped my seat belt to retrieve the letter. As I picked up the letter, our Kia Sportage spun out of control. The last thing I heard my father say was, "God help us!" My mother screamed and the terrible grinding of metal colliding against metal was the last thing I remember. It's amazing I can remember everything about that day up until the accident with such clarity because, for the next month, I could remember nothing at all.

morning hell is called Normandy, and I'll be seeing you there.'"

Hank fell silent and his lower lip quivered. He reached over to start the car but Joan placed her hand on his. "Please, you've come this far. What happened?"

He turned to face her for the first time since climbing into the wagon. Like a fish out of water, Hank gasped, trying to speak, but only great sobs rose from deep in his throat. Joan grabbed his hands and squeezed. The big man's shoulders heaved and shuddered.

"I'm so sorry," Joan said. "I shouldn't have been so nosy. I only wanted to know about...you know...the woman and her unborn child."

"Lord, forgive me," Hank stammered. "Forgive me."

Joan squeezed his hand once more, then let go. "You don't have to tell me any more if you don't want to. As a matter of fact, we can split if you want to." She moved to turn the ignition key, but Hank pulled her hand away.

"I need to finish telling this story, Joan. You are the only one I have ever told this part of the story to—except God."

Joan put both hands in her lap. "Really, you don't have to."

"Please, Joan, I need to tell someone."

"Okay, I'm listening."

Hank grabbed the bloody handkerchief, once used for his forehead, from his back pocket, blew his nose, then wadded up the handkerchief. "We drew enemy fire as we approached the beach. Bullets pounded the loading ramp as it was lowered for us to disembark. Before the ramp splashed into the water, three men in front of me were blown away; their blood spewed across my face. We did not know until later that a strong current pulled us off course, causing us to land on the wrong section of beach. Chaos ruled as we scurried off the boats. We trudged through waist-deep water toward shore. Machine-gun fire from the top of the bluffs cut down two men in front of me before they could reach dry land. Once on the beach, about 300 yards of sand lay between me and a seawall high enough to provide shelter from the bullets raining down from above. A group of us raced across the sand toward the wall, when there was an explosion."

Hank turned from Joan, opened the car door, and vomited. He tilted his face toward the dark sky. After letting the cleansing rain wash over him, he vigorously shook his wet head and slunk back into the seat. He pointed towards the glove box. "Open it up, and hand me the bottle please."

Joan put both hands over the door to the glove box. "Don't you think you've had enough to drink already? I want to hear the rest of the story before you pass out like Grandma always does."

"It's only mouthwash. Pastors are expected to have fresh breath and, besides, I hate the taste of bile." He motioned again for her to open the compartment door.

"Sorry," she said sheepishly. She pulled out the bottle, unscrewed the cap, and smelled the contents before handing it over.

He spit out the oral disinfectant and put the cap back on. Handing the bottle back to Joan, he said, "I must be more of an inebriant than I realized, resorting to smuggling booze into my car camouflaged as Listerine mouthwash."

"It's become a habit of mine to smell anything before I drink it. At home I find alcohol in everything from bottles of soda pop to bottles of cough syrup." She put the mouthwash back into the glove box. "Are you feeling better?"

Hank wiped his mouth with the back of his shirt sleeve. "I will be once I get through this story." He rubbed both eyes before continuing. "There was an explosion, then I was tossed through the air and landed hard. I faded in and out of consciousness several times, but I vividly remember thinking I would die. While conscious, I wondered whether I would end up in heaven or hell. The next thing I remember was being picked up and carried to the seawall.

"Someone was talking to me, but I was too woozy to respond until I inhaled a sobering jolt of smelling salts.

"'About time you woke up. I thought you were going to sleep through the party,' Stan said while removing my pack and placing it under my head like a pillow. My confusion turned to fear as machine-gun fire ricocheted off the top of our precarious shelter.

"'Where are your injuries?' Stan asked.

"'I'm fine, I'm fine,' I answered while shaking so hard my helmet did a tap dance on my head. 'Where's my Browning?' I attempted to stand to look for my rifle.

"Stan grabbed my shoulders and yanked me down. 'I'd say you were injured up here,' he said, rapping his knuckles on my helmet, 'but all this blood you're sitting in tells me your keister took some shrapnel.'

"I looked with dread at the patch of crimson sand spreading out from under me.

"Stan forced me to lie down. 'Listen to me, football player,' he said. 'Some of our buddies out there are in worse shape than you. They need my help, and I need your help. I need you to pray for me while I'm dodging bullets on my way back to them.'

"I pleaded with him to stay, but he shook me with both hands. 'I don't have a lot of time to shoot the breeze, but I do need your prayers.'

"As he turned to leave, I cried out, 'I'm afraid to die, Preach'n Man."

"A bomb exploded fifty feet away. Stan hovered over me like a protective mother eagle as sand rained down on him from an angry sky. His cheek pressed against mine as he yelled over the horrific screams of bullets and men. 'Don't worry. I prayed for you harder than anyone this morning, but you'd better start worry'n about being born again before you start worry'n about die'n.'

"Stan took off across the sand in a zigzag pattern toward our fallen buddies. Puffs of sand from machine-gun fire chased him as he lumbered down the beach. The pursuing bullets miraculously stopped when he reached the first injured soldier. I whooped and hollered as Stan scooped up the G.I. and draped him over his shoulders like a sack of potatoes. Instead of the zigging and zagging, he made a beeline straight back. The German snipers missed the easy target of a big, slow man carrying another on his back.

"'You're home free, Tony.' Stan set the moaning young man against the base of the wall next to me. 'Take care of him Hank,' he said while heading back out into the hailstorm of bullets. Again he zigzagged; again he picked up a fallen soldier; again he trudged straight back.

"Stan staggered to the wall, collapsed face-first into the sand with the injured man strewn across his back, then rolled over to examine him. 'You're home free, Scott,' the Preach'n Man wheezed while reading the G.I.'s name from the dogtags wrapped around the soldier's neck. 'Jesus protected us today.' Stan turned to me while I was making a feeble attempt, with a torn shirt, to stop the bleeding in Tony's arm. 'Wish I would've taken your advice and ran a little harder in boot camp.' He patted me on the shoulder and said, 'Keep up the good work and keep pray'n.' He stumbled out toward another injured soldier sixty yards away.

"The Preach'n Man brought two more wounded soldiers *home free*. I did my best to tend to their injuries, but I was no medic. Leonard and Harold were more dead than alive when Stan delivered them to me. I wanted to believe I had been too busy to pray for him as the Preach'n Man had wanted me to. Every time Stan told an injured soldier that Jesus had protected them, I wanted to scream, 'Stan, are you blind? Look at us. Me and the boys are trapped in a patch of quicksand oozing with the stench of our own urine, blood, and feces. Like angry African killer bees, swarms of bullets buzz over our heads searching for our flesh. I don't need this kind of protection any more than I needed it when my Bible-thumping father beat my mother, sister, and me.'

"I was jolted awake by Stan's exhausted voice calling to me over the drone of the metallic bees. I looked up to see him with another injured man. He was only thirty feet from the safety of the wall but staggering like a punch-drunk boxer about to go down for the count. 'Keep...on...pray'n...Hank!" Stan gasped.

"'Forget about prayer!' I bellowed. 'It doesn't work! Just get over here!' At that instant shock spread over his face—the kind of expression reserved for a man betrayed by his brother. He shook his head and adjusted the living cargo on his shoulders. Before he could take another step, a bullet hit him in the chest, knocking him off his feet and flat on his back.

"I bolted out to him, ignoring the relentless buzz from the bees around my head. I dropped to both knees, digging my arms beneath him into the cold, damp sand, but he weakly pushed me away. Bubbles of dark red blood oozed from his mouth as he struggled to talk. 'Father, forgive him, for he knows not what he does,' he said and coughed frothy red mucus over my face. 'Go help *him*.' He motioned with his head to the injured soldier Stan had dropped when he was hit.

"'Please help me,' the injured GI pleaded. 'I can't move my legs.'"

"With every laborious breath, Stan coughed up more blood. The paralyzed soldier began to scream and the horrible *zing...zing...zing* of those incessant bees continued to torment us. I froze with indecision and fear until one of those bees brushed against the side of my helmet, knocking it off my head with a loud *thud*.

"'Come on, Stan,' I said, putting my hand behind his back to sit him up. 'I am bringing you home with the other guys.'

"Stan's eyes rolled lazily in his head as he looked at me. The grimace on his face turned to a painful smile. Gurgling noises, mixed in with words, bubbled up his throat as he said, 'Jesus is here. He'll take me home.' The words had barely left his lips when his head snapped back from the impact of a bullet penetrating his helmet into his forehead."

A few minutes passed before Joan noticed that Hank had quit talking. "I'm sorry," she said. "That was an awful thing to go through...but what about the mother and her unborn child?"

"My story is not finished yet." Hank turned the key. bringing the station wagon to life. "I will tell you the rest on the way to the church and when I drop you off at your Grandmother's house."

"Is that how you won your Purple Heart?" Joan asked.

Hank waited for a car to pass by before answering. "The Purple Heart is not something to be won like a blue ribbon for the best strawberry preserves

from the twenty-five Native Americans at the Lummi Indian Reservation to the five-hundred or so that packed a small gymnasium in Spokane.

The governor also knew Hank's disappointment over not pulling in more people to his crusades. The governor suggested Hank needed a drawing card, a well-known face on the program to attract a more diverse crowd. At the time, Hank was using the choir from Soundview Cathedral as worship music at his crusades. On occasion, McCoy used to sing baritone for the Seattle Opera House. He was given the nickname "The Baritone Baby-kisser" for his penchant to end his political speeches by belting out a few lines from a play or song that strategically fit his message.

The governor suggested he could do for Hank what George Beverly Shea did for Billy Graham's young ministry: be that drawing card. He could sing some hymns, tell several holy jokes, introduce Hank, and shake a few hands on his way out to his limousine. He was a busy man, so of course he couldn't be expected to stay for the entire crusade, but his mission would be accomplished. He guaranteed Hank that his appearance at the crusades would at least double but would probably triple or quadruple the overall attendance. McCoy would get the positive exposure his campaign desperately needed. After thrashing his opponent eight years ago, he narrowly beat him the last election.

It was two years ago, this past November, when Joan walked down the stairs after putting Johnny down for a nap. She heard the loud *thud* of a fist being pounded onto the kitchen table. Stopping in her tracks, she listened as the governor barked at Betty, "What was Hank thinking? His first crusade with the black community of Seattle as the target audience, and I know nothing about it until the last day of the event!"

"Daddy...," Betty began but her father wasn't finished.

"He's been planning this event and others with the black community behind my back, not thinking I would eventually find out." Joan heard a fist slam into the table, knocking something to the floor with a crash. "And to add salt to the wound, he's hoping to tie one of these events in with the first visit by Martin Luther King Jr. to the State of Washington."

"Daddy," Betty said weakly, "you always told Hank you didn't need the black vote."

McCoy's response rumbled through the kitchen like a clap of thunder. "I didn't when I won the '56 election by over 20 percent!" The kitchen fell silent as the verbal storm passed through. When the governor spoke again, his voice was calm. "The '60 election was a different story. The bleeding heart liberals stole 19 percent of my people. It's time I steal some of theirs. The last time I

29

looked, a black vote counted the same as a white one."

"How are you going to do that, Daddy?" Betty sounded nervous to Joan, like a whimpering puppy expecting a beating after being caught chewing on her master's slipper. "I mean, you haven't made many friends among the black community."

McCoy laughed, catching Joan off guard, but it must have been like seeing a rainbow after the storm for Betty. "Have you forgotten, my dear, that all us politicians have a little chameleon in our blood?"

Betty's laughter was a little too loud, a little too forced.

"Oh well, what's done is done. As your mother always used to say, 'No use crying over spilled milk.'" The mood in the kitchen grew instantly dark again as McCoy said, "Your husband is a fool, Betty. His recent success with rising attendance at his events has made him shortsighted. While it's true that his ministry has expanded to other states and into Canada, my involvement has been limited to this state, and for good reason. This is the only state I need to win for re-election."

"And you'll win again in two years," Betty said. "Just wait and see."

Joan heard a loud sigh from the governor. "'The Lord giveth and the Lord taketh away,' Betty. The good Lord and I are both giving a lot to your husband right now, and I'm not going to let his shortsightedness take the upcoming election away from me. If I lose the '64 election, I won't be his drawing card any longer. If I lose he loses, and even you will lose, my dear."

"What are you talking about, Daddy?" Betty's voice was weak and fragile.

Joan heard someone pour themselves a glass of water. She assumed it was McCoy, because there was a long pause before he answered, allowing the weight of his edict to sink in. "Besides the pay I receive as a servant of the state, there are many other financial perks I would lose by having the election fall into the hands of the Democrats. I might have to sell my house I have most graciously allowed your family to stay in for free."

"No, Daddy—you wouldn't."

"I would also have to significantly raise the rent on the church your husband now uses for practically nothing."

Betty began to cry. "Please, not our house. Think of Johnny."

"Betty, stop crying. To look at you, one would think I'd lost the election already." Joan's disgust toward the governor quickly turned into a rage at the threats the man was making toward Hank and Johnny. She even felt a twinge of empathy toward Betty. "All's not lost yet," McCoy said. "I'll do what I can from my end to make Hank see the light, but you are the one he really listens to. If it wasn't for your influence over Hank, I might not be a part of his ministry to begin with."

"What if he won't listen to me?" she blubbered.

"Oh, he will. If it comes right down to it, just withdraw some of his marital privileges from him. Can you do that, Betty?"

Betty was quiet for a second but softly answered, "Yes, I can do that."

"Betty, what is Hank thinking?"

Before she could stop herself, Joan flew down the final few stairs and stood at the entrance to the kitchen with her finger pointed at the startled governor. "Hank's thinking he wants to distance himself from a carpetbagger like you."

Betty sprang from her chair, ran to Joan, and slapped her face. "How dare you listen in on our private conversation. You have a lot of nerve insulting my father and your governor like that!"

"How dare you slap me after what I heard?" Joan pushed Betty and she fell, skidding across the freshly waxed floor on her bottom. "You don't deserve Hank as a husband."

Betty scrambled to her feet ready for round two when her father picked her up and roughly deposited her on a chair. "The both of you settle down." A sly grin crawled across his face. "The way you two are carrying on reminds me of how we used to settle things on the floor of the Senate." He motioned Joan toward an empty chair. "Please have a seat, little lady."

"I'd rather stand," Joan replied.

The governor eyed her smugly. "Of course, I've known this for quite some time from our past talks about politics, but you have adopted some very dangerous liberal ideologies."

"What does that have to do with anything I heard?" Joan snapped at him.

"You shouldn't have heard anything, babysitter," Betty said with a hiss and rose from her chair.

McCoy held up a hand with his palm toward Betty like a traffic cop, prompting her to plop back down and bite her fingernails in frustration. He walked over to Joan, placed his hand gently on her elbow, and attempted to lead her to the kitchen table. She jerked her arm away. "I need to get out of here," she said and turned to leave.

"Joan!" McCoy called out after her. "Do you think I'm an evil man for doing what needs to be done so I can be re-elected?"

Joan turned to face him. "Why do you care what I think?"

"Because, like you, I'm a Christian who would, if given the chance, do anything to remain in a position where we could influence our world for the Kingdom of God."

Joan clasped her fingers of both hands together and pressed them against her forehead. "I'm not anything like you. As a Christian, I believe in an unconditional love that wouldn't allow me to turn my back on family members because we don't agree on everything. Unlike you, I'm not a lizard who changes colors to match his environment."

Once again Joan turned to leave and once again McCoy grabbed her elbow, a little more firmly this time. "Don't be so sure your spiritual values match your politics, my dear. Remember, it was your liberal friends who took prayer out of the public schools and are now trying to make killing babies legal. What Bible verses did you learn in Sunday School to justify those actions? No Joan, we are all chameleons. We live in a fallen world and it's a dogfight sometimes just to survive. Sometimes the end really does justify the means." He let go of her arm and made a gesture toward the door. As she reached the door, the governor called out to her. "I'm sure you remember one of the greatest patriarchs in the Bible, Abraham, lied and said he was Sara's brother instead of telling his hosts the truth; he was actually her husband. He did this to protect himself from harm so he could later be used of God."

⌘⌘⌘

Joan jumped as something brushed against her knee. It stung. She opened her eyes to find Hank dabbing her bloody knees with a wet cotton swab. "Hydrogen peroxide," he said apologetically and held up the antiseptic in a brown bottle, she assumed, to convince her he wasn't dabbing her knees with gasoline. "Sorry I startled you. Did you fall asleep?"

"Are you kidding? I was only resting my eyes." She wiggled to sit up straight and the wet pew squished like she'd sat on a pile of juicy grapes. "I still have an unfinished story to listen to."

Hank knelt and gently blew on her knees before applying the butterfly bandages. A warm feeling, like the sensation from the vodka, spread through her belly. This feeling traveled much faster than the alcohol. It began as a small pebble dropped into the very depths of her abdomen and radiated out, building momentum, like a speeding tsunami leaving in its wake a trail of goose bumps until crashing into the tips of her toes, fingers, and scalp in an explosion of tingling sensations.

"I bet Mrs. Johnson goes ape when you blow on her knees." Joan wanted to grab the words and shove them back in her throat. Instead they clung to the air like toilet paper clinging to the back of a skirt.

A smile tugged at one corner of Hank's mouth. "Actually, I have a lot

Administration with the hopes of managing his company someday."

"Is that when you went to the University of Washington?" Joan asked, fighting back a yawn.

"Mr. James McCoy paid for both Betty and I to get business degrees at the U. Betty made the cheerleading squad, and I started all four years at tight end as a nonscholarship walk-on for the Husky football team." Hank brought both palms together and placed his hands against his lips as though he were praying. "Betty was happy back then. No, she was more than happy. She loved life back then; she loved me back then."

"What happened?" Joan sat up straight. Another yawn was the furthest thing from her mind.

"After graduation, I was drafted in the first round by the Chicago Bears of the NFL. Betty was ecstatic, but I had made a commitment to her grandfather to learn the business. After all, he had invested a lot for my education, and I fully intended to repay his financial investment in me with loyalty and dedication."

"What did Patrick think?"

"He was running for his first term as governor so, as usual, was too busy with politics to bother himself with anything else. Mr. James McCoy, on the other hand, being a huge sports fan, was thrilled his son-in-law might play professional football. He told me he was not planning to retire any time soon, so there would be plenty of time for me to learn the business. I was to work for him that summer and then report to the Bears' training camp in August. I could work for McCoy during the off seasons if I made the team. Two weeks before that first training camp, Mr. McCoy took me to a bank he did business with in downtown Seattle to meet the manager. After our meeting, the manager was walking Mr. McCoy and me back through the lobby when two masked people burst through the front door. One was wearing a bulky, hooded sweatshirt, the other a gray trenchcoat. Both wore ski masks pulled down over their faces."

Joan was on the edge of the platform now. "A bank robbery?"

"The taller and thinner of the two bandits pulled out a sawed-off shotgun hidden inside his trenchcoat and screamed for everyone to get on their bellies with arms and feet spread. A shorter robber with a huge pot belly, carrying a pistol, went to a teller window with a note and empty bag." Hank shifted uneasily. "Mr. McCoy and I were on our hands and knees when a street cop, who had been in the lunch room visiting his wife, popped up from behind a partition. He drew his revolver and hollered at the bank robbers to drop their guns."

Hank fixed his gaze directly into Joan's eyes. "Have you seen a movie where everything in the scene is slowed down?" Joan could only nod as Hank continued. "That's cinematic trick photography. What happens, though, when that phenomenon occurs in real life? As you watch such a scene unfold before your eyes, you realize your thoughts must be processing information much faster than your body can react. That seems to be the only logical explanation. Some people call that indecision, others may call it uncertainty, but for me I now believe those times are moments of revelation. Our sovereign God, the author and director of the universe, gives us free reign over how we play our parts in the movie of our life."

"I'm confused. Whenever I've been bummed out over something in my life that seems to be out of my control, you've tried to comfort me by saying, 'God's in control of all circumstances.'"

"Like a director of a movie, God is in control of all the scenes in our life. He allows us to have the creative freedom to choose how we act out each circumstance." Hank shifted his gaze away from Joan and stared at his hands folded on his lap. "Joan, I believe there are defining moments in each of our lives; scenes where we come upon a fork in the road. What path we choose will bring us to a scene entirely different than if we had chosen the opposite path. You see, God is in control of every scene: the weather, the location, the people we meet. Do we listen to our heavenly director as he guides us through each scene, or do we rely solely on our own instincts and desires? We are in control of how we act out each scene that will lead us to a new fork and another decision and yet another scene."

"Which leads us back to the bank robbery," Joan said motioning with her hands for Hank to get back to the story.

Hank smiled. "Sorry. You know us pastors. Any conversation can lead to a mini-sermon."

His smile faded as he resumed telling the story. "The guy with the scatter gun was extremely nervous and agitated. He swore threats at the policeman while aiming his weapon at the officer. The fat robber was quiet and held the revolver pointed toward the floor. Several people were standing close to the officer. Without taking his eyes off of the trenchcoat guy, the officer directed everyone to slowly move away from him. Trenchcoat screamed at everyone to stay put and for his partner to point his pistol at the officer."

"Why didn't the policeman put his gun down and let the robbers take the money?" Joan asked. "Why provoke a confrontation?"

Hank made eye contact. "That's what was going through my mind at the very instant the officer put his hand on the bank manager to push him away and Trenchcoat squeezed the trigger. Do you know how a scatter gun works, Joan?"

"No," she whispered.

"A shotgun barrel is sawed off to allow the pellets to spread apart quicker or to scatter over a broader area. It's a very effective and deadly weapon at close range. The main force of the blast instantly killed the officer but also hit the bank manager and a female teller standing close by. "

Joan covered her mouth with her hand.

"Not completely lost in the terrified screams of customers and employees was the pitiful moaning and crying of the two injured bank personnel. Mr. James McCoy leaned over and whispered for me to pray for him. Then he stood and while cautiously walking backward toward the injured people, began to talk to Trenchcoat."

"What did he say?" Joan asked.

"Trenchcoat screamed at him to get back down. Mr. McCoy told them to hurry up with their business, but he was going to tend to the injured."

Joan could hardly wait to hear how Hank had saved the day. "What did you do?"

"This is the part of the scene where everything slows down but my mind. Many options ricocheted through my head, but in the end I simply watched the scene unfold before me. Trenchcoat marched over to my father-in-law, put the gun within one foot of his chest, gave him one final order to get down, and then pulled the trigger."

Hank flinched as he relived that awful moment again. "As James hit the floor, his body landed by the dead officer's revolver. Trenchcoat kicked the revolver in the direction of his partner but forgot I was between the two. At that moment everything around me speeded back up to normal. I picked up the revolver at the same instant Trenchcoat pumped another shell into the barrel of his shotgun. My shot hit him in the forehead. I spun around on my back and leveled the gun at Sweatshirt, who already had a pistol pointed at me. I fired off two quick rounds, the first hitting the huge belly of Sweatshirt, the second ripping into Sweatshirt's chest."

A sick feeling deep in the pit of her stomach began to grow as a horrible realization materialized in Joan's mind.

"I scrambled on my hands and knees over to Mr. McCoy, but he was gone. So was Trenchcoat. The whole bank was eerily quiet until I heard Sweatshirt faintly sobbing in a growing puddle of blood in the middle of the lobby. One of the bank's loan officers met me as we cautiously approached Sweatshirt. I reached down and yanked off Sweatshirt's ski mask. Sweatshirt was a woman—a baby-faced, teenage girl to be more exact."

Joan absentmindedly put a hand on her abdomen. "She was pregnant, wasn't she?"

"As I yelled for someone to call an ambulance and the police department, the teenager wailed at me, 'You killed my baby, you killed my baby!'"

"The loan officer picked up the pistol in his handkerchief. 'Mister, you should look at this.' He handed me the weapon. It wasn't a weapon at all but a harmless cap gun."

"Oh Hank," Joan said as she wrapped her arms around him and laid her head on his shoulder. "I'm so sorry."

"The police found the girl's terrified younger sister hiding in a nearby alley. Come to find out their father was Trenchcoat. He had lost everything gambling in Vegas. He panhandled his way up the coast, ending up in Seattle, homeless and walking the streets with his two daughters, whom he was sexually abusing. The girl's unborn baby was dead by the time the ambulance arrived and the girl died two days later."

Her head was still on Hank's shoulder as she asked, "What happened to the girl's younger sister?"

"The police found a relative for the little girl to live with." Hank looked down at Joan, his eyes wet and red. "Well, there it is, Joan—the end of the story. Do you even remember the question that led me to spend all night in a meandering attempt to retell that awful story?" He pulled himself away from Joan's embrace. "I bet you're glad my sermons don't ramble on like that story."

Joan grabbed Hank's hand and stared into his sad eyes. She had never felt closer to any human being than she did toward this tormented man right now. "The question I wanted answered was why you murdered an unborn child and its mother, but you didn't murder them. What happened was horrible, but you were a hero, you..."

"The question you originally asked me was why Betty did not know I would be a pastor. When I walked out of the bank that day, Betty lost not only a grandfather she loved more than her own father; she lost the man she married. A part of me died in the lobby of the bank that day, and a stranger walked through the door into Betty's arms that night."

"What are you talking about?" Joan asked.

"My whole life has revolved around protecting others. Growing up, I protected my mother and sister from my father, who expected perfection from his family. He wanted us to make him look good in front of his congregation, and he beat us when we failed. In football, on the offensive line, my job was to protect the quarterback; as a soldier in Europe, my duty was to protect my country. After that day at the bank, I started to protect myself by drinking the pain away."

Joan rested her other hand on Hank's shoulder. "You did nothing wrong. You couldn't have prevented it from happening."

Hank grabbed her hand and held it tight. "Both Stan and James McCoy asked me to pray for them. At the time they both requested it from me, praying was the last thing on my mind. All I was thinking, on both occasions, was how I could protect everyone around me...and I failed. Twice, two good men asked me to pray for them, and they both died because of my lack of faith."

"It would have happened anyway." Joan squeezed his hand.

Hank pulled a little brown book from his pocket. "After Stan died, all his personal items were boxed up and shipped to his parents in Nebraska, including his diary." He opened the diary, pointing to the last entry written, and handed it to Joan. "Read this."

The journal entry was scribbled in pencil on a dog-eared page worn and smudged with fingerprints and tears.

June 5, 1944
God, why can't you leave me alone about this football player? Now you have even put him in my dreams. I'm so tired of you telling me how this man will be a rock, like Peter. When you speak to me in my dreams, I always obay you, like Joseph did, like Daniel did. This time, Lord, you ask too much. You ask me to prepare a sacrafice for him. What do I sacrafice? My pride? I have alredy done that for him. My honor? I have spent four days in the brig for two fistfights with him after trying to talk to him about you. Lord, I know if you can change Saul into Paul you can change this man, but what do I have left to sacrafice except my own life? Is that it, Lord? Am I to die for him so he can live? I want to see my beutiful Jenny again. I want to hold my son who I haven't even seen. I want to feel the warm, rich soil of Nebraska between my fingers again. I'll pray for him, Lord, and that will have to be sacrafice enough.

Hank took the diary from Joan and put it back into his pocket. "I received this in the mail from Stan's parents the same day of the bank robbery. They wrote a note to me with the diary. Because of their grief, it had taken them four years before they could go through any of their son's belongings which had been shipped home from France. After reading his diary, they felt Stan would have wanted me to see it, so they contacted the army and found my last known mailing address."

"So you read it and gave your life back over to God?" Joan asked.

"No. The incident at the bank consumed my life. Betty did not even show me the diary until almost two weeks after it had come in the mail. By then the guilt and remorse over what had happened was ripping my guts out. I shoved the diary in a kitchen drawer and did not see it again until three months later. After reporting to the Chicago Bears' training camp out of shape and hung over, I only lasted until the first cut. I arrived home and drank until I passed out. Later I awoke in a puddle of my own vomit. Stumbling to the knife drawer, I reached inside, looking for the sharpest blade I could find to slit my wrists. Instead of a knife, I latched onto Stan's diary with the note from his parents tucked inside."

"Is that what prompted you to go to Bible School and become a past—?"

Hank put a finger to Joan's lips. "Actually, reading Stan's diary made me feel more guilty and then angry that I felt so guilty. I missed more days of work than I was there, and even when I did show up, I was too drunk or hung over to do anything well. Although Betty had graduated with her degree in Business Administration, she had not taken school seriously enough to apply what she knew to the business. She ended up being almost as worthless as me but was too full of pride to allow the employees, who really knew how to run the business, run it. The cash cow Patrick McCoy had inherited was quickly drying up, and he did not waste any time before he found a buyer with deep pockets to cash him out."

"What did you and Betty do?" Joan asked.

"Part of the sales agreement between McCoy and the new owner stipulated that Betty and I would be hired back on and could not be let go for five years without a cash settlement. Betty couldn't type worth a darn but with her pretty face she was hired on as a receptionist. I had to hit the road as a salesman and drum up new business as well as win back some of the business we had lost since Mr. James McCoy died."

Joan leaned back onto her elbows; her eyelids were heavy. "What made you decide to become a pastor then?"

"One day, I came upon a homeless man with his two young children on 1st Avenue in Seattle. They were looking for food inside garbage cans down an alley. I was on my way to the closest tavern when the youngest child looked up from inside one of the cans and made eye contact with me. She had the same expression as the little four-year-old daughter of Trenchcoat: fear, hunger, but more than anything else, hopelessness. I drove around the block and knew I had to stop. I asked them if they would like a home-cooked meal.

At first, the father refused until I mentioned I would also pay him to rake some leaves in my yard."

Joan giggled. "Did Betty have a cow when three homeless people showed up for dinner?"

"She had a bigger cow when I invited them back the next night."

"What did you do—adopt them?" Joan giggled again.

Hank leaned back, stuck his hand in the baptismal pool, brought it back out, and splashed his face with the still cold water. "No, but I got the father a job at the lumber mill, and I started helping out at the downtown homeless shelter. The more I helped, the less pain I felt. The less pain I felt, the less I drank, until one night I told Betty I wanted to go to school to become a pastor."

"Just like that?" Joan snapped her finger.

"No, not just like that, but I don't have time to tell you another long story." He tried unsuccessfully to stifle a yawn. "I have a church service to get ready for, and I might change my mind and take a little nap before too long so I don't fall asleep giving my sermon."

Hank stood and Joan stood beside him. She touched his arm. "Why isn't Betty happy?"

Hank cradled Joan's head in the palms of his big hands, bent over, and kissed her forehead. Joan felt goose bumps pop out all over. She held her breath as Hank kissed her cheek. He abruptly stopped and, with a confused expression, ruffled her hair. "Another question that needs a long answer." He backed away from her a few steps. "My little dove, it seems the closer I get to God, the further Betty pulls away from me. The day I quit drinking for good was the day she started. The faith that saved me physically and spiritually is killing Betty. Ironic, isn't it, but in the end it all comes down to those forks in the road. I only pray that one day she chooses the right one before it's too late."

Joan took a step toward Hank and let the choir robe fall to the floor. His eyes grew as round as saucers and his Adam's apple jumped up his throat. "Baptize me, Pastor Hank."

"Holy smokes, Joan." He coughed up a nervous little laugh. "Thank God you remembered to put on my T-shirt. "Get baptized later in the morning with everyone else." He picked up the choir robe and held it out to Joan. "I can give you some ideas for your testimony, if you need help."

She walked over to the edge of the baptismal pool and stepped over the side onto the submerged top step. The water was still cold. More goose bumps. "Baptize me now."

He stepped forward, still holding the robe out to her. "Remember what baptism is. It is the believer's act of obedience that you have died to yourself and are taking a public stand to announce your allegiance to Christ. Where are all your witnesses? Where are the ones to hear your testimony?"

"You know my testimony, and I love you more than all the other people in the congregation added together." The water was cold, but she was determined. "You and God are the only witnesses I need."

In frustration, Hank ran a hand through his curly black hair. "I am still intoxicated, Joan. God will not bless this sacred rite if I perform it in my present condition."

"This is *my* fork in the road," Joan pleaded. "Please, Hank, I want this now."

Silently Hank bent over, removed his shoes and socks, and climbed into the pool alongside Joan. They walked down the steps to the bottom of the pool. With his slacks still on, in thigh-deep water, Hank recited the baptismal liturgy and spoke a short prayer. Gazing into Joan's eyes, he said, "My little dove, from the day you first came into my life, you have been a blessing. You have become so much more to me than Johnny's babysitter. You are family." He flashed her a shy smile. "You have been a blessing to Betty, even if she doesn't realize it yet. As a nine-year-old I watched you give your life to Jesus Christ on your knees in my study, and every year I watch your walk with God grow deeper." Hank guided her left hand up to her face so she could plug her nose. He placed one hand at the small of her back, the other behind her neck, and leaned her back into the cold water. "Joan Butler, it is my pleasure to baptize you in the name of the Father, the Son, and the Holy Ghost."

As she was pulled out of the water, the weight of Hank's wet T-shirt pulled the neck opening down over her shoulders where it clung to her body like a tight-fitting, white strapless dinner gown. She gasped from the shock of the cold water and began to shiver. Hank picked up the choir robe and draped it over her. With one hand around her shoulder, he led her back to his office.

"Stand by the heater." He turned up the thermostat. "I'll get you a towel."

Joan grabbed him by the arm. "Thank you."

Hank put both arms around her and squeezed. "I am proud of you, little dove."

Instead of bending over to hug her like he normally did, he pulled her to him. She knew she must be getting him wet, but his hug was warm and she melted into it. A slight tremor shook through Hank as her body pressed against his. With her head resting on his chest, she could feel the rhythmic pounding of his heart speed up with each passing moment. She didn't dare

44

look at him for fear any movement might wake her up from this wonderful dream. Instead, Hank cupped her head in his hands and leaned over to give her a kiss. She bowed her head, expecting his familiar peck on the brow, But with only his finger, he tilted her head gently up towards his. He paused as another tremor shook his body. She instinctively opened her mouth to receive his as their lips met. She let the white robe fall silently to the red carpet as they slowly made their way to the couch.

⌘⌘⌘

Joan woke to a scream. She bolted upright on the couch next to Hank, with only the choir robe covering their naked bodies. Betty was standing in the open doorway to Hank's office. She covered her mouth with both hands, but another scream escaped. Behind Betty, wearing his Daniel Boone pajamas and coonskin cap, was Johnny.

Hank leapt from the couch, threw on his wet slacks, and pulled Betty down the hall, away from Joan. Johnny stood alone in the hall, sucking his thumb and staring at Joan. She slipped on the robe and motioned for Johnny to come to her. He took one step backward. Tears welled in her eyes. She called out softly to him. He took one more step back into the hall.

As Joan reached her hand out again to the boy, another hand grabbed Johnny from the waist and pulled him down the hall. She fought back the tears. The only thought piercing through her numbness was how she was ever going to find her way back from the fork in the road she had chosen.

4

I've seen movies where someone is talking to a coma patient, convinced that patient can hear what's being said to him. Let me tell you from firsthand experience that's a bunch of bologna, at least in my case. From the moment of impact until I awoke at Harborview Medical Center in Seattle thirty-three days later, it was if I'd fallen into a dreamless sleep one night and awakened the next morning. I opened my eyes to the startled expression of a thin, white-haired, black man sitting next to the bed I was in.

"Oh my gosh!" He almost fell out of his chair. "You're awake. Ryan, you're awake!"

I tried to speak, but my mouth felt full of stale cotton balls. Long tubes stretched out from behind me into my arms and the only thing I could hear was the beating of my heart. Only instead of going *thump...thump...thump*, it made an alien *beep...beep...beep* from somewhere in the room. I truly believed a black Frankenstein had brought me back from the dead and was deliriously running around the room screaming, "He's awake! He's awake!" The last thing I remember before doctors and nurses stampeded into my room was yanking the tubes from my arms and trying to squeeze enough air through the cotton balls to scream.

I fell back to sleep but was awakened to the muffled talk of two people.

"I think I scared him."

"Are you sure he tried to speak?"

"Yes—yes, I'm sure. And as I moved around the room, he followed me with his eyes.

"What does this mean?"

"It means he could be coming out of his coma."

"Then he's going to be okay?"

"You have to remember, he sustained a very serious head injury and up to this point, Ryan had not made any progress since the surgery to remove the blood clot. We won't know the long-term extent of damage the epidural hematoma may have caused for quite some time."

"Can you take another CT scan or EEG to see how he's doing?"

"Pastor, while those tests are essential in determining a diagnosis for physical and neurological damage, to truly measure the extent of any permanent impairments we'll need to test how his brain functions once he is fully awake, and even then it may be years before we know how he has responded to rehabilitation."

"How long before he wakes back up?"

"That's entirely up to Ryan. Pastor, just because Ryan opened his eyes and moved doesn't mean he is out of the woods. His GCS rating has been a 4 since he was first evaluated the afternoon he was brought in. While what you described definitely shows a dramatic change in his condition, the first thing we will check is to see if he experienced a seizure."

I opened my eyes and looked at the two men. "Don't bother; it wasn't a seizure." The doctor dropped his clipboard, and the other man smiled so big, I thought he would swallow his ears. "What's a GCS rating?" I asked through rusty vocal cords. "Before you answer that, I really need a drink of water."

The doctor gave me a thimble-full of water, which I complained wasn't enough until I gagged on it. He promised more later, in small doses. The pastor stood off to the side cupping his hands over his nose and mouth.

"A GCS rating is an acronym for The Glasgow Coma Scale," the doctor began. "It's a rating system used to measure or give a number to the severity of a brain injury. Ryan, you were brought here over a month ago registering a 4 on the GCS scale. A 3 denotes the deepest level of a coma; a 15 the lightest stage. You wouldn't open your eyes, even to pain; you wouldn't vocalize any sounds; and your only response to painful stimuli was that your body automatically stretched out and became rigid. On a 6 point scale for motor responses, your response to painful stimuli earned you 2 points. On eye opening and verbal response you graded out a 1 each for a total of 4."

"You tortured me?"

"Only when you ignored me, Ryan." He picked his clipboard up off the floor, checked a monitor, and wrote something down.

With much effort and a little pain, I lifted my arm and pointed toward the man leaning against the wall. "You called him a pastor."

"He is a pastor," the doctor said while still writing on his clipboard.

"So why is he here? If I needed a pastor to give me the sacrament of last rites, I would want my father—even if he isn't Catholic."

The two men exchanged uneasy glances, and the doctor said, "I'll be back in a few minutes, Ryan."

"Don't leave me alone with him. Where's my parents? If I need a pastor, I want to talk to my dad."

The tall black man drew closer and placed a bony hand on my foot. "You don't recognize me, do you?"

"Am I supposed to?"

"It's okay, Ryan," the doctor said. "It's very common for a person with a head injury to experience post-traumatic amnesia. You might wake up tomorrow and not remember having this conversation." The doctor put his arm around the other man's shoulder. "Pastor, I think we've stimulated Ryan enough for now. Why don't you go home, get some rest, and come back tomorrow afternoon? We should know a little more about the boy's condition by then."

The pastor was ushered from the room, and the doctor came back beside me. With the clipboard by his side, he brought his other hand to his face and massaged his hairy chin. He studied me, staring into my eyes and cocking his head to one side.

"What?" I said, annoyed at being stared at like a lab experiment. "Do I have a booger hanging out of my nose or is my face melting?"

"Amazing," the doctor said and wrote something else down.

"You know, Doc, you're about as annoyingly cryptic as my parents were the day...the day...of...of the..."

"Of what, Ryan?"

The human mind is a funny thing. It's filled with millions of different rooms, each filled with many memories. I could see into many different rooms at once, but all the rooms with memories covering the past thirty-two days have doors with locks on them. The only difference is the thirty-second day. There is a lock on that door but a key is in that lock. I am afraid of that room. For only a brief second, I dared to open that door but the traumatic crashing of metal against metal, the terrible screams of a woman, the cold blast of snow in my face, and a green envelope, whipping through the whiteness of a blizzard was more than I wanted to experience right now.

"What do you remember, Ryan?"

"I remember you haven't told me where my parents are," I croaked. "Are they in another room in the hospital? Are they injured like me?" I tried to sit up, but the doctor firmly but gently pushed me back down.

"Careful—you don't want to yank out all your monitoring lines again after the nurses just had them reinserted."

"Why aren't my parents here?"

"Pastor Tom will talk to you tomorrow afternoon about their condition."

"You're the doctor!" I tried to yell but could only muster an angry whisper. "I want to know right now!" I fought weakly to get out of bed, but I was no match for the doctor and the three nurses who came to assist him. They strapped me down and gave me a shot.

As I drifted off to sleep, I remember floating toward that unlocked door. It was now opened a crack, and a bright light escaped from it. That terrible screaming filled my ears, and with a spray of snow, the green envelope blew through the small opening in the door and landed at my feet. *Hurry and close the door before you let the abominable snowman through as well. Wonder if anybody's ever told that white ape he screams like a woman.* I closed the door, and the screaming stopped. With caution, I picked up the envelope; it was cold. I had trouble opening the flap because my fingers were freezing. Inside was a folded piece of bonded typing paper.

While I unfolded the letter, my fingers trembled not only from the cold, but from the possible revelation of the mystery behind the door. It dropped from my hands as if it were on fire. The paper did not physically burn my flesh but seared my mind with fear. Not one word was printed or typed on that page, but instead it was the letter itself I heard scream at me. The door suddenly blew open, and the shrieking paper was sucked back into the frozen wasteland of my mind.

⌘⌘⌘

Normally I'm a very light sleeper, but maybe I developed a new trait over the past thirty-three days. Sleep was heavy and uninterrupted last night, which I know, from past experience, is unusual in a hospital. My last hospital stay was for an appendectomy. When I complained about being smothered with attention every two hours in the middle of the night, a nurse told me, "a hospital is the last place on earth to catch up on your sleep." I must be the exception.

Today, though, the whole hospital staff made up for lost time. I felt like Frankenstein's monster on an examination table. Instead of being poked and prodded by the townfolk with pitchforks, butcher knives, and clubs under the glow of torches, I was injected, scoped, scanned, pulled, twisted, pricked, interviewed, analyzed, assessed, monitored, and bathed. After the hospital shrink finally ran out of questions and left me alone for the first time in eight hours, I succumbed to my new favorite pastime...sleep.

The room was semi-dark as I opened my eyes. The only noises were the eerie electronic beeps from the monitor and the shuffling of pages being turned in a book. To my left sat the black preacher, reading the Bible using light filtering in from the hallway. He glanced up from reading and smiled. *Be careful of that smile, Ryan. Only the Cheshire cat smiles like that.*

"Hello, Ryan." The pastor put down his Bible. "You've become quite the celebrity around here."

Don't answer him. You of all people know that unless you're a good friend or relative, there's no middle ground with pastors or doctors; they either come to bring you good news or bad. He may claim to know you, but you sure as heck don't know him.

The pastor stood. "The good doctor told me you are a modern miracle of medicine."

I kept quiet.

"Don't feel like talking?" He picked up his Bible and tucked it under his arm. "I'll go grab a bite to eat and come back later."

"Where's my parents?" I asked through gritty vocal cords.

"The doctors told me you would be asking me that."

"So you've had time to prepare a sermon for me then."

The black man pulled his chair closer to my bed. "What do you mean?"

"I'm a P.K. and, as a pastor's kid, I know all the tricks."

One of his bushy eyebrows arched high on his forehead. "Such as?"

"Such as giving me a sermon to tell me an answer to a question in a roundabout way."

"And why would I do that?"

"So I can either give God the glory for good news or for bad news spend the next few days looking up the Scripture references you give me from the book of Psalms."

The pastor leaned toward me. His white hair glowed like a halo around his dark face. The Cheshire cat smile disappeared behind thick lips, while his eyes glowed like burning coals. He grabbed my hand.

"How bad are my parents' injuries?"

"What do you remember about the day you were brought here by helicopter?"

"I remember how I've been asked this question so many times today that if I have to say, 'nothing' one more time, I'm gonna puke."

Both eyebrows shot up, giving their best impression of McDonald's golden arches. "If you remember nothing, then why do you assume they must be injured?"

"Because I am, and you're sitting here holding my hand, instead of them."

The pastor leaned back and nodded. "You remind me of your grandmother. Under trying circumstances you're confident and level headed, but you also bring a red-hot chip on your shoulder to any conversation. Arguing with her was like eating ice cream smothered in tabasco sauce. You are a little more sarcastic than she was, though."

50

"So, you knew my grandmother."

His smile was back. "The most incredible person I ever met."

"Too bad I never met her, then."

His smile faded. "That *was* a shame."

"And you're using another famous trick to keep from answering my question."

The pastor closed his eyes. Why was he stalling? *He's either silently praying for God's wisdom on how to tell you some very bad news, or he's counting on Scotty to beam him aboard the* Enterprise. *Looks like you lose either way, ol' buddy.* The pastor opened his eyes and stood.

"From the police report, your family was traveling west on I-90 during blizzard conditions over Snoqualmie Pass. About one mile west of the summit, your parents' vehicle went into a skid and hit an oncoming pickup head on. You were not strapped in and were thrown from the car through the side window, dislocating your left shoulder and shattering your left kneecap. You landed in a snowbank and struck the trunk of a tree, which was believed to be the cause of your head injury."

"And my parents?"

"They both died from the injuries sustained in the accident. I'm sorry, Ryan."

When my best friend, Brandon, lost his mother to breast cancer last year, he told me that, even though he had time to prepare for her death, preparation didn't ease the pain he felt when she died. My instincts warned me this was what I was going to hear, but the shock of it felt like ice water flowed through the IV drip into my bloodstream. A reservoir of tears, collecting behind a dam of frozen emotions, was about to overflow when I noticed the pastor was weeping. Perplexed and slightly annoyed that his emotional release delayed my own, I picked up a paper cup full of water and threw it at him.

"Hey!" I yelled. "I'm the one who lost a family here. I can cry on my own without you priming the pump."

The pastor hung his head. "I'm so sorry," he said, while wiping the tears from his cheeks. "You still don't know who I am, do you?"

I slammed the palm of my hand against the railing of the hospital bed. "You tell me my parents are dead, then *you* cry, and after that, you want me to play a guessing game with you. I may have amnesia about the events from the accident until I woke up yesterday, but I remember everything about my life before that. And, mister, you weren't part of it."

"Oh dear God, I should have been." He reached for a tissue from my meal tray and blew his nose.

"What do you mean?"

"I made the mistake of letting your mother and father walk out of my life, and I won't allow that to happen with you."

"You know," I said, pointing my finger at him, "you're really starting to freak me out." I pushed the nurses' call button. "It's time for you to go and never come back."

"Who do you think will look after you once you recover?"

Tell him you know Mr. Rogers is dead, but you would still choose his neighbor over him. "Well, for some reason I'm beginning to suspect you would, but I haven't given it much thought since I found out I'm an orphan only two minutes ago."

A male nurse poked his head into the room. "You need something, Ryan?"

I nodded, and he walked into the room. His huge shoulders and thick chest tested the stretchability of the blue uniform he wore. "You seem big enough to act as my personal bodyguard."

He playfully flexed his biceps and struck a familiar body builder pose. "At your service."

"Would you please show the pastor his way out of my room?"

The nurse glanced uneasily at the man seated beside me. "Uh, hello, Pastor Tom."

Tom stood and patted the nurse on the shoulder. "Didn't see you in church last Sunday. Shift change?"

"Well...no...uh." The poor boob began to blush. "NFC championship game. Had a party at my house. You know."

"You don't need to explain to me, Ted. If I didn't have to preach, I would've been parked in front of the TV myself. Just give me another minute with Ryan and I'll see myself out, okay?"

"Anything you say, Pastor." Superman turned into the incredible shrinking man as he backed toward the door. "If you need anything else, Ryan, just holler." He bumped into the door and fled from the room.

"So, do you always carry around a spare chunk of kryptonite in your back pocket for occasions such as this?"

He held up his Bible like a shield. "No, this works much better than kryptonite."

"Why are you here, besides being the bearer of bad news?"

"I'm here to take care of you."

"I don't know you. I'm sure I could live with my basketball coach until I go off to college."

52

made half as much money as she had babysitting and had to pay twenty-five dollars a month for room and board.

Then President Kennedy was assassinated by Lee Harvey Oswald—Camelot was over—and Joan was over one week late in getting her period. She was never late.

Joan was sweeping the dead Christmas tree needles into a pile when Sue entered the room. "So, has your ugly red-headed aunt paid you a visit yet?" Sue held the dust pan for Joan to sweep the needles into.

"No." Joan answered.

Sue dumped the needles into a brown IGA grocery bag. "Don't get bummed out over it; my period's always late."

"I've never been late," Joan replied while loosening the screws to the Christmas tree stand. "Never!" She stood and stuck one foot on the stand. Grasping the tree with both hands, she yanked, and it pulled free, sending hundreds of needles exploding from its parched branches.

"That's one dry tree." Sue said.

"Not as dry as me." Joan angrily shook the evergreen, dislodging more needles, and flung it to the ground. She walked to the couch and plopped listlessly onto it.

Sue ran over, jumped on top of Joan, and tickled her. "You wouldn't be so bummed out unless you think you have a bun in the oven. Am I right?"

Joan shook her head no, so the bigger girl kept on tickling. "Have you been on the make and didn't tell your best friend about it?"

"Stop it! No, no!" Joan shrieked.

"Liar!" Sue continued relentlessly. "Who have you been intimate with down at the passion pit?"

Joan squirmed away and pointed a finger at Sue. "You're the only girl I'd let do that to me."

"That's because I'm the only girl in the school who can kick your butt." Sue laughed.

The kitchen door opened and Sue's mother walked in, a tissue pressed to her nose. She had been crying. "What's wrong, Mom?" Sue asked. "You're home early. Is everything okay at the store?"

Mrs. Olson dabbed at her eyes as she entered the living room. "Joan, come here and have a seat, sweetheart." Joan glanced from Mrs. Olson to Sue who shrugged and asked again, "Mom, what is it? Tell us."

"It's...it's little Johnny Johnson," she stammered.

A cold vise squeezed Joan's heart.

Mrs. Olson took Joan's hand. "Johnny's nanny fell asleep while reading him a book last evening. Johnny and the family dog were both missing when the pastor and his wife came home. A search party looked all night with no luck—until this morning."

"Thank God, they found him!" Joan's optimism couldn't melt the cold dread crushing her insides. "He's safe at home, right?"

Mrs. Olson hung her head. "One of the searchers found his coonskin cap on a mud bar in the Stilly. They followed the dog's tracks to a patch of cattails along the riverbank."

"No, please dear God, no," Joan pleaded.

"They found Johnny facedown in a foot of water, the dog sitting by his side, guarding him." With a wistful expression, she added, "The dog wouldn't let any of the rescue workers get close to Johnny until Pastor Johnson arrived."

Blackness closed in around Joan. Mrs. Olson's face faded; her voice was a balloon, released and drifting over distant tree tops. The last thing Joan remembered was a vision of Johnny walking in the dark along the riverbank with Moses at his side.

Johnny patted the big Labrador on the head and said, "Come on, Moses, we're gonna find sister Joan."

⌘⌘⌘

January was cold and wet. Snow would have been a welcome sight, covering the dreary gray of winter with a bright blanket of white. Instead, it seemed to rain every day with the thermometer never falling below 36 and never climbing over 45. Every dull day the same wet, soggy blanket dampened her spirits enough to fear spring would never come.

Joan didn't go to the funeral. She had loved little Johnny with all her heart, but funerals were held for the living, not the dead. She was afraid Betty would make a scene, so out of respect for the Johnsons, she volunteered to work at the IGA the afternoon of the funeral. People assumed she didn't go out of the grief she was going through. She didn't care what they thought.

As a desolate January turned into a depressing February, Joan still did not get her period. She made an appointment with a gynecologist in Seattle. Sue gladly skipped school to drive Joan to the doctor.

After her examination, Joan walked back to the waiting room. *Dead man walking*—Joan had heard that expression used to describe a convict's long march to his execution. With the doctor's confirmation that a new life was growing inside her, she could not help but feel a big part of her was going to die after she completed her nine-month march. Sue sat on the edge of her seat, her jaws working frantically on a wad of bubble gum as Joan approached. Joan patted her stomach and nodded, causing Sue to gag on her gum.

The two sat in silence as Sue drove away from the Greenlake Medical Center toward Highway 99. Joan didn't know what to tell her best friend. She hated lying to Sue, but what could she do? She hoped she could be ambiguous with Sue and hope her friend would understand.

Sue pulled into Dick's Drive-In. Joan pulled her knees up to her chest in the bucket seat. She wondered how many more months she would be able to do that before her belly would get in the way. "I'm not hungry," she said dully.

"Well, I am." Sue walked up to the window, ordered, and returned with two hamburgers, two fries, and two chocolate shakes.

She put a sack on her lap and set the other on Joan's.

"I told you," Joan said, putting the sack between the bucket seats, "I'm not hungry."

Sue unwrapped Joan's hamburger, pried open her friend's hand, and shoved the burger into it. "Don't forget—you're eating for two now." Sue grabbed the fries and forced them between Joan's legs. "Maybe you aren't hungry, but I bet your baby is."

A small grin touched Joan's lips. "Okay, Mom." She picked out one French fry and put it into her mouth. "You can be a real dweeb sometimes, you know that?"

"I've been so worried about you. With you having to put your Grandmother in the home...losing Johnny...not getting your period...having to live in our basement...well, you've been acting like a zombie and not confiding in me like you used to." As she leaned over to hug Joan, Sue's milkshake spilled over her skirt. "Oh, crap on a stick," Sue blurted out. She jumped out of the car and the rest of the shake spread across the seat. "Cooties—double cooties," she stammered.

Joan bent over in laughter, spilling her own milkshake.

She was still giggling when Sue stopped at the last light heading out of Seattle. "That's what I needed today—some comic relief."

Sue flashed a plastic smile. "Anything for a friend."

"I know I haven't been much of a friend lately." Joan put a hand on Sue's shoulder. "Johnny's death has been...hard."

"Why didn't they hire you to be the nanny?" Sue kept her eyes straight ahead. "You would have been the natural choice."

A knot tightened in Joan's throat. "The Johnsons wanted someone for the long haul. I let them know I wanted to pursue college, so they found someone else. It's that simple."

Sue chewed her thoughts before spitting them out. "Why won't you tell me who knocked you up? I'm your best friend. Do ya think I'll announce it at the next pep assembly or something?"

"I don't want to hurt him."

"You've got to be kidding." Sue gagged on each word. "Are you wiggin' out on me?" She snapped her fingers in front of Joan's face. "Wake up, Joan. Some fat cat got you pregnant. Do you even love him?"

"Yes."

"Does he love you?"

"Well—yes."

"You hesitated."

"It's complicated."

"That's a bunch of bull."

"I can't tell anyone who he is," Joan said. "Not even you. I'm sorry."

Sue's tone softened. "So, what are you going to do?"

"You have to help me get an abortion."

⌘⌘⌘

Joan sat in her car staring blankly out the side window. She never prayed so much in her life as she had leading up to tonight. The church parking lot was dark and empty, except for a Ford station wagon with a long scratch along the right rear panel. It was Thursday night, and Joan knew Hank would still be here putting the finishing touches on his next sermon.

Her heart pounded as she opened the door leading into the sanctuary. Joan willed her heavy feet to move down the middle aisle, where she paused at the rear pew. A water stain marked the spot on the upholstered bench where Hank had placed her rain-soaked body three months ago. Had it really been that long?

She longed to wake up from this nightmare, but the real whammy was all the events in her life since that Sunday morning when Betty had found her and Hank on the couch together. Joan hadn't attended any church service since her adulteress act. She knew in her head that God had forgiven her the first time she prayed for it, but after thousands of shed tears, she was drowning in guilt.

Because of the choices she made that night, her relationship with Hank was dead, Johnny was dead, and her chances of obtaining an academic scholarship were dead because of failing grades this quarter. The only thing alive in her was the unwanted growing mass of living tissue—a relentless reminder of her sin.

"Hello, Joan."

Startled, Joan looked up from the pew to find Hank standing by his podium. "Hello, Pastor."

Hank held up a few typed pages for Joan to see and awkwardly proclaimed, "My sermon notes." He slid them in a drawer on the back side of the podium and inched toward her, measuring each step as he measured her. Stopping two pews from her, he gathered himself with a deep breath. Before tonight, she had never noticed the gray in his temples, the crow's feet etched around his eyes, or how his clothes hung from him like rags on a scarecrow. "I am so sorry." He stared at the floor for an eternity before lifting his gaze. "I am so very sorry."

"Me too," she said, choking back years of memories creeping up her throat.

Hank began to take another step toward her but thought better of it. "In my mind I have formulated a million different ways I have wanted to apologize to you, and when I actually have the opportunity to do so, I can only muster a pathetic, 'I'm sorry.'"

"I didn't come here for an apology," she said, standing as tall as she could. "I came here to ask my pastor for some spiritual advice."

"Do you still trust me with giving you sound advice?"

Joan held her gaze. "I not only still trust your advice over any other man I know, I still love you more than any man I've ever met. I realize now, though, that it would have been far better for the both of us if my love for you would have remained like that of a father rather than what it had become."

Hank turned to the pew, leaning against it with both hands. "What advice can I give you, Joan?"

She reached into her pocket and pulled out a sealed envelope. "Before I say anything more, I've been waiting to give this to you and Betty." She held the envelope out toward Hank. He didn't make any attempt to take it, so she added, "It's a card I picked out for Johnny's funeral. I...I just couldn't go, so I'll give it to you now."

Hank bit his lower lip as he received the card from Joan. "Thank you. I know it must have been hard on you, too."

"Yep," she replied fighting back the tears. She coughed several times into her fist. "Pastor?"

"Yes, Joan."

"Is there any sin God would not forgive?"

Hank pushed himself away from the pew and faced Joan once again. "Guilt over what happened between us and the pain it has caused you and Betty has ripped me up. I have to deal with the consequences of my sin as King David did after his affair with Bathsheba. Keeping this in mind, we must never forget why Jesus died for us on the cross. The author of 1 John writes, 'If we confess our sins, he is faithful and righteous and to forgive us our sins and to cleanse us from all unrighteousness.'"

"Even abortion?"

The word hit Hank like a right hook from a heavyweight prizefighter. He staggered and stumbled into the pew. "You are pregnant?"

"Tough break for me, isn't it?"

Hank ran a trembling hand through his hair. "Let me think about this—are you sure? I mean, Betty had a couple of false alarms before she had Joh..." Hank brought both hands up to cover his face and wept. "I miss him so much." He met her intense gaze and, with tears streaming down his face, said, "I loved him so much. Don't murder your baby."

Hearing Hank say the word *murder* was now an upper-cut to her chin. Joan and Sue had talked about the few options she had: keep the baby and quit school; desperately look for a husband; find a job; have an abortion and run the risk of regretting it for the rest of her life; have the baby and put it up for adoption. She had seriously thought of this option. Her reputation in Soundview would be shot, but she planned on leaving anyway, and she could still go to college. The only thing she feared about this option was knowing she would become emotionally attached after carrying it for nine months. Already she constantly wondered if it was a boy or a girl, what color eyes and hair it would have, and what other physical qualities it would share with both her and Hank. The attachment had started already, so she knew after another six months, giving up the baby might prove impossible. The third option was abortion. At first, Joan resisted this option. The more Sue insisted, the more she realized this was the only option if she were to pursue the life she had dreamt about: college, travel, career, marriage and family—on her terms. The only stumbling block was God. In her heart, she already knew that answer before asking Hank. She supposed she came not so much for his opinion but out of respect to inform him in person what she planned to do.

"Murder's a strong word, Pastor Hank."

"Premeditated murder, Joan."

Joan stepped toward him. "Your sermons have always told of a forgiving God. You talk of a God full of mercy and compassion. The Bible is full of

this. She doesn't know it was you, I swear."

Hank was looking at Joan, but she realized he didn't see her as the girl he had thought of as a daughter. She was now the girl he had made love to on his couch—a problem he was trying to dispose of like an unwanted litter of kittens. "Listen to Patrick. This plan really is the best thing for you, Joan."

"Focus," McCoy said, snapping his fingers in front of Joan's face. "In two weeks, I will fly you back east to a private school, where you will live and finish out your senior year. A part-time job will be waiting for you that will more than compensate you for your living expenses. I will also make arrangements to get you accepted and registered at a college close by."

"What about the baby?" Joan asked warily.

"Ah yes—the baby." The governor placed the cigar back into his breast pocket and tapped it once to push it all the way down. "As you know, my family has suffered a terrible tragedy with the loss of our little Johnny." Hank abruptly opened the door and stormed down the hallway. "Hank and Betty are still tormented by the loss of their son." McCoy pulled his chair to within inches of Joan's. "So far, little lady, all the benefits of this plan have been placed on your side of the scales." He grabbed her hands and had Joan hold them out in front of her, palms up. He then snapped up a handful of pencils from Hank's desk. He placed a pencil in her right hand. "You will get to travel." Another pencil. "Finish high school in a prestigious private academy." Another pencil. "Great paying, part-time job, a free four-year college education, and delivery of your baby, free of charge." Pencil...pencil...pencil.

"What happens to my baby?" Tears misted her eyes.

The governor snatched a Bible from the desk and placed it in her left hand. "Your baby, whom *you* were planning to kill, in less than a week, will be given to Hank and Betty to raise."

Tears streamed down Joan's face. She dabbed at them but couldn't wipe them away fast enough. "What if I change my mind? What if I want to keep the baby?"

"You said yourself that you couldn't go to school and raise a child. Hank tells me a college education has been a lifelong dream for you. This dream is within your grasp, Joan. Don't throw it away." McCoy placed his hands under her outstretched ones and adjusted them so they looked level. "I believe the scales appear to balance, don't you?"

6

I was discharged from the hospital nine days after my "miraculous" awakening. Getting discharged and being fully recovered doesn't mean the same thing unfortunately. After being subjected to more tests than any lab rat should ever have to endure, I was released to Tom. To be completely truthful, if I didn't drag my left leg behind me like the mummy Boris Karloff played, I would have tried to rehab back in Spokane and live out my senior year with my coach. As it was, the team of doctors at Harborview wanted me to rehab close by so they could keep tabs on my progress. Besides the therapy needed for my leg and shoulder, a clinical psychologist was assigned to help me work through my recurring nightmares.

Tom lived in a small resort town on the north end of Camano Island called Bayview. He said from Bayview, on a good day, it took seventy minutes to drive to Harborview and on a bad day, which was the norm, the drive equaled the duration of two Sunday morning services endured back to back. Fortunately, I only had to return to the hospital once a week for four weeks and then once a month if all went well with my rehab.

Tom pulled his Toyota Corolla into a driveway next to a small A-frame house built on a bluff overlooking Bayview's marina and beyond that, Utsalady Bay. I could never remember a trip west of the mountains and seeing the sun; the rain yes—the sun no. Maybe that was part of the reason there was a certain amount of bad blood between us Eastern Washingtonians and our jealous neighbors to the west. General consensus was that all west-siders looked down upon their country cousins from east of the mountains with as much contempt as Microsoft has for computer viruses. I suppose the contempt goes both ways.

At the age of ten, in my first AAU basketball game in Seattle, I was half expecting the other players to be decked out in $200 Nikes and wearing authentic Seattle SuperSonics uniforms with gold chains dangling from their necks and cell phones attached to their ears. Their expectations of us weren't quite as cool. During the game, the Seattle players were constantly trash talking, asking why we weren't wearing bib overalls and straw hats. When one kid said he thought all Eastern Washington kids played basketball in their bare feet, I answered, "Well, at least my feet aren't webbed." He pushed me, and I pushed him, and we were both ejected from the game before half-time. I had to admit, my views of Western Washington have been negative ever since. But seeing the sun reflect like a sparkling jewel over the brilliant blue waters of Puget Sound had me admitting I could never see a sight like this back in Spokane.

Tom opened the door and led me into his living room.

"You still have your Christmas tree up?"

He took my letterman's jacket and hung it on a coat rack. "I didn't think it seemed fair that you slept right on through Christmas so I thought, why don't we celebrate it today?"

I limped over to the tree and touched its needles. Flashes of memories darted through my mind: My parents putting up our Christmas tree in their pajamas; me sitting on my mom's lap, opening presents while Dad took video pictures; Dad and I shooting hoops in the driveway with my new basketball.

The sadness I felt was as intense as the flocked noble fir was beautiful. I turned toward Tom, fighting back tears. "I'm sorry. I'm not up for this today."

"I understand. That's why I thought you might need some prodding."

"Merry Christmas, Ryan." A heavy-set, black woman approached me with a wrapped present held out before her.

"Thank you," I said. Even though this woman was much darker complexioned and heavier than my mother, I could see past the padded layers of skin and wrinkles to see my mom's face; her large round eyes, the gentle slope of her jaw and lopsided smile. "You must be Cathy."

I held out my hand, but she brushed it aside and threw her arms around me.

"Careful, Sis. I don't want to take him back to Harborview the first day we bring him home."

She looked up at me with wet eyes. "You're even taller than your grandfather. Welcome home."

From behind, I heard a ball bouncing. I turned to see my basketball coach dribbling a ball in the kitchen. He tossed over a leather basketball autographed by all the members of my high school team. "The official game ball from our last contest," he commented. "We miss you, Ryan. We've been struggling without our Mr. Everything."

"So you didn't bring any of the guys with you?"

He ruffled my fuzzy head. "Hey, you're not *that* important. I can't just dismiss the whole team from school and drag them over 400 miles so they can masquerade as some globetrotting get-well card."

The words had barely escaped his lips when my eleven teammates stormed in from the outside deck and surrounded me. They gave me gifts, exchanged high-fives, made fun of the bald spot on my head from surgery, and generally hooped and hollered like a pack of hungry coyotes. The celebration lasted until I hobbled to a chair. The room fell awkwardly silent.

"What?" I implied. "None of you ever see an injury before?"

Coach spoke up first. "Sorry, Ryan. We had heard you were doing great; we hadn't heard about your leg."

"I was in a coma for a month; I had surgery on my freak'n brain; both my parents are dead." I slammed the ball off the floor catching it on the rebound. "I don't need a machine to help me breathe; I can eat without half the food dribbling down my chin; and I can figure out the only reason you all came was to hopefully haul me back to Spokane so I could save your pathetic season."

My best friend, Brandon, cautiously stepped away from the pack toward me. "Hey buddy—chill out. Out of everyone here, I know what you're going through. Remember how hard it was last year for me to get over my mom dying from cancer? You gave me some good advice, though. The sooner I started to focus back on sports, the less it hurt."

"You lost one parent. Try losing two."

"You're not alone," Brandon assured me. "We're all here for you. Just begin to focus, get that leg healed, and things will get better."

"Better for who—you, so you don't have the weight of the entire team resting on your shoulders? Is it getting too heavy for a football player to handle?"

"What's got into you, man?" Brandon replied. "All we want to do is encourage a teammate and you go freak'n out on us."

Freak'n out was the mode my brain was embracing at the moment. Funny how I had been kidding myself about aliens taking control of my parents because now I felt infected. Tendrils from some foreign origin were rapidly germinating anxiety and anger throughout every fiber of my being. *Do you really think they care about you, Ryan ol' buddy? You're nothing but a freak in tennis shoes to them. The gift they brought—a bribe. Look at them. Now that they know you're damaged goods, you're worthless to them.* A spark of mistrust ignited a nuclear reaction I couldn't shut down.

"You know what would make me feel better, Brandon?" I whipped the ball behind my back, and it bounced off his thick chest. "Showing everyone here, with only one leg, I can still take you and your sorry jumpshot in a game of one-on-one."

Coach and the boys all looked at me like I had sprouted another head and in a sense, I had. Two voices inside my skull were having a shouting match with each other. The angry voice was winning the battle while the other was relegated to a spectator.

Tom put an arm around my shoulders. "Calm down, son."

"I'm not your son!" I reacted by pushing Tom. He stumbled backward, falling over a foot stool, and landing hard on his hip. Cathy and coach hurried to Tom while I glared at Brandon. "Come on, you flabby side of pork! I saw a hoop outside by the driveway."

"I'm not playing you," Brandon replied. "You've got nothing to prove to me. You've always kicked my butt in basketball but by beating you today, I'd only be taking advantage of a cripple."

"I'm not crippled; I have an injury! I can play through pain, unlike you."

Brandon was massive at six-foot-six and 270 pounds. I felt the gravitational pull from his all-state-defensive-tackle body overpower me as he loitered too long in my personal space. "Yeah, I missed four games last year when my mom died. I was hurting—bad—but you helped me get through it. Are you too cool to let me help you?"

"I don't need your help!" I screamed past Brandon at the other ten players. "I've never needed any of you!"

The football player pressed closer. "I always knew you were cocky but not stupid."

I lunged at him, but he shrugged me off like a pit bull on a bucking bronco. Pain shot through my healing shoulder as I hit the floor. Every swear word I knew erupted from my brain to my vocal cords but met a dead end at my tongue. My tongue was a useless chunk of meat filling space in my mouth. I tried to sit but felt a small tremor course through my body. I tried again but was paralyzed by a series of much larger tremors that, if they had been earthquakes, would have measured at least a 9.0 on the Richter scale. The last thing I remembered was coach sticking a pencil in my mouth and yelling for someone to call the ambulance.

7

The basement was cold and damp this morning. The burnt-out light bulb in the corner, by the washer and dryer, fed the spaces of the cellar where it smelled like dirty, wet socks and the shadows collected darkness. The lone basement window had accumulated so much condensation, Joan wasn't able to see clearly outside, no matter how many times she wiped it off.

She didn't go to school this morning with Sue and never would again. She told her friend she was ill—probably morning sickness. Sue understood, but Joan felt like a traitor. After making the bed, Joan lugged her two suitcases upstairs and set them down by the front door. She took a letter from her purse, walked into Sue's room, and placed it on her pillow. It wasn't hard to write the letter because it was mostly bologna: I can't take it anymore in Soundview...I'm going far away...Don't bother looking for me...I've got to follow my dream...thanks for being such a good friend...yada, yada, yada. What *was* hard was taking one last look at her best friend's room: Pink ribbon and lace...yearbooks...dried flowers...the photo collage of all the birthday parties Sue put on for Joan because Joan's grandmother never would. Still hanging on one wall were both of their old Poodle Skirts, stained with red paint from forgetting to wear aprons during art class in sixth grade.

Joan picked up the receiver to Sue's pink telephone. She was so tempted to call the school and make up any excuse to get her friend out of class; to talk to her one last time. She quickly placed the receiver back in the cradle. She couldn't say good-bye—it was too hard. That's why she wrote the note; that's why she was sneaking away. If she had to tell Sue good-bye, she would never be able to leave. She picked up the envelope, kissed it, and placed it back on Sue's pillow.

After throwing her suitcases in the trunk and settling into the front seat of her car, she pulled out another envelope from her purse. This one she had found taped under the passenger seat four days ago, as she had been told it would. Inside was 300 dollars for abandoning her car at the airport, her airline ticket, and a note explaining to her what to do once she arrived in Chicago.

She had always dreamt of this day when she would drive away and leave Soundview in her rearview mirror. Her infatuation with Hank had always stopped her from leaving before. Now the ties were severed and she was free, but the more she tried to convince herself to be excited, the more bummed she felt. As she rubbed her hand over the small bulge in her abdomen, total freedom would not be realized until this final link to Hank was delivered from her five months from now.

Patchy fog grew from the earth like giant mushrooms as she pulled her car onto Poplar Drive and headed east through the mist toward Interstate 5. She turned on the radio but decided to turn it off and pray. "Lord, this isn't the way I wanted to leave this town. I wanted to leave under my terms and by my timetable. I wanted to travel—but not to Chicago. I don't even know if I ever want to have children, and now I have one growing inside and I'm not even married. My future seems as hard to see as this road in front of me. Help—I'm scared."

She was driving by Soundview Cathedral as she finished up her prayer. The church was shrouded in a soupy haze and took on the ominous appearance of another she had seen in a horror movie. Hank was walking from his car toward the church. Through the fog, he reminded her of the tormented hunchback, Quasimodo of Notre Dame. He walked slowly, shoulders slumped and head bowed. He appeared to look her way as he opened the front door. She wasn't sure if he saw her or not, because his face was obscured by the gloom of the morning's gray shroud.

⌘⌘⌘

Not far from SeaTac Airport, the fog lifted, as did her spirits. She reached into the envelope and touched her airline ticket. Maybe things would work out after all. Once the ordeal of having this baby was over with, she could get on with the rest of her life. Let Hank and Betty raise the baby; it was Hank's responsibility as much as hers. She would then be free to move forward. Free to pursue her dreams.

A Boeing 707 roared skyward as she approached the parking area. The ticket in her hand would put her on a plane like that and send her soaring to a new life. Yes, she was going to be fine—just fine.

⌘⌘⌘

She was petrified disembarking the airplane into O'Hare International Airport. The note from McCoy simply stated someone would contact her at the airport. How would they know her? How would she know them? The airport terminal was a sea of nameless strangers. Joan struggled against the relentless flow of people. She desperately sought a lifeline thrown her way to keep her from drowning in this tempest of flesh and cloth. Out from the waves of humanity appeared a harbor of hope. A tall, thin, dark-haired woman with a cigarette dangling from one corner of her mouth, held up a big sign: *Joan from Soundview—Welcome to Chicago.*

The woman threw down the sign and her cigarette as Joan warily approached and gave her the biggest bear hug Joan had ever received. "Hello, Joan. My name is Mrs. Barletti." The woman held on to Joan's shoulders and took one step backward. She eyed Joan from the soles of her shoes to the top of her head. "You're the first girl we've taken in from the state of Washington. God sure makes them pretty up in the northwest."

"Were you expecting me to have webbed feet and hands?" Joan responded with a little more sarcasm than she had intended.

"Oh, heavens no," Mrs. Barletti answered graciously. "I only expected gills."

Joan blushed. "I'm sorry; that was rude. My past few months have been a real bummer."

The woman rubbed Joan's back. "Don't worry about it. I've received worse greetings from some of the girls I take in. That just comes with the territory."

"What do you mean?" Joan asked.

Mrs. Barletti pulled a pack of Winston cigarettes from her fake leopard skin purse. She lit one and shoved it in the corner of her mouth. "Well, honey, when you run a home for wayward girls, you don't expect them to be as refined as Jacqueline Kennedy."

"I don't understand," Joan said. "I thought I was being sent to a prestigious boarding school."

The lady pulled her cat's-eye sunglasses down her nose and peered over the top of them at the lanky, button-nosed blond standing in front of her. She pulled a piece of paper from her purse and read from it. "Are you Joan Butler from Soundview, Washington?"

"Yes."

"It says here you lived with your elderly grandmother until she sold her house and moved into a nursing home, at which time you moved in with a friend."

"Yes, that's true."

Mrs. Barletti removed her sunglasses. "It says you were an A student until your move and then things began to unravel for you. You began to skip school, flunked two classes, started drinking alcohol, got pregnant, and don't know who the father is."

Joan had to bite her cheek. "Yea, it's something like that."

The older woman put an arm around Joan. "We can talk as we walk to baggage claim." As Mrs. Barletti began to walk, Joan had a hard time keeping up with her. "You don't have any known living relatives, except for a grandmother in a nursing home, you've given up on school, started drinking, and you're pregnant. Sounds like a candidate for our school to me."

"I was under the impression this was a highly esteemed and respectable private school where I would get a good education."

The older woman abruptly stopped. She took a long drag on her cigarette and exhaled with a sigh. "As far as the type of institution I run, this is the best you're gonna find. As long as you don't run away and as long as you give me even half the effort you gave in Soundview, I promise you will graduate in June with a high school diploma." She put her sunglasses back on. "You'll also learn a lot about relationships and survival from living with thirty-four other girls who will look at your resumé and think you were born with a silver spoon in your mouth. You know, in a way you were. I would sure like to meet this anonymous sugar daddy who will be paying all your bills for the next four years." She pulled down her glasses, winked at Joan, and began to fast-walk down the concourse again.

"I thought you were a Mrs.?" Joan asked, spotting the older woman's bare ring finger while trying to keep up with her.

"Oh, I am," she replied, "but my Mr. walked out on me, and I haven't seen hide nor hair of him in over ten years. I figure the statute of limitations on my patience has all but run out for that bum. I think I deserve to be treated as fair game for any male newcomer—don't you?"

After collecting Joan's suitcases, Mrs. Barletti made Joan open one and dig out her heaviest coat. Joan understood why as they stepped outside to hail a cab. Despite the bright sunshine, a bitterly cold wind howled from the north, biting into Joan's cheeks and burning her eyes.

On the ride from the airport, Mrs. Barletti filled Joan in on the history and rules of Joan's new residence—The South Side Home for Wayward Girls. The school was started by a husband and wife who both taught public school but saw a need for the girls who would get in trouble and drop out. This couple bought a small, rundown hotel on the south side of town and successfully ran the school for the next twenty-five years.

After Mr. Barletti left his wife, she had to find work. She found a job at the first place she applied—the same place that had taken her in as a troubled youth and taught her how to read and write but also how to survive in a man's world. After four years of teaching girls how to sew and cook, Mrs. Barletti was asked if she would like to be the institution's next headmaster, when the couple who had run the school the past twenty-five years retired. She accepted and had held the position for the past six years.

The rules were similar to the ones in high school, except for a few differences. No alcohol was allowed on the school grounds...period...no exceptions, but the girls *were* allowed to smoke cigarettes, as long as Mrs. Barletti was the one to purchase them and the girls only smoked them in the game room or outside. No boys were ever allowed in any room except the main lobby, where girls could be seen making out with their boyfriends on the furniture day and night. There was no dress code as long as what you wore was clean. You had to shower at least once a day and brush your teeth twice a day. Everyone took turns cooking meals and cleaning up afterward. You were required to attend every class every day unless you were sick, in which case it was presumed you were also too sick to leave your room to smoke, see a boyfriend, watch television, play games, or use the telephone in the lobby.

Prestigious was definitely not how Joan would have described her first impression of the school. While Mrs. Barletti paid the cabby his fare, Joan took in the exterior of the three-story building. The brick facade was crumbling like Silly Putty left out in the sun too long. All the windows were barred like liquor windows back in Washington. The cement stairs, leading up to a weathered front door, were cracked and chipped. A overweight black girl sat on the bottom step smoking a cigarette. A large, round mound of kinky black hair protruded from her hooded sweatshirt. The girl stood and addressed Mrs. Barletti as she and Joan approached. "Is this her?" the black girl asked.

The headmaster motioned toward Joan. "Cathy, this is Joan. Joan, this is your roommate, Cathy."

Cathy flicked her cigarette to the sidewalk and crushed it with the heel of her boot. She stuck out her hand to Joan. "Hey."

Joan set down her suitcases and hesitantly took Cathy's hand. The black girl's grip was powerful, and Joan felt her hand go limp like a mouse in a trap. She looked back at Mrs. Barletti for reassurance.

"How long have you been out here in the cold?" the older woman asked Cathy. Before Cathy could respond, Mrs. Barletti pushed both the girls up the steps. "We are all going to end up like a frozen dinner if we don't get inside."

Cathy opened the front door and the aroma of pot roast made Joan's stomach growl. She hadn't eaten all day.

"Cathy, show Joan upstairs to your room. Let her get settled and then come down for dinner." She breathed in deeply and exhaled loudly. "Smells delicious."

Joan followed Cathy across the threadbare carpet toward the stairs. They passed a girl and boy tangled in all arms and legs on a couch. As Joan started up the stairs, she heard Mrs. Barletti talk to the couple on the couch. "Billy, would you like to stay for dinner tonight?" The two quickly untangled and Joan heard the boy mutter something with a muffled "Thank you" thrown in. Joan was at the top of the stairs when she heard Mrs. Barletti add, "and of course, you will help with the dishes afterward." The boy jumped off the couch, mumbled something about "stink'n woman's work," and stormed out the front door. The last thing Joan heard before heading down the hall toward her room was the boy's girlfriend screaming at Mrs. Barletti.

By the time Joan had lugged both suitcases upstairs and into the room, she was weary and a little miffed the black girl hadn't offered to help. "That's your bed over there." The girl pointed to a single bed whose mattress looked as if an elephant had been the tired bed's last occupant.

Cathy sat down on her own bed, which didn't sag even with the heavy girl on it. She pulled out a record from its jacket and positioned it on a turntable placed on top of a weathered desk. The desk was once painted white, but more of the natural wood showed through than the paint. The rhythm of big band jazz jumped from the little speakers. A smooth female voice soon accompanied the band.

"Aretha Franklin," Cathy stated flatly.

"Never heard of her." Joan answered while putting clothes in a small dresser beside her bed.

Cathy bobbed her head to the music. "Girl—she'll be more famous than Elvis or Sedaka or Anka."

"At least you've heard of them." Joan's clothes were not all going to fit in these four shallow drawers.

Cathy was silent for a moment. "You don't recognize Aretha, because she's black."

"I could care less if she's black, purple, pink or blue. I don't know her and just from what I hear so far, you won't be listening to *her* on American Bandstand."

Cathy sat up in bed. "I saw the way you looked at Mrs. B. when she told you we were roommates. I know what you were thinking. You were thinking, 'Please don't put me in the same room as that Nigger.' When I shook your hand, it was like grabbin' hold of a wet noodle. You didn't even want to touch me. What are you afraid of? Maybe you never seen a person with black skin before?"

"What's your bag, anyway?" Joan asked. "I've just flown halfway across the country. I'm tired, I'm hungry, and all I really would like is a little peace and quiet." Joan had filled up her little dresser and still had her socks and underwear left. "And for your information, once a month I would volunteer to feed people like you down at the homeless shelter in Seattle."

Cathy climbed out of her bed and opened a drawer that was empty in her dresser. "Well I guess it's my turn to volunteer and help out you white folks because, girl, in this place we are all finally equal." She turned and walked out the door, leaving the drawer open.

After putting on fresh but somewhat wrinkled clothes, Joan made her way downstairs. The lobby was deserted, but she followed her ears and nose to the dining room. The room was set up restaurant style with girls seated in folding chairs set up around circular tables, each covered with stained table cloths. Faded silk flowers, protruding from empty soup cans, graced the tops of each table.

Between three to five girls sat chatting away at each table and didn't notice Joan as she entered. Cathy sat alone at a table closest to the kitchen. Joan made her way to the back of the room and sat down at Cathy's table. "Thanks for letting me use one of your drawers."

"You don't have to sit with me just because we're roommates," Cathy said while pushing her fork around the table with her finger.

Joan grabbed the fork. "You were right."

"Give me my fork." The black girl snatched the fork out of Joan's hand.

"You make me feel uncomfortable," Joan said. "I was hoping for at least one thing here that would seem familiar—that would make me feel like I was back in Washington."

"And it sure ain't me, is it?" Cathy pointed toward the kitchen. "Well, if it would make you feel any better, pretend you're at the homeless shelter and go dish up some food for me, and give me your portion while you're at it."

Joan got up and walked through the swinging doors into the kitchen. Mrs. Barletti and a handsome, young black man were dishing up plates with food while the Beach Boys' *Surfin USA* blared over the radio above the stainless steel sink.

Mrs. Barletti turned to Joan as she approached. "What are you doing back here, sugar?" She placed a big spoonful of potatoes on a plate.

"Need any help?" Joan asked.

The headmistress passed the plate to the man standing next to her. He grabbed it without looking at Joan and put a generous slice of roast beef on it.

78

"We never give a new girl any responsibilities her first week," Mrs. Barletti said. "Go find a seat. Meet some of the girls. I know you're starving, so we'll make sure to serve your table first." She gave Joan a quick, one-handed hug and turned back to her potatoes.

"Mrs. Barletti?"

The older woman turned back to Joan, patience still plastered across her face, but her voice betrayed her true feelings. "I'm really very busy, sugar. What is it?"

"I don't need my food yet, but would you mind if I served Cathy her food myself?"

The young man peeked toward Joan.

"If you're trying to score brownie points with Cathy, this isn't the way to do it." Mrs. Barletti handed her helper another plate. "She'll only think you're trying to patronize her."

"I was rude to her upstairs," Joan began. "She's sitting all by herself, and I bet she does every meal. This would be my way of saying, 'I'm sorry—let's be friends.'"

Before Mrs. Barletti could respond, the young black man handed her a full plate of food.

"Go ahead," he said and smiled. He had the most beautiful smile Joan had ever seen.

"Thanks," she said. "I won't bother you two anymore."

She pushed back through the swinging doors, strolled over to the table, and set the food down in front of Cathy. Instead of looking pleased or even smug she had coerced Joan into submission, the black girl looked upset. "Quick, take it back before they see what you did," she whispered to Joan.

The words had barely left Cathy's lips when someone hollered in a Southern drawl, "Look, I believe that Nigger got served before any of us."

Four girls from one of the tables got up and approached Joan and Cathy. The black girl pushed the plate of food across to Joan. "It's not mine; it's hers."

The blond with the Southern drawl spoke first. "I distinctly remember seeing your friend here set this food down in front of you." She reached over and pushed the plate back in front of Cathy. "Yes, that's how I remember it."

Joan's gaze darted from the troublemaker in the sunflower print dress to Cathy. The black girl's eyes burned with anger as she chewed on her lower lip.

Joan stood and extended her hand to anyone who would take it. "Hi, I'm..."

"You're Joan, we know." A brunette in a short bob spoke up. They all ignored Joan's outstretched hand. "Since you're new around here, we'll cut ya some slack. You don't want to eat with this black pig." The brunette grabbed Joan's wrist to lead her away, but Joan wouldn't budge.

She yanked her hand away. "What's wrong with all of you?" Joan asked, staring down all four girls.

"No nigger is gonna get her meal before the rest of us," the brunette said.

Joan noticed Mrs. Barletti backing through the kitchen's double doors while carrying four plates of food. Her kitchen helper was right behind with four more plates. With a tilt of her head, the Southern belle addressed Joan. "If you insist on eating with pigs, don't let us stop you." With that said, she pushed the plate of food off the table into Cathy's lap.

Cathy jumped to her feet, her large belly catching the edge of the table, tipping it over. Her mouth agape, she spread her arms out and bent her head, examining the potatoes and gravy running down the front of her blouse.

"Tom!" Mrs. Barletti yelled. "Quick!"

Cathy began to shake. A low moaning rumbled from deep inside her. It suddenly erupted into a savage roar, and she lunged toward her tormentors. From behind, Tom wrapped his long arms around Cathy and pulled her away from the four smiling girls. He held on tight and talked into her ear. "Don't let them beat you," he said loud enough for everyone to hear. "Don't let them win, baby. Don't let them."

Mrs. Barletti pointed at Joan. "Help him take Cathy up to your room."

The four girls defiantly stood their ground as Joan walked beside Cathy, who had turned her back to them and was being hugged by Tom. He looked over her shoulder at the four and said harshly, "Shame on you girls."

The blond stepped toward him and put her hands on her hips. "She doesn't belong here, and neither do you." She leaned forward and spit in his face.

The black man did nothing. With spittle running down his chin, he simply put an arm around Cathy's shoulder and said, "Come on, baby. Let's get you cleaned up."

Joan gently grabbed Cathy's hand, but the black girl shoved her away. "Go away. You've helped me enough already."

Tom looked over his shoulder at Joan. "I'll take care of her. You go help Mrs. B."

⌘ ⌘ ⌘

Joan was exhausted. Everyone had been served, tables cleared, dishes washed, dishes put away, and floors mopped. Mrs. Barletti excused the other girl who

her mouth.

"Shhhh!" a voice whispered. "It's Tom. You don't want to be putting your hand on that hot heater."

Joan didn't know Tom—didn't know anything about him except he was Cathy's brother.

She struggled to pull his hand away from her mouth, but he kept it firmly in place. "I'm sorry I startled you," he whispered. "All I wanted to tell you was that my sister is asleep, and I'm going to leave so you can have your bed back." He cautiously removed his hand from her mouth and knelt beside the couch.

Joan slapped him on the side of his head. "You scared me half to death."

Tom wasn't as dark as his sister, but he still blended in with the shadows. His eyes, though, were bright and kind, and when he smiled, those teeth almost lit up the dark room.

She could see him rubbing the side of his head. "For my own safety, I won't ever do that again."

"How can I help her?" Joan sat up, pulling the wool blanket to her chin.

Tom settled on the armrest. "That's a good question. I left home three years ago for college when she was a beautiful thirteen-year-old so full of life I thought she would explode." He moved onto the couch so he could lower his voice. "Every summer when I came home, though, she was heavier and more sullen. I tried to talk to her, but she wouldn't open up to me like she used to."

Joan could see a wet sheen in his eyes as he continued.

"At first I thought she was upset I had gone away to college. I thought maybe she was feeling abandoned, even though I'd write her at least once a week."

"What about your adoptive parents?"

"They loved her—and me. We couldn't have asked for better parents. They have done everything for us despite losing friends, clients, and the respect they had in the community we grew up in because they adopted two black kids."

"Why is she so negative of white people when the people who raised her are Caucasian?"

"This place hasn't helped her perception none, but we grew up with many people in our hometown never accepting us. Not fitting in always bothered me more than her. She was the positive one. What you see upstairs is not the sister I grew up with. Something happened while I was away at college that's changed her."

A car's horn blared, followed by angry voices, reminded Joan she was not living in her friend's house in the country. "So you have no idea why she's all bummed out?"

Tom stood. "That's the thing driving me crazy. I don't know." He pointed toward the front door. "I'd better split. My first class is in five hours. You'd better lock the door behind me; it's a rough neighborhood, especially this time of night."

Joan rose from the couch, securely wrapped her blanket around her, and followed Tom to the front door. He unlatched the dead bolt and turned toward her. The porch light filtering through the frosted glass on the front door glowed around Tom's head like a halo. "You seem like a nice girl. There aren't too many around here."

"Please tell that to your sister." Joan motioned toward the stairs with her head. "I don't think *she* believes that."

Tom folded his arms and leaned against the door. "You started to say something to my sister earlier tonight about how God would give her the grace she would need."

"Yeah, and she almost bit my head off for mentioning it."

Tom shook his head slowly and stared past Joan. "Cathy believes God has turned His back on her. Deep down in their hearts, all the girls here feel betrayed by God in one way or another."

"To tell you the truth," Joan said, "I'm feeling more than a little bummed about being here myself."

Tom returned his gaze back upon Joan. "The Cathy I knew when I left for college would have looked at this as a divine appointment from God. This would be an adventure to explore and figure out what special task God had called her to."

"Don't you think you are being a little too copacetic?"

"All these girls feel God has turned his back on them, when in reality, it's each of them who have turned their back on God." He lifted his head slightly and the porch light glowed on his face, igniting a flame in his gentle eyes. He tapped his finger against her forehead. "I see Christ in you." Tom sniffed the air. "You smell like Christ." He cupped his hand to his ear. "When you speak, I hear Christ."

"You sound like a pastor I once knew."

"I'm not attending seminary to sound like one. I hope someday people will see Christ in me like I see Him in you."

Joan took a step backward. "You don't know anything about me. You don't know the awful thoughts I think. You don't know the awful things I've done. If I am so wonderful, then why am I here?"

"To set the captives free."

86

Joan stifled a laugh. "So now you make me out as God's feminine version of Moses."

"One day Cathy will see in you what I see, and then she will allow you to be a friend." He opened the door and a frigid wind pushed past Tom, into the lobby, like an uninvited guest. He pulled the hood to his jacket over his head and stuck out a hand to Joan. "I'll see you again soon."

Joan took his hand and shook. "I'll see you again, Pastor Tom."

Joan closed the door enough to keep most of the wind out but open enough to still allow her to watch Tom descend the stairs two at a time. At the bottom he stopped. After pointing a finger toward the night sky, he slapped his hands together before shoving them into his jacket. She could hear him whistle an unfamiliar tune as he strolled down the sidewalk. Joan then closed the door and set the deadbolt.

She snatched her pillow from the couch and made her way toward the stairs. The temperature seemed to drop with each step she climbed. At the top of the stairs, she was tempted to turn around, run back down, and snuggle up in the couch by the heater. Joan froze as she heard a muffled cry drift down the dark corridor. The only light in the long hallway was directly above her head, so looking down the hall was like looking into the mouth of a black cave. She heard a door creak open and forced herself to step away from the light. Without the glare of the overhead light, her eyes began to adjust. She heard it again; a muted cry and a shuffling in the hall straight ahead. Her legs turned to ice pillars. She leaned forward, wanting to see but hoping not to. Hearing movement ahead, she leaned against the wall for balance but not too far from the security of the light behind her. Indiscernible gray shadows gathered in the darkness twenty feet before her.

Five ghostly figures materialized from the depths of the cave. She gasped as she heard something escape from the black hole and skitter towards her across the wood floor. A small object slid into her slipper; it was a pair of scissors—scissors with unclean blades. She let her blanket drop to the floor and with trembling hands picked up the scissors. Covering her mouth with one hand, she held the cutting device in the other. The blades of the scissors were covered with long, kinky black hair clinging to moist, red blood.

Turn and run. Run down the stairs, out the front door, and keep on running. That's what her mind demanded of her. A stronger force pushed her forward—into the dark hole—toward the phantoms. Instead of repulsion, she clung to the scissors for protection and carefully felt her way down the hall. With each deliberate step she took, the ghostly apparitions receded further into the darkness until they vanished around a corner.

She ran blindly to her room and pushed open the door. Joan placed a trembling finger on the light switch but hesitated. Fear grabbed hold of her hand. Images of Cathy's slit throat, resembling a ghastly smile drooling blood from the corners of this second mouth, paralyzed her. It was all those horror movies and books she had read over the years while babysitting. She heard the same frantic, muffled cry come from Cathy's bed. She was alive!

Joan flipped on the light switch. Cathy lay naked in bed. She had been bound on her wrists and ankles with duct tape. Several more strands of silver tape stretched across her face holding in a sock shoved into her mouth. Her nearly bald head rested in a pile of her own sheared hair atop a bloodied pillow. Fresh blood flowed from a gash in her ear and several more on her head. Cathy's terrified gaze fell from Joan's face to the bloody scissors clutched in Joan's hand. The black girl fought against the tape like a trout in a fisherman's net.

Joan tossed the scissors aside and dropped to her knees beside her roommate. She attempted to peel the tape from Cathy's mouth, but the frightened girl continued to recoil and squirm. Joan climbed on top of her and, grasping a corner of the tape, yanked it off with one sudden pull. Cathy began to gag. Joan reached in to pull out the sock but was bit. She tried again and the black girl clamped down harder, drawing blood this time. Joan pinched her roommate's cheeks hard enough to force her to open her mouth. She pulled one of the socks from Cathy's mouth and the black girl screamed. Without help, Joan knew she couldn't control her roommate's rage, so she left her bound up. While still straddling the frightened girl, Joan leaned over and with both arms embraced Cathy, whispering into her ear, "It's okay, scream. I won't leave you." Joan heard doors open and footsteps pad down the hall toward her room. Cathy continued to scream as Joan continued to whisper into her roommate's ear, "I won't leave you."

⌘⌘⌘

Joan was exhausted. She hadn't slept a wink the night before her flight to Chicago and had only slept about three hours last night. She now sat in Mrs. Barletti's office, her head resting on folded arms spread out over the headmistress's desk. The midmorning sun shone through a grimy window onto Joan. She soaked in the warmth like a cat by a flaming hearth. The smell of stale cigarettes and bitter coffee filled the air, so she filtered the funky odor by breathing through her shirt sleeve.

Mrs. Barletti burst into the room while filing her long nails. As Joan

⌘ ⌘ ⌘

Joan took the math test in the hall the following day. Fortunately, there was an overhead light right above the cot Mrs. Barletti set up for her. Joan talked Mrs. B. into letting her sleep a second night in the hall as Cathy still refused to let her in. Tom brought two plates of food for dinner the second night along with Joan's math, history, and English books to read. Again, Cathy refused to let Joan in but begged her brother to bring in her food. He refused but sat down on the cot next to Joan instead. He held out a plate of food toward her. She bit her lip and shook her head.

"Please don't tempt me, Tom. I'm so hungry I could eat the hind end off a skunk."

Tom set the plate down and turned toward Joan. He smiled, but it wasn't one of his blinding, put on your shades smiles. He didn't even show his teeth. This smile was as tender as filet mignon. "I appreciate what you are trying to do, but you don't have to do it."

"Have you ever seen the *Wizard of Oz?*" Joan asked.

"Has anybody not seen it?" Tom replied.

"Do you remember how at the beginning of their journey to find the Wizard, none of the characters got along? They didn't trust each other at first. It wasn't until they had gone through the trials of defeating the wicked witch that they learned to trust one another."

Tom flashed his ear-to-ear grin. "I think I'll start having you write my book reports."

"Do you understand why I have to do this?"

Tom patted Joan's hand. "Yeah, but don't you go killing my baby sister to show her how much you love her. That might make me mad."

"What if it killed me?" Joan asked. "Would you still be mad?"

Tom blinked rapidly and fumbled to get the words out. "I...well I...I don't think I would ever be able to forgive myself for letting you do it."

"Do you have any homework to do tonight?" Joan picked up her English book.

Tom pointed down the corridor. "I left it in the kitchen."

"Would you like to come back and study with me? It's kinda lonely down this hallway."

"I'll be back before you can say chicken-fried steak."

Joan laughed and plugged her ears. "I can't hear you." She unplugged her ears and pointed towards the plates of food. "Take them back with you. I can't be trusted with them alone."

Tom picked them up. "Can I bring you back anything?"

Joan pressed her hands against her stomach as it grumbled in protest. "Yeah, bring me back two or three glasses of water. I don't have a faucet out here like Cathy does in her room."

⌘⌘⌘

The third day, Joan saw curious girls taking the long route from the dining room to their classes. Instead of leaving the dining room from the west door, which would exit directly to the corridor all the classes were on, the girls took the north exit through the lobby and left down the hall where only Mrs. Barletti, the crazy black girl, and her even crazier white friend resided. Some girls genuinely wanted to know why Joan would do what she was doing for a black girl. Others would tempt Joan with leftovers from the kitchen. But most heaped taunts and ridicule upon her.

Most of the third day Joan tried to study or read from the Bible but because her stomach was empty, her mind filled with thoughts of food. Mrs. Barletti reluctantly allowed Joan to continue her quest and eagerly brought breakfast and lunch, only to leave as frustrated as a mother trying to force spinach through her child's locked lips.

In the afternoon, after writing a paper for English, three girls approached Joan. They all continuously glanced over their shoulders as though being caught with Joan was the equivalent to being caught buying beer from an older friend in the church parking lot. They introduced themselves as Bobbie, Karen, and Jill. Jill, a redhead with a distinct Irish accent, did most of the talking.

"Most of the girls here think you're just acting the maggot," Jill began, "but we think fair play to ya."

"Thank you—I think," Joan said and shook Jill's outstretched hand while the other girls nodded their approval.

"Tell me now," Jill said, peering nervously over her shoulder, "did ya really reef on the KKK with a bloody knife or is that all a horse's hoof?"

Joan frowned, puzzled.

Karen pushed past Jill to translate. "Did you really go after the KKK with the knife used to stab the nigger, or are you trying to con your way up to the queen's table?"

"If you expect to sit at the queen's table," Jill said, pointing toward Cathy's door, " ya are a right idiot to try to make that black one in there yer friend. Her royal highness hates her with a passion, she does."

Bobbie, a short, stocky girl with no neck, piped up. "When you're done playing babysitter, you're welcome to eat at our table."

Joan began to speak but Jill interrupted her. "Begorra! The royal banshee is coming." She put her arms around her friends. "Just keep up the blather. I'll have a little talk with 'er."

The Southern Belle, who had dumped the food in Cathy's lap strutted toward the group. "My, my," she said, "we must be having a little party."

"Howya, Claire," Jill said.

"You surely know how I love parties so." Claire playfully grabbed the taller girl by the wrists and squealed. "Did you smuggle in some Irish whiskey like you did before?"

Jill turned toward Joan and shoved her hard against the wall. Her head snapped back and knocked loose some plaster onto her lap. "The other birds and me was only having a little fun with 'er, that's all."

"Now that's no way to treat our host," Claire said, squeezing between the other two girls to have a look at Joan. "I must say Joan, you do have a lot to learn about how to host a party. You didn't even provide any food for your guests."

Joan wiped the plaster from her hair and flashed an angry gaze toward Jill, who backed up a step behind Claire, mouthed, "Sorry," and shrugged.

Claire pulled out a tissue from a pocket in her dress, wiped the plaster off a corner of the cot and sat down next to Joan. "While I am very disappointed I wasn't invited to your party, and proper etiquette deems it deplorable to not provide some form of food for your guests, I will, out of the goodness of my heart, find some food to smuggle up here to you."

"I'm not eating until Cathy does." Joan gingerly touched a lump on the back of her head.

Claire gracefully stood. "Well, by all means then, I shall waste no effort in bringing back two plates full of food." She ran to Cathy's peephole and looked in. "And if that little black tramp won't open the door, I know where Mrs. Barletti keeps her spare keys." Claire pounded mercilessly on the door. "Once we get inside, Cathy, there are enough of us to force your mouth open and shove the food down your throat 'til it comes out your—"

"Claire!" Mrs. Barletti called from the entrance to the lobby. Her cigarette shifted from one side of her mouth to the other. "Get away from that door!"

Jill grabbed her friends. "Time for us to skedaddle." She pointed at Joan and, with a wink said, "Mind yerself now."

Jill and her friends were around the corner before the headmistress stopped in front of Claire, who stood defiantly before her.

Mrs. Barletti set down the plate of food. She stared down at the girl six inches shorter than the older woman. "What are you doing here?"

"Why, helping Joan to get that little ol' door open, of course." Claire batted her eyes mockingly. "Why must you always be so suspicious of me?"

"Suspicion is having doubts about someone's intentions, and I have no doubt your intentions have nothing to do with good will." The headmistress pointed toward the lobby. "Go eat your lunch, and then you can enjoy clean-up duties all by yourself today."

Blood rushed into Claire's ivory face, transforming it into a dark mask. "That would take me all afternoon."

"I don't want to find out the queen bee has coerced one of her worker bees into doing her dirty work for her, either." Mrs. Barletti pointed again toward the lobby. "Now get out of here."

As Claire stomped away, she warned, "My daddy's gonna hear about this—about all of this."

"So, who's her daddy?" Joan asked.

Mrs. B. plopped onto the cot. "He's some bigwig, real-estate developer from Alabama who spent way too much time developing his business and not enough time developing his daughter."

Cathy still refused to open up for lunch and dinner, Tom spent another few hours studying on the cot with Joan, and day three slipped into blackness as Joan dreamt about food all night.

⌘⌘⌘

Early in the morning of the fourth day, Joan awoke with a start to a strange sound. She swore she had heard the low rumble of thunder, but it had sounded close—very close—so close she peeked under her cot. *Must have been a dream,* she thought, until a clap of pain shot through her stomach. Grumbling stomach and hunger pains...thunder and lightning. She had never understood hunger like this before, although she had seen it in the eyes of the homeless while serving them dinner once a month at the shelter in Seattle.

She closed her eyes and prayed, "Dear Heavenly Father, I know Your Son fasted for forty-days in the desert and in His weakened condition was then tempted by the devil, but He resisted temptation. I know this is only the beginning of my fourth day, counting the day I flew here, but don't let me be tempted today. Cathy just has to open that door when Mrs. B. brings breakfast, or I'll fall and crack bigger than Humpty Dumpty." She hesitated, then added, "and forgive me for thinking I was better than those homeless people I served food to. You know my thoughts, so I guess You know the only reason I helped was so I could be with Hank and make myself look good in his eyes."

Joan sat up and listened. She heard voices but not the kind that echoed and bounced off walls announcing the impending arrival of their owners. Instead she heard secretive voices that clung to walls and lurked in shadows.

Thrusting her hand into her front pocket, she clutched the security of two keys. She carefully slid off the cot and tip toed to Mrs. B's door. She pulled out one of the keys and slipped it into the lock; it wouldn't turn—wrong key! She heard another noise—something was closer. She stole a peek to her left. Three phantoms dressed in white, with red crosses painted on their robes, stood twenty feet away. She shot a glance to her right. Two more phantoms, holding packages wrapped in tape, blocked the hall in the other direction. Silently, the phantom figures inched forwards. The ghostly apparitions appeared to drift through the air toward Joan.

While attempting to shove the wrong key in her pocket, it fell to the floor. She frantically fumbled for Mrs. B's key with her other hand. As she yanked the key from her pocket, it slipped from her jittery fingers onto the side of her foot and bounced halfway between her and the floating sheets. She banged repeatedly on the headmistress's door until the figures loomed around her in a tight semi-circle. She slowly quit pounding on the door until the only noise she heard was the pounding inside her chest. She rested her forehead against the door while her racing heart threatened to gallop out of her chest. It was only then that she heard another noise—the distant sound of the radio playing in the kitchen. Mrs. Barletti was already up helping Tom with breakfast. They would be busy for at least an hour and, as long as the radio stayed on, wouldn't hear a tornado blow through this corridor.

"We brought you some food, Joan." The voice was male.

Someone grabbed her and roughly spun her. The tallest of the costumed KKK members had a hold of her. He tilted his head as he examined her. Looking past the hood into his eyes was like staring past the eyes of a jack-o-lantern into an unquenchable fire. He pulled her over to the cot and forced her onto it. Taking a package wrapped in butcher paper from another phantom, he tossed it in Joan's lap.

"We tried to warn you," the male voice said, "but you wouldn't listen." He bent over, and Joan could smell vapors of alcohol seeping through the fabric of his hood. "We knew you haven't eaten for a while, so we brought you a present. Open it."

She grabbed the package and reared back to throw it. The man caught her arm and twisted it until she yelped in pain. The bundle dropped onto the floor. He swore and slapped her face. "You are an ungrateful little wretch, aren't you?"

"I haven't done anything to you," Joan pleaded. "Please let me go."

The man shoved the package back onto her lap. "Open it!" With trembling fingers, she worked at the tape. The man continued. "You think you are this nice little Christian girl trying to be a hero. What you really are is a threat to the chosen race of God. You need to quit attempting to help one of His enemies." He pointed toward Cathy's door. "Satan is the exact opposite of God. God is good; Satan is bad. God is love; Satan is hate. God is light; Satan is darkness. Not only is Satan darkness, all his children represent his darkness. The black thing behind that door you are trying to befriend is a daughter of Satan."

She unenthusiastically tugged at the tape, hoping Mrs. Barletti forgot to bring her cigarettes to the kitchen with her. Maybe Tom would stop by to check up on her and Cathy.

The man pushed the bundle up to her face. "The tape can't be that hard to tear. Use your teeth if you have to."

With the butcher paper pressed against her mouth, she inhaled a faint smell of meat. Could it be these pretenders of the faith actually brought her something good to eat? Her stomach, not her mind, now controlled her actions. She tore cautiously at the tape with her teeth until the scent of meat intensified. Then she ripped recklessly at the tape with both her fingers and teeth until the butcher paper was finally free to be unwrapped. She quickly unfolded the paper. The aroma was very strong now, and her stomach growled with anticipation as she lifted the bundle of meat out from the man's shadow. While her sense of smell had been distorted from hunger, her sense of sight was as keen as ever. With a shriek, she dropped the quivering mass of rotting matter to the floor, watching cockroaches and maggots swarm over the indiscernible heap of brown flesh.

"Are you missing these?" He held up the two keys she had dropped. "Let's see which one will open that nigger's door, so we can bring this yummy food inside and watch you two eat it all."

Joan jumped up, but he pushed her against the wall. "Hold her," he commanded the other sheets. The four other KKK members held on to Joan as the man walked over to the door and inserted a key. He twisted the key and turned the doorknob—still locked. Cursing he threw the worthless key to the floor. He promptly slipped in the second key and turned—still nothing. He roared and whirled, throwing the key at Joan. "Where is it?"

"I don't have it." Joan struggled against the eight hands holding her.

The man stormed across the hall and seized Joan around the throat as the other sheets held her arms and legs. She gasped for breath but instead heard a sound like a giant spring unwinding inside her head. Her sense of sound unraveled. She heard the commotion around her, but she heard it from her past. She heard her angry grandmother call out to her while she hid under the water in the bathtub as a little girl. The edges of her field of vision grew fuzzy and dark. She willed herself to focus but could only see down a tunnel past the man at Cathy's door. The tunnel narrowed, but then the door swung open.

Cathy sprang into the hall carrying a sword. She felt the weight of the man leave her as he turned toward Cathy. She jabbed the weapon into the man's hood. His hands went to his face, and he toppled to the floor. One of the sheets let go of Joan to assist the man curled up in a ball on the floor. Another hood popped in front of Joan's field of vision, and the sword was thrust into that sheet's side. With a shrill cry, the sheet grabbed its side and stumbled over the injured sheet already on the floor. Another sheet let go of Joan to confront Cathy.

The last hood appeared inches in front of Joan's face, and a new set of hands clenched her throat. She could clearly see bright blue eyes with long curly lashes inside this hood. A feminine voice spewed out obscenities concerning the missing key. Joan flailed at the hands around her throat but couldn't pry the determined pit bull loose. Frantically she clawed at her tormentor's face until the two fingers of her right hand found the girl's eyes. With a shriek, the sheet fell to the floor, writhing like a worm on a hook.

Joan gagged, sucking air into her hungry lungs. Two sheets were on the floor to her left. One was trying to stand while holding its blood-soaked side, and the other was still impersonating a squirming worm. To her right, the smaller sheet was helping the male sheet to sit up. The man removed a bloody hand away from his face. A large red stain saturated one eye hole. For a moment his good eye was riveted on Joan and she shivered. Then his attention diverted to Cathy. She was fighting off a sheet with what appeared to be a broom and, keeping his gaze focused on her, the man attempted to stand.

Joan reached for the closest weapon she could find—her math book. She threw it, hitting him flush across the front of his face. With a howl, he clutched his face once again. Joan scrambled to Cathy, pushed the other sheet from behind into the wall and pulled Cathy into her room. They closed and locked the door just as a fist slammed into it from the other side. Both girls leaned against the door with their backs not trusting the deadbolt to keep out the angry sheets.

When the only thing they heard was their own panting, Joan noticed the broom handle still clutched firmly in Cathy's hands. The tip had been whittled to a sharp point.

Joan nodded to the broom tip. "You must have been pretty hungry," she whispered. "I know my pillow was starting to look like a marshmallow."

A faint smile crossed the other girl's face, and she pulled a Swiss Army Knife from her pocket. "Tom gave it to me for protection, but I feel better with this." She held up the broom; the sharp tip was red.

Cathy looked through the peephole. "See anyone?" Joan asked.

The black girl shook her head but leaned back against the door. "They could be hiding out there, just waiting for us to come out."

"What took *you* so long to come out?" Joan stared at the ceiling as she asked the question.

"I thought it would be a good time to lose the sixty pounds I gained the past three years."

"Hey, I mean it." Joan said. "Why didn't you let me in?"

"I don't trust no one."

"You can trust me. I want to be your friend."

Cathy stepped away from the door and sat on her bed. She pulled out her toothbrush from under her pillow—the handle tapered to a sharp point. "I don't need any friends." She waved the deadly end of the toothbrush at Joan.

"If you don't trust me, then why did you risk your own neck to help me out in the hall?"

Cathy jumped off the bed and held the sharp toothbrush under Joan's chin. The black girl then reached in Joan's back pocket, pulled out a room key, and backed away. "I saw Mrs. B. give this to you and watched as you put it in your back pocket. There was no way I was gonna let the KKK find it and trap me in my own room."

"That key proves I don't want to hurt you. I could have entered this room any time I wanted to, but I didn't. I wanted to wait until you invited me in."

Cathy backed up to the barred window and glanced nervously into the back alley. "Girl, that proves only two things. That you're stupid to think I would want to be your friend after starving me...and to want to be my friend when you know the KKK is after me."

"Looks like I need a friend worse than you do."

Cathy skirted past Joan and stared out the peephole again. "I would rather know who my enemies are. I can at least protect myself from them." She jabbed the pointed end of the toothbrush into the door. "It's people who say they are your friends who stab you in the back."

Someone kicked the bottom of the door. Cathy pulled the toothbrush from the door and peeked through the peephole. She screamed and stumbled into bed. Joan cautiously looked into the hole in the door. A giant eye was staring back at her. Her heart beat in Morse code as she imagined the man holding his severed, bloody eyeball up to the peephole,.

"Hey sis, what's going on in there?"

Joan exhaled and looked through the peephole again. Tom stepped back from the door and held up a plate of food in each hand. Joan threw back the dead bolt and opened the door. As soon as Tom crossed the threshold, the girls attacked him.

"Whoa, whoa!" he said, holding the plates above his head. "Where's your manners?"

Cathy punched him in the stomach. He doubled over, and Cathy grabbed both plates of food. "Thank you," she said sitting on the bed with both plates on her lap. "There's my manners."

Tom walked over to the bed holding his stomach. "What was that for?"

"That's for not bringing me any food for the past three days," Cathy answered while shoving three pieces of bacon into her mouth.

As the smell of breakfast wafted up to Joan, her jaw ached with saliva pumping through glands, rusty from neglect. Joan shut the door and set the deadbolt again.

"What's wrong with you?" Tom asked Cathy. "One of those plates is for her." He turned to Joan. "Thanks for shutting that door. It smelled like something died out th—" Tom placed his hand gently on her cheek and then ran it down her throat. "What happened, Joan?" He looked at Cathy. "Did my sister do this to you?"

"Sure, blame me for everything." Cathy picked up a handful of hash browns. "She was entertained by the white clowns this morning."

⌘⌘⌘

The police notified the area hospitals to report any emergency room activity regarding all eye injuries and puncture wound injuries to the chest. All the rooms at the school were searched, and the only thing found were two packages of putrid meat decaying under Joan's cot in the hall. While Joan didn't have a clue who the male sheet was, she was surprised to find out no girls from their school had reported eye or chest injuries. The police found no sign of a forced entry, so Mrs. B. had stronger locks installed on all exterior doors, which also required a key to be opened from the inside to keep an alarm from sounding. She kept that key on her at all times. She also imposed a nine o'clock curfew and removed the radio from the kitchen. The police added the school to their security patrol hot list. Another week passed while Cathy still refused to join everyone in the dining room.

Joan marched down the hall to Cathy's room like she had done three times a day for the past week, except this time she carried no trays of food. The only thing in her hands was a safety razor and a can of shaving cream. Cathy stumbled back into her room, tears welling in her eyes as she saw what Joan carried with her. The terrified girl reached under her pillow and with trembling hands produced the lethal toothbrush. Joan said nothing, but instead sat on the floor in front of the full-length mirror, massaged shaving cream into her scalp, and with one stroke cut a swath down the middle of her head with the safety razor.

8

"Okay, Doc," Tom began, "before you send us home again, let's go over this one more time." Tom sat at the foot of my hospital bed massaging his temples. "So there is no connection between Ryan's seizure and his violent outbursts—correct?"

The doctor glanced at his watch, making sure we both knew he was on a tight schedule. "Even if they were connected, the treatment of each condition is not dependent on the other. Ryan will take the anti-seizure medication prescribed, and the latest assessment from the neuropsychologist will give us a new game plan to improve Ryan's behavioral skills."

"So you can't just give me a 'chill out' pill?"

The doctor glanced at his watch again. "That's called a lobotomy."

"Oh great, now I'm going to end up like Jack Nicholson in *One Flew Over The Cuckoo's Nest*."

"I'm sorry, Ryan." The doctor walked to the side of my bed. "You're recovering from a very severe head injury. You've made remarkable progress, but your brain has not fully healed yet. Structurally, your knee is healing well but something is damaged up here," he said tapping the top of my head, "blocking the messages you give your leg, telling it to walk. Also, neurological damage from a head injury may accentuate that person's personality traits. For example: in your case, being an athlete involves intense competition, a desire to dominate an opponent, aggressiveness—all desirable characteristics for a basketball player during a game but not for someone who has just received gifts and the fellowship of friends who hoped to only bring some cheer into your life."

"Guess that makes me a despicable reincarnation of Ebenezer Scrooge."

"Nonsense," the doc said while looking at his watch again. "I told you this not to make you feel guilty but to challenge you. All athletes need goals—right, Pastor? Tom, I hear you were quite the football player in your day, so you'll understand what I'm trying to say." He backed his way toward the door as he spoke. "Tom, understand that Ryan's judgment has been impaired by this injury. You'll have to retrain him, like a young athlete learning to play a new sport. Start with the basics."

"What about his leg?" Tom asked.

The doctor was now at the door. "Let the physical therapists teach him to walk again. You and the counselor I recommended will teach him how to treasure life again."

"What do you mean by that?" I asked, but the doctor was gone.

Tom patted my leg. "I believe the good doctor was reminding us of God's greatest commandment."

"You mean the one in Proverbs that says, give the orphaned, crippled boy anything he asks for so he won't have a seizure, swallow his tongue, and die?"

Tom smiled. "I'm not familiar with that particular passage, but I was referring to the one in Matthew that reads, 'Love the Lord your God with all your heart and with all your soul and with all your mind...and love your neighbor as yourself.'"

"I think I like my commandment better." As Tom continued to talk, I closed my eyes and drifted back to my dreams of that green envelope and the screaming letter with no writing on its white pages. My mother didn't want me to see that letter or any of the journals in that suitcase—why? Because of the contents of that suitcase, my parents dropped everything to come over on this side of the Cascades—why? I was told all my grandparents had died—why?

I drifted further back: riding in the back seat of the Kia, arguing with my father about the journals...outside the vehicle, everything is white...the green envelope drops...I hear screaming...

"No!" I bolted upright in bed. "The suitcase!"

Tom stirred in a chair next to my bed. "Ryan?"

"There was a suitcase in my parent's car."

"Yes, there were four suitcases."

"Where are they?"

"It's okay," he said, placing a hand on my arm. "They're at my house."

"Are you sure there are four?"

Tom rubbed his pointy chin. "Yes, I'm sure. There are three blue ones and a brown one that is locked shut."

I relaxed back onto my pillow. "How soon before I'm discharged?"

He smiled. "We should be home in time to watch the Sonics game on TV this afternoon."

⌘⌘⌘

The Christmas tree was still in the middle of the "great room," as Tom called it. The autographed basketball, along with a dozen or so wrapped presents, were scattered under the fir's bottom branches. I limped past the tree toward the far end of the room. A large fireplace flanked by floor-to-ceiling windows revealed a sweet view of Utsalady Bay. A long banner stretched across the stone chimney and was taped to the windows. The cloth banner was yellow and white with the rattlesnake mascot of my high school entwined between the words **GET WELL SOON, RYAN...WE MISS YOU!!!** painted in black letters.

They're diss'n you, ol' buddy.

I ripped the banner down and tossed it on a brown leather couch. The two-headed monster was battling itself for superiority inside my head again. However much I wanted the gentle monster to win, I seemed to be only a bystander helplessly watching as the evil head was too strong.

"I know we've only had one counseling session together," Tom said as he approached me, "but I think I'm supposed to ask you what emotion triggered that action."

"They're diss'n me. Yeah, they miss me all right. They miss my sweet jump shot; they miss my rebounding; they miss my lock-down defense."

Tom put a hand on my shoulder. "No, Ryan, they miss more than that. They miss their friend."

"What do you know, old man?" I pushed his arm off my shoulder. "They were all jealous, every one of them. If they weren't jealous, they only pretended to be tight with me. They were all gold-digging groupies."

"Have a little faith in your friends."

"You know, old man—for all I know, you could be just like them. How do I know you really are my grandfather anyway? What reason would my parents have to lie about you?"

"I can prove I'm your grandfather."

"Whatever—but the joke is on you, because according to the doc, I'm not really the same person I was before the accident. That tree I hit turned me from Dr. Jekyll into Mr. Hyde." I scrunched up my face and showed Tom my best Mr. Hyde impersonation. "Everyone including you misses Dr. Jekyll but he doesn't exist anymore," I snarled.

Tom smiled. "I never knew Dr. Jekyll, and I don't see Mr. Hyde. All I see is my grandson. And I have a lot of catching up to do with him."

I didn't know what to make of this man. *He seems sincere. He says he has proof...but you can't really trust him, can you, Ryan? Your parents thought it was necessary for you to think he was dead, so why should you trust him? Your parents were desperate to answer the secret those diaries held. What if they were written by Tom? Maybe your mom stole them from him, and he wants them back. Whether those are his diaries or not, one thing is for certain—he must not know what's in that suitcase.*

"Where are the suitcases?" I asked.

Tom walked to the Christmas tree and plugged it in. The lights were all white, accentuating the snow-covered branches of the flocked tree. I blinked away the fleeting image of lying in a blanket of snow—of a kaleidoscope of white swirling around me and a green envelope floating into the branches of a white tree above my head and...

"I put them in your room." Tom pointed to a door off of the great room. "They're in the closet."

"Did you snoop around inside them?"

Tom stood beside the tree, his black face in stark contrast to the white background. "No, I didn't snoop inside your suitcases."

"You swear, old man."

"I'm a pastor and your grandfather. You can trust my word."

"Judas Iscariot was one of the apostles, and that didn't stop him from ratting on Jesus. And where's this proof that you're my grandfather?"

He waved his hand to follow him. I trudged along, dragging my left leg behind me to the bottom of a steep flight of stairs. Tom was on the first landing, halfway up before the stairs veered left up to the loft.

"Come on up," Tom called. "This will be your physical therapy for the day."

What if Tom had broken into the brown suitcase? Whatever secrets my parents were attempting to solve might be important enough for Tom to keep me from finding out. *You know what would really bite, ol' buddy? It would suck to struggle up those stairs, only to have him push you back down.* "I don't think my leg is ready yet to drag it up Mt. Everest."

"I want to show you a photograph on the wall up here."

"Think I'll just head to my room."

"The physical therapist doesn't want you to 'drag' your leg anywhere. You're able to put weight on it." He motioned again for me to come up. "Remember, the therapist said stair climbing would be good for you."

"Easy for him to say."

Tom took a framed photo from the wall and carried it down the stairs. He handed it to me and pointed to a beautiful, golden-skinned, teenage girl with curly black hair and a big smile. I had never seen any photographs of my parents as teenagers, but there was no doubt that the young teen seated between Tom and a white, middle-aged, blond woman was my mother.

"I don't know," I said. "I need to go to my room."

"Take the picture with you." Tom pointed back up the stairs and added, "I have some more proof. I'll bring it to your room."

I opened the door to "my room" while Tom climbed back up the stairs. The small room had a single bed, a white dresser, a round wooden table and chair next to a sliding glass door. A large bookshelf, crammed with hundreds of paperback books, was next to a door which, I assumed, must open to the closet the suitcases were stored. I pulled a blue curtain across the sliding door, sat on the bed, and stared at the family photo in my hands.

So, my grandmother was white. Guess I'd never thought about it much since neither of my parents talked about my grandparents. Made sense, though, since my mother was so much lighter-skinned than Tom, and I was lighter still.

I set the picture down and stared at the closet door. *What freaked you out so much about the contents of those journals, Mom?* I stood and limped to the closet. My hand was clammy as I reached for the doorknob.

Tom knocked, and I yanked my hand away from the closet as if I'd been bitten by a charge of electrical current.

"May I come in, Ryan?"

"It's your house."

Tom entered and placed a handful of white envelopes on the table. "Come over and have a seat." He pulled a padded, folding chair out from the table.

I sat, and he pushed five envelopes towards me. They were all addressed to Tom. My name and address was written on the top left-hand corner of each envelope. "What are you trying to pull, old man?" I tossed one of the envelopes at him and he caught it. "I never wrote anything to you, and this isn't even written in my handwriting."

"You're right." He set the envelope back down in front of me. "It was written by your mother—all of these were written by your mother *pretending* to be you."

I snatched the letter from the envelope and noticed my name signed at the bottom of the page. I had practiced forging my mother's handwriting enough to recognize the large, looping, left-slanted letters written in cursive on the page. It was her handwriting all right.

"You recognize the handwriting, don't you?" Tom declared.

"It's hers—but why?"

"I didn't recognize it until I was cleaning out drawers after your grandmother died. I found a handmade birthday card given to me by your mother over twenty years ago." He picked up another envelope and ran his hands across the address. "Her handwriting is quite unique."

"Does your wife have something to do with this?"

"Your grandmother is dead, Ryan."

"How long ago did your wife die?"

Tom put the envelope back on the table. "You don't remember?"

"How am I supposed to know? Until a few days ago, I thought both of you were dead."

Tom rubbed his chin before responding. "Your mother never told you she went to your grandmother's funeral the day before the car accident?"

"No, but she was acting really strange when she came home that night."

"I wonder if it has anything to do with this." He reached into his coat pocket and pulled out another envelope—*the green envelope.*

"Where did you find that?" I asked seizing the envelope from his fingers.

"The paramedics found this resting on a branch of the tree your head struck."

"This one is addressed to me with *your* name typed in the upper left-hand corner."

Tom strode to the window and pulled back the curtains. "Ryan, I wrote to you six times over the past two years and for some reason your mother wrote back, pretending to be you."

"What would she say?"

Tom closed the curtain. "The letters were always very short—to the point. They basically told me to quit writing; that I was wasting my time."

"But you kept writing anyway?"

He turned again to the window. "I loved your mother, and I wanted a relationship with my only grandson."

Both the green envelope and the letter were typed instead of written freehand. "You type all your letters?"

Tom nodded. "According to the postmark, that must be the last letter I sent to you."

I ripped open the envelope which haunted my dreams. "Well, let's see what you wrote to me." I sat back in my chair and began to read.

November 24

Dear Ryan:
Hello, my dear grandson. It feels very awkward and sad to say you don't know me, but that's the truth, isn't it?

108

Tom took the letter from me. "I didn't write this." The expression on his face, as he read the letter out loud, changed from confusion, to disbelief, to indignation.

> It feels very awkward and sad to say you don't know me, but that's the truth, isn't it? I wouldn't blame you at all if you felt like wadding up this letter and flushing it down the toilet—especially when the reason I have written is to ask a favor from you. If you are still reading this, I want to thank you in advance even if your motivation is strictly for curiosity's sake.
>
> I don't know what you know about me, but it doesn't really matter because nobody really knows me. All my life I have demanded the truth from everyone but myself. There are so many things I need to say, but unfortunately I don't have much time left to say them and the time I do have left I want to be uncomplicated for me and your grandfathers.
>
> I have written and telephoned your mother many times, but she refuses to write back and darn that caller ID you have. I am writing you, Ryan, to convince your mother to come to my funeral. In the spare bedroom on the table is a box wrapped with duck tape. Tell her not to open it until she gets back to Spokane. I will leave a note in an envelope addressed to you, next to the box. This note will explain the importance that your mother sees the contents of that box.
>
> I'm sorry I never knew you.
> Grandma Fisher

Tom let the letter slip from his hand and drop onto the table. "What was in that box?"

"Diaries and journals—lots of them."

"Where are they now?"

I pointed at the closet. "They are all in that brown suitcase."

Tom spun and opened the closet door. He pulled out the three blue suitcases and flung them on the bed. Dropping to his knees, he crawled under a wall of ladies' coats hanging from a metal rod. My heart almost stopped when he backed out from the closet without the brown suitcase.

"Where is it?" I hopped over to the closet and dove through the coats as Tom was brushing himself off.

Tom hollered through the wall of leather and nylon, "I was about to ask you the same thing."

Coats exploded from the closet as I lunged back into the room. "My parents died because of that stupid suitcase!" I grabbed Tom's shoulders and shook. "What did you do with it, old man?"

He slapped me hard, seized my wrists, swung me around, and wrestled me to the bed. I struggled, but he pinned my arms by climbing on top of me. "I know the counselor said you could become easily angered and for me to validate your emotions." Tom was breathing with difficulty, his spit spraying my face as he spoke. "We both lost people we loved who were withholding secrets from us." His face was only inches from mine, his voice edgy but controlled. "I want to know what those diaries said just as much as you do."

Once more I swore at him and struggled to get him off me, but I was too weak. "I hate her!" I screamed. Hot tears streamed down my cheeks. "She killed my mom and dad!"

He threw his arms around me and pulled me up into a hug. "To lose loved ones is painful; I know that all too well. Your parents died searching for the truth about their past—your past as well." Tom squeezed harder while talking into my ear. "We will not let that search be in vain. We will find that suitcase and uncover the truth."

He wiped my tears with his handkerchief, but I pushed his hand away. "You're not my mother."

He held out the handkerchief. "You have snot running down your upper lip."

"Thanks," I said, grabbing the hanky.

Tom stood and held out a hand. "Let's search for that suitcase. It's gotta be around here somewhere." I reached out my hand, and he pulled me to my feet. "By the way," he added. "Don't ever call me 'old man' again. That will be your first lesson in proper manners."

"Would 'Gramps' be okay?"

Tom flashed a huge smile. "That would be just fine."

9

The dining room was buzzing with worker bees attending their queen. A new girl, Asian in descent, sat alone at the table closest to the kitchen door. She was petite with long, black hair. She shrunk into her chair as Claire approached with three of her friends.

Claire stood across from the Asian girl while the worker bees hovered close by. She leaned against the table and said, "I heard your daddy was flying one of the Zeros that attacked Pearl Harbor?" A smattering of boos and jeers arose from the other side of the room.

The tiny girl timidly shook her head back and forth. "That cannot be true," she said in a small voice.

One of the worker bees flew around the table and slapped the Asian girl. "Are you calling Claire a liar?" A resounding cheer erupted from the spectators.

"No," she answered. "I wasn't born yet, but my father, mother, and older brother were all interned during the war."

"Whatever." Claire dismissed the girl's response with a wave of her hand. "I suppose it would only be proper to welcome you with a gift." One of her stooges handed Claire a shoe box wrapped with a red bow. "Welcome to the Home for Wayward Girls." She set the box down in front of the girl. "Don't be shy. Go ahead and open it."

The girl warily untied the bow, lifted the lid, and with a startled cry shoved the box onto the floor. The crowd behind Claire stood screaming their approval as a snake slithered out of the box and across the floor. With dramatic flair, the queen bee turned and curtsied to her royal subjects. She was into her second curtain call when the entire room fell silent. With annoyance she glared into a sea of frozen expressions. Impatiently placing her hands on her hips she turned to see what they were all gawking at.

Standing arm-in-arm at the entrance to the lobby were Joan and Cathy. They were both bald. The two girls walked to the table with the young Asian. Her large almond-shaped eyes grew round as the two hairless girls took a seat beside her.

With a snort, Claire broke the silence. "Are you two supposed to be the chrome dome twins?"

The room was very quiet.

"Whatever." Claire spun around to return to her hive.

Without looking up, the Asian said, "This must be your table. I'll move to that one." She pointed at an empty table by the entrance to the lobby.

"I don't see my name carved into this table. Is your name carved into this table, Cathy?"

"Nobody's name is carved in any of these tables that I know of," Cathy responded. "And if they are, then they can be scratched out."

Joan stuck out her hand to the timid girl. "You must be Yoko, the new girl."

"Yes."

Joan patted her shoulder. "Wait right here with Cathy." Joan raced to the kitchen. A moment later she returned with three plates of food. "I goofed this up last time." She glanced back toward the kitchen and nodded at Tom, who was watching them with folded arms from the double doors.

Later, Mrs. B. and Tom joined the three girls. Joan couldn't remember the last time she laughed so much. The kicker was when the cleanup crew ran out from the kitchen screaming that the snake had crawled under the oven. Everyone erupted when Mrs. B. informed Claire she had to capture it and make sure the snake was returned to wherever it came from. They talked and laughed until they were the last ones in the dining room.

Before getting up to leave, Cathy asked Yoko a question. "Why are you here, girl? This place is for bad girls and, as far as I can tell, you don't have a bad bone in that little body of yours."

Yoko looked hesitantly at Mrs. B. Mrs. Barletti pointed at Yoko with a cigarette between her two fingers. "You're free to tell them everything or nothing. It's up to you."

Yoko searched every face at the table before deciding to speak. "I am a geisha."

"What's a geisha?" Cathy asked.

Yoko moved her arms and hands in a graceful, fluid motion like flowers swaying in a gentle breeze. "Geisha means 'person of the arts.'"

Joan slapped her hands together. "You're one of those Japanese entertainers who paint their faces white and carry painted fans and wear the most beautiful bathrobes in the world."

"Yes, we call the bathrobes a *kimono.*"

"So, why are you here?" Cathy asked. "Did you get caught stealing another girl's kimono?"

Yoko closed her eyes and inhaled a long, slow breath.

112

Tom reached across the table and touched her arm. "The headmistress is right. You don't have to tell us anything, and if my presence here is uncomfortable for you, I'll leave."

She opened her eyes and once again studied the faces of everyone at the table before speaking. "I wish for all of you to hear my story. You, at this table, are my new family. If you do not know my past, you cannot know me as family."

She stood, stepped a few feet away from the table, and turned. As she began to talk, her body told a visual story to compliment her words. Without the sensations these sensual movements aroused, her story would not be complete.

"My mother, and her mother and many mothers before them were all geisha. My father was a businessman who fell in love with my mother, and to start a new life, they move to San Francisco. In March of 1942, very close after my older brother was born, the United States put all Japanese into internment camps. My brother die two days before my father and mother were released. My father lost his business and his house to the government. My father become very bitter and swore to move back to Japan someday. To make money my father started a hanamichi..."

"What's that?" Cathy asked.

"A hanamichi is a house of the geisha. My father purchase young girls from Japan and ship to San Francisco to be train by my mother. After I was born, I train along with other young girls in the ways of the geisha. My father and mother intend for their business to focus on the dancing, the singing, the playing of musical instrument. But the reality of what is geisha follow them from Japan. While the geisha is an entertainer, often more is expected of her. She not only train to entertain with her voice, her dance, and her music—she train to please her male client with her body."

"A geisha is a prostitute?" Cathy asked.

"No." Yoko said. With grace and dignity she removed her outer clothing and shoes. Slowly, deliberately she handed each article of clothing to one of the mesmerized people around the table. She snatched the checkerboard tablecloth from our table and wrapped herself in her makeshift kimono. Yoko then plucked silk flowers from several soup cans and told a story not with words but with dance. With a deliberate pace, and delicate grace she moved, the flowers becoming her fan, tastefully concealing her secrets, freeing the mind to see the story and not her.

Joan stole a glance at Tom. His elbows were propped on the table with his head in his hands. He was in a trance and a teardrop of slobber drooled from a corner of his open mouth. She pushed his elbows out from under his head, and he jerked awake from his daydream.

Yoko froze in place. She was a beautiful statue, chiseled from pure ivory and polished to perfection. Her head swiveled on her motionless body toward Joan and, as she spoke, her lips were as motionless as stone. "Any female can sell her body for a profit like a farmer sells eggs at the market for money. For a geisha, her only purpose is to create a fantasy for her client. For the prostitute, her work is sex; for the geisha, her work is art."

After dressing, Yoko sat back down. "I become my father's best geisha. On the day of my fifteenth birthday, my mother take me shopping as is our custom. She bring along an empty suitcase, which she fill with new clothing she purchase for me. Then she bring me to the airport station and purchase me a ticket to Chicago." Tears welled in her eyes as she continued. "As we stand waiting for me to board the plane, she explain she had teach me the way of the geisha too well. A wealthy businessman from Japan see me perform and outbid other men in the ancient ritual of 'mizu-age' for me." Yoko rested her head in her arms and wept.

Mrs. B. hurried around the table and put her arms around Yoko. "Her Mother told me, over the phone, that she did not want for her daughter the same fate she had gone through." She stroked the long, silky hair of the Asian girl. "The ritual of 'mizu-age' involves an auction where the virginity of a geisha is sold to the highest bidder. In Yoko's case, the wealthy Japanese businessman had not only purchased her virginity, but he planned to take her back to Tokyo with him as an entertainer and personal geisha."

"I'll be tarred and feathered." Tom ran his fingers through his short, kinky hair. "Her own father was selling her into slavery."

⌘⌘⌘

The next evening, the dining room was again buzzing with anticipation. Another gift-wrapped box sat on the outcast's table. Unlike yesterday, when everybody saw Claire give Yoko the snake, nobody saw who placed this gift on the table. Claire even denied knowledge.

The commotion deadened to a hushed murmur as fingers pointed toward the entrance to the dining room where a bald Yoko stood between Joan and Cathy. Arm-in-arm they ran to the table together. The girls stumbled into their chairs, laughing and giggling while rubbing each other's smooth heads. Joan picked up the small box. Something inside rolled, like a marble, against the side of the package. From the kitchen, the thick smell of split pea soup clung to the air. Her palms began to sweat, and her stomach rolled. She put the box back down onto the table.

"Open it!" someone yelled.

"Yeah, are you chicken?" another hollered.

Cathy jumped up. "If you are all so brave, why don't one of you come and open it." She stared at Claire, who shrugged and turned her back on them.

Jill stood, shoved her chair aside, and rode on a wave of applause to Joan's table. She snatched up the box. "Just for a laugh, let's open this together." Her green eyes bore through Joan. "Come on, don't be a namby pamby. Probably just a wee spider is all." Something rolled inside the box. "We'll open this together." Snickers floated from the other side of the room. "Who did that?" She bellowed. "I've got a notion to come over and eat your heads off!"

Joan stood beside Jill and grabbed the box. Something moved again but with effort, like a marble rolling through honey. "Hey, it's my gift, so I get to open it."

She untied the bow and, holding the box out at arm's length, removed the lid. Nothing jumped out...nothing crawled out...nothing squeaked or fluttered inside the package. With the fingers of one hand pressed firmly against her lips, Jill took a step and peeked inside. Her brow furrowed as she examined what was inside. The contents shifted as she poked at something with her finger. She shrieked and hit the package out of Joan's hands onto the floor. A red and white marble squirted out. It rolled across the linoleum, stopping at the foot of a plump, acne-faced girl. The girl screamed hysterically, and another girl at her table cried out, "It's a bloody eyeball!"

No one confessed. After dinner, most of the girls scurried silently to their rooms and whispered behind locked doors. The plump girl with acne and her three friends stayed behind and sat at Joan's table. The headmistress put her arm around the plump girl, while snuffing out her cigarette in the dirt of a large potted fern, and spoke softly to her. A shy smile spread across the acne-filled face as Mrs. Bartelli hugged her. They talked until Mrs. B. had to shoo them all out of the dining room.

⌘⌘⌘

The next evening at dinner no gift-wrapped package could be found. The only surprise was the sight of four freshly shaved, bald girls pulling their table from one side of the dining room to the other.

⌘⌘⌘

The police called Mrs. Bartelli the next day and told her the eye she had brought in to them belonged to a sheep. She was assured they would beef up their patrols throughout the day and night. Mrs. Bartelli didn't notice any difference in the police presence, though.

Early in the afternoon, as the pastel sun peeked through the bars across Joan's window, someone knocked on her door. She set her Bible down and rose from her cross legged position on the floor. She peeked through the peep hole. A freckle-faced girl with green eyes and red hair rapped on the door again.

"Howya, Joan." Jill whispered from the hall as Joan opened the door. She was alone. The redhead's eyes darted nervously to the shadows in the far corners of the corridor. "I've noticed o'er the past few days, some of the birds have been flock'n to yer nest here 'bout this time of the day." She stood on her tiptoes to look over Joan's shoulder into the room. Six bald girls sat on the carpeted floor, their attention resting fully on the young man sitting on Cathy's bed reading from a black, leather-bound book. "Begorra! Even the black lad is in there."

"Would you like to join us?" The door opened wider.

⌘ ⌘ ⌘

Six weeks passed without any more snakes or eyeballs. No more girls had shaved their heads. No one else had moved their table from one side of the room to the other. For a few weeks, life at the School for Wayward Girls had been measured out and sifted through a strainer but had now settled into a familiar pattern. The evening dinner was about to be served, and the room was a lion's den full of hungry stomachs and sharp tongues.

The group of bald girls who called themselves The Chrome Dome Club entered together and sat at their two tables. Hair of various lengths and color were beginning to grow back on their heads. Joan carried a package wrapped with ribbon and a bow. She stood holding the package under one arm and nodded to Cathy, who, put two fingers in her mouth and whistled. The restless room calmed from a boil to a simmer.

"What do you have in the package, Joan?" Claire called out. "All your hair?" The girls at her table laughed, but the rest continued to quietly gossip.

Tom and Mrs. B. strolled out from the kitchen and sat with The Chrome Domes. Joan held out the present, offering it to the group. A muffled gasp arose from the back of the room. Jill stood and pushed chairs aside as she lumbered through the crowded tables.

As Jill walked past Claire, the blond reached out to stop her. "What do you think you're doing, you Irish pig?"

"I'm accepting a gift, if ya don't mind." She shook Claire's hand from her wrist and marched to Joan. Mrs. B. approached Jill and hugged her. Jill pulled out a chair from the table and sat down facing the queen bee and her royal hive. Joan handed her the gift-wrapped box. With a shrill squeal, Jill became a little girl ripping and tearing at the ribbon until the lid was removed and she pulled out the contents.

Joan heard a few girls chuckle; she heard some whispers. Then, after several seconds of nervous expression, she heard nothing. Jill handed a can of shaving cream, a safety razor, and scissors to Joan. The last thing Jill pulled out of the box was a Bible. She held up a trembling left hand to Mrs. B., who latched on with both of hers. With her right hand, Jill set the Bible in her lap and opened it. With a quivering voice, she spoke as Joan snipped off the first strand of hair and placed it in the gift box.

"Me sitting up here and talking like this is scary, it is." She shifted in her chair and drew in a deep breath. A lock of red hair fell onto her lap. She picked up the rust-colored strand between her fingers and held it up. "I know some of you are mortified to think I would let these birds do this to me because...I love me hair." With a snip, a long piece of hair fell to the floor. "Truth be told, me hair was the only thing I could say I loved about meself. I hated me freckles, I hated me crooked nose, I hated me bony body, but most of all I hated me insides."

A girl sitting at a back table stood up. "What kind of garbage have they been filling your head with?"

From the kitchen, the three girls on cooking duty all peeked their heads over the four-foot-high swinging doors.

Another girl at the same table yelled out, "If you go through with this, don't expect to come crawling back to us after you look in the mirror!"

"That's the problem," Jill said. "Every time I looked in the mirror, I'd get cheesed off at what looked back at me. All you birds out there were also mirrors to me. Every time I would take a gander at Claire or Holly or Joan or any of you, I would hate meself."

"Well Jill, you're really gonna hate what you see in the mirror now," Claire said to chuckles around her table.

"No, I won't." Jill held up the Bible. "This be the only mirror that matters to me now."

Claire made a circular motion with her finger around her head. "I think all your brains were in the hair that's piling up on the floor."

"The mirror in me room only shows me what's on the outside. This book shows me what's on me insides." One tear fell from her cheek onto the Word of God nestled in Jill's lap. "As I have been reading this book, I found I hated me insides more than me outsides."

Joan snipped off the last long strand. Jill ran her hand over what was left. "You ready?" Joan asked.

"Mow that field of clover," Jill answered.

While Joan massaged the shaving cream into the uneven patches of hair, Jill remained silent. Deep green eyes followed the path of the razor as it ascended to wipe clean her past. "Me Da used to belt me around when I lived in Ireland, so Me Ma brought me to New York when I be ten. First day here she has her purse stole. All our money is gone. She asks a fella directions to a police house. He takes us to some manky alley; tells me Ma to take off her clothes. She tells him off, and that's when he stabbed her."

Joan guided the razor and wiped clean the first swath of Jill's scalp.

"Me Ma screamed at me to run just as the git reefed on her with his knife a second time. She screamed again—so I ran. I ran 'til I thought I couldn't hear her screaming anymore, but since then, every time I see meself in a mirror I hear her scream."

Another swath clean.

"For a spell now, I be watching The Chrome Dome birds. They seem to be always happy and never mean-spirited to the rest of us—even when we had no problem pulling shenanigans on them. So I started keeping tabs on the birds. I wanted what they had, whatever that be. Unbeknownst to me I was being drawn to them like a drunk to a pub."

Another patch wiped clean.

"I followed them to Joan and Cathy's room awhile back. They invited me in, but I let on I wernt interested see, but I kept returning day after day, knocking on their door. One fine afternoon I had already made plans to skedaddle as soon as they invited me in, only this time 'twas if the whole weight of the Blarney Stone laid upon me shoulders. I couldn't move a twitch. Tom said it be the Holy Ghost keeping me from leaving, and I should do what the Spirit told me to do. I was afraid and didn't know what to do."

Another patch.

"Then Tom read from this book." She held up the Bible and read. "'For God so loved the world, that He gave His only begotten Son, that whoever believes in Him should not perish, but have eternal life.'" She laid the Book back on her lap and turned a couple pages. "Love always meant pain to me. My Ma told me that me Da loved me, but his love meant doing things

118

perfectly. There be no middling with him. Do it his way, or he'd belt me one. Me Ma died loving on me. Her screams in me head reminded me that love will always hurt, so I hated instead."

She picked up the Bible again. "God be showing me what true love is. This be what God says about love:

> Love is patient, love is kind, and is not jealous; love does not brag and is not arrogant, does not act unbecomingly; it does not seek its own, is not provoked, does not take into account a wrong suffered, does not rejoice in unrighteousness, but rejoices with the truth; bears all things, believes all things, hopes all things, endures all things. Love never fails. But now abide faith, hope, love, these three; but the greatest of these is love.

...wiped clean.

A frail girl with a chalky complexion and greasy hair raised her hand. "It's okay, Peg, what is it?" Mrs. Barletti asked.

The girl rubbed her hands furiously, trying to remove an invisible filth. "I was gang-raped when I was fourteen. When I told my parents, my mother called me a..." The girl shivered and wrapped her own arms around her brittle body. "Two nights later, my father raped me in my bed." Tears rolled down parched cheeks. "My mother found a suicide note next to his body telling her I had seduced him and now couldn't live with his guilt. She hated me after that and sent me here." She grabbed a napkin from the table and blew her nose. "My mother hates me, everyone here hates me, and I hate me. How can I find the love 'that never fails'? There's got to be more to it than just reading it in a book."

Jill's emerald eyes sparkled. "You must be born again."

...clean!!!

The headmistress scurried over to Peg and wrapped her arms around the weeping girl.

Claire's chair toppled angrily to the floor as she stood. "Why, that's plain silly. How can Peg climb back into her mother's belly and be born all over again?"

The girls at the two tables behind Jill failed at stifling their giggles.

"What's so funny?" Claire folded her arms and cocked her head to one side.

"Two thousand years ago, someone asked Jesus the same question." Joan wiped the last bit of shaving cream from Jill's smooth head with a kitchen towel. "Jesus wasn't talking about a physical rebirth but a spiritual rebirth."

Tom stepped beside Joan and put an arm around her shoulder. "Claire—all of you. Listen to me now. When Jill read that Scripture about love, she skipped over a verse that might help clear things up." He knelt down and took Jill's hand in his. "This world is a messed-up place. I think all of you can agree to that—am I right?" Jill looked into Tom's big brown eyes and nodded. A low murmur stirred from the rest of the girls. "There's a lot of imperfection in this cesspool we call earth. That's including how we perceive love."

"What do you know about love, black man?" Claire snorted.

"Everything I know about love I learned right here." He took the Bible from Jill's hand, stood, and held it high. "The verse Jill did not read says, 'For now we see in a mirror dimly.' Everything we see in this world, ladies, we see through glasses smeared with dog doo-doo."

Joan heard a few girls laugh. *This man knows; he understands.*

"You live in this filth every day. It's not all your fault, but the stench from livin' rubs off on you so when you look in that mirror what do you see?"

"I hate what I see," Peg cried out from the arms of Mrs. B.

Tom pointed toward Peg. "But it's not your soul you hate. You see the contamination from this world clinging to your flesh like a sucking leach. It robs the light from within you, 'til when you do see your reflection in a mirror, it's a dark imitation of who you were meant to be." He pointed throughout the crowd of girls. "You can shower and scrub and powder and primp all you want, but when you look in this mirror—God's Word—you look past the outside to see what's within." He took a step closer to the center of the room. "What's inside you ladies?" He pounded his chest with his finger. "Is it love?" He gestured throughout the room to no one in particular. "No, you're filled with anger and jealousy and fear and malice and..." He made an exaggerated sweep with his finger until it stopped at Claire. "...and pride."

"Don't you point that black finger at me, nigger," Claire screamed. She picked up a soup can of silk flowers from her table and threw it at Tom. The can bounced off his lanky body and Claire stormed from the dining room.

Tom swooped up the disheveled flowers and handed them in a bouquet to Peg. "'Don't be overcome by evil, but overcome evil with good.'"

"What's with the bald heads?" a voice from the crowd called out.

Joan patted Jill on the back. "Do you want to answer that one?"

Jill ran her hand across her smooth scalp. "I may have hated just about everything about me, but I loved me hair." She picked up a handful of her ginger-colored locks from the floor. "I must be a bloody dreadful sight, but I did this—we all did this—to remember someone who sacrificed more than His hair for us."

"Hey, I'm hungry!" someone yelled.

As Tom walked past Joan toward the kitchen, he winked and flashed his 100-watt smile. "I hope they're hungry for more than just food tonight."

⌘⌘⌘

Joan looked at herself in the mirror. It was amazing how much a body could change in nine months. Her belly felt like a rubber band, pulled and stretched to the limit of its elasticity. She now wore a bra two sizes larger than before. Her jeans hadn't hugged her hips for close to three months now. With the summer heat wave entering its second month, she was glad her roommate didn't need her size sixteen dresses anymore. Cathy had lost forty pounds in the past five months.

Her hands explored the bulge below her breasts. She turned and smiled as she massaged her protruding belly button. Did she always have an outie? Grabbing a comb from her dresser, she returned to the mirror to brush her thick, shoulder-length hair. With each strong stroke, she counted the girls who had shaved their heads and moved their table to the other side of the room. When Jill shaved her roommate Karen's head tonight, that would make nineteen girls who belong to the Chrome Domes. They would now be the majority in the house.

The South Side Home for Wayward Girls had definitely undergone a primo overhaul since she had arrived six months ago. Yes, the brick facade was still crumbling, the cement sidewalks still had cracks, and the windows still let in more of the weather than they kept out. The change had come from within. A new creation was growing inside the dilapidated school. While past demons desperately sucked at the hollow nipples of hate and fear this new life was gorging itself from the umbilical cord of love.

Angry girls who used to fight over the back-row seats in class were now pushing and shoving to get the front-row seats to hear Tom preach. Girls who would scream and fight over the telephone were now singing to Cathy's rendition of *Amazing Grace* she pounded out on the school's piano. Instead of tearing out each other's hair over petty differences, many were now publicly shaving off their hair.

Tonight will be the first time the dining room tables wouldn't be divided by fifteen feet of bare linoleum. It didn't take much convincing to have Tom rearrange the tables in the dining room to form one large circle. King Arthur promoted equality among the knights by having them sit at a round table. Joan hoped placing all the tables in a big circle would stop all the minor cliques and more importantly stop tables from crossing the imaginary dividing line between The Chrome Domes and nonbelievers.

The most dramatic change occurred when three policemen showed up with an arrest warrant and dragged Clair, screaming and cursing, out to their vehicle in handcuffs. The police received a tip from a hospital in Champaign about a husband and wife both receiving treatment for eye injuries. The couple was Claire's parents and very active KKK members. They and their two daughters were wanted for the murder of a black family back in Alabama. The last Mrs. B. had heard, they had been released on bail while waiting for their trial. Joan figured that would account for four of the five sheets who attacked her that night in the hallway. Who was the fifth?

A little foot or hand pushed hard against her bladder and she winced as the little bugger rattled its tin cup along the jail cell bars of her ribs. She hoped this kid would pop out before college classes started two weeks from tomorrow.

The door knob shook and the voice of her roommate called out from the other side of the locked door, "You'd better only be standing in front of the mirror gawking at yourself and not lying in *my* bed and having your baby."

While trying to pull up her underwear, Joan bounced around the room on one leg like a beach ball on a pogo stick. She fell back onto Cathy's bed giggling. Cupping her hand to her mouth, she began to loudly moan.

"That doesn't sound like someone in labor," Cathy called from the other side of the door. "I think you either snuck a boy in the room with you or you ate chili at the Corner Café again."

"If a boy expects to get anywhere with me, he would need to bring mountain climbing gear."

"What about the chili?" Cathy asked. "That sounded a lot like chili groans to me."

"No, it will be a longgg time before I..." Joan gasped as real pain exploded in her lower abdomen.

Cathy banged on the door. "Okay, enough is enough. You're going to have to let me in; I forgot my room key again."

Joan leaned on her elbows to push her way off of the bed and felt a rush of fluids leave her body. Her panties were soaked, along with Cathy's quilted bedspread cover. Cathy banged on the door again. "Stop fooling around, girl. It's gotta be 100 degrees in this hallway. Let me in."

Joan unlocked the door and Cathy rushed in. She took one look at Joan and one look at her bed and exclaimed, "Oh! Your water broke. What do we do? Look at my bed!" She quickly ripped the quilt off her bed and threw it on the ground. "Lay down. No...wait...put on some dry underwear first."

Joan grabbed Cathy's forearms. "Don't have a cow. Go get Mrs. Barletti. Tell her my water broke."

By the time Cathy ran back into the room, Joan had dressed and thrown a few items into her suitcase.

Jill followed close behind. "I can't believe you still haven't got a crib yet for yer new babby," she said with her hands on her hips. "And you don't have no babby bottles or babby powder." As Joan and Cathy headed out into the hall, Jill stepped in front of Joan and said, "Yer don't even have any babby diapers."

Joan was agonizing over how to explain coming home from the hospital with no baby. "I must have left her in the taxi," or "He didn't fit in my suitcase" just didn't work, but how could she tell everyone the truth? She was now the spiritual leader all the girls looked up to. By each of them sharing from their sordid pasts they had cleaned out the skeletons from the closets of their heart to make room for Jesus to take up residency. By not revealing *her* past, she had allowed herself to be adorned with a crown she didn't deserve but dreaded removing for fear of losing her friends back to the enemy.

Joan doubled over with another contraction. "Wow! I thought I wouldn't hurt this bad until the baby was really close."

"Take this!" Cathy handed the suitcase to Jill as she pushed Joan past the red head. "Maybe she is close." Cathy turned off the alarm system with the headmistresses' key, opened the door, and ushered Joan down the steps to a waiting taxi.

"Where's Mrs. B.?" Joan asked.

"She told me to ride with you because she had to take care of some disciplinary problem."

Jill handed the suitcase to the taxi driver who, with a snort, took it from her in his beefy hands. "Well, I got the notion to tag along meself."

"No," Cathy called out while helping Joan into the back seat. "Mrs. B. said she would need you here."

"I'm all done with me classes. I have no kitchen duties this afternoon. I want to go."

Cathy whispered something in her ear. The redhead threw her arms in the air and walked away. At the top of the stairs she wagged her finger at Joan and said, "Mind yerself now."

⌘⌘⌘

The taxi hit a pothole as it pulled up behind another cab alongside a neglected two-story house in the south side of Chicago Heights.

"You sure this is the right address?" Cathy asked. Ignoring her, the robust cabby rolled out the door and opened the trunk. Cathy kicked away shards from a broken beer bottle with her foot and held her hand out to Joan. "Is this where you've been going with Mrs. B. for your checkups?"

"No, she'd take me to a nice clinic in Hyde Park but yeah, this is the place my wealthy benefactor chose for me to have my baby." Joan noticed the graffiti spray painted across the front door and plywood nailed over several broken windows.

Cathy pulled on her arm. "This looks more like an abortion clinic than a place to have a baby."

"Thanks—you're so encouraging." While placing one foot out of the cab, Joan's abdominal muscles clamped around her womb with the same intensity she imagined it would take to throw up a watermelon.

While waiting out the painful contraction, she considered the ache in her heart. Why had she spent so much time naked in front of the mirror the past six months, closely following the progress of her ballooning belly? Why had she spent so much time writing down first names for the baby with the last names all ending with Johnson? Why had she spent the time learning to knit a blanket she would never get a chance to wrap her baby in?

Cathy put an arm around Joan. "Those contractions must hurt like heck." Cathy wiped a tear from Joan's eye using the back of her hand. "I don't think I've ever seen you cry."

"Actually, these are tears of joy," Joan said. "Tomorrow I'll be able to give you back your old size-sixteen dresses, and I can shake the dust off my jeans."

The front door opened with a high-pitched squeal. The two girls entered what they assumed was a waiting area but looked more like a living room. It smelled like musty disinfectant. The room was lit by two table lamps,and a well-dressed young couple sat together on a worn plaid couch. The man was reading a *Playboy* magazine and wore his hair slicked back with a D.A. in the back. The two were holding hands, but the woman looked old enough to be his mother. He peered over the top of his magazine at Joan. They made eye contact, and the woman nudged him hard enough that he dropped the magazine, exposing the centerfold page.

The sparsely furnished room had two interior doors: one was closed, while the other was covered with a stained white sheet. The walls were bare except for a picture of Martin Luther King Jr. on one wall and a picture of Malcolm X on another. Joan didn't see a receptionist but found a bell with a wooden handle on a tall table by the closed door. A handwritten note told her to ring for service. She picked up the bell as another contraction bent her over in pain.

Cathy rushed over to her. "They're getting closer together. You're gonna plop that baby out right here on this dirty carpet." She snatched the bell out of Joan's hand and shook vigorously until the door opened. A thick black man in a white surgical gown, mask, and cap filled up the doorway. He reached over and plucked the bell from Cathy's hand. "Her contractions are only about five minutes apart. This baby's gonna plop out any time now."

"Are you Joan Butler?" She nodded, holding her belly with one hand and reaching out to grab the doctor's pudgy fingers with the other. "I'm Dr. Brown. Let's get you back to the delivery room. Your friend can stay out here with your suitcase."

Cathy hugged Joan. "I'll be pray'n for you, girl."

Dr. Brown pulled aside the discolored sheet for Joan. Her heart pounded wildly in her chest as she waddled down a dimly lit hallway that opened into a large kitchen. Everything in the room was painted white, including the two windows. A hospital bed was set up under two bright lights in the middle of the room.

The doctor pulled a hospital gown from a drawer to the right of the stainless steel sink and handed it to Joan. He pointed toward a door. "That's the bathroom. You'll find a bar of soap, a washrag, and clean towel. Do you have a powerful urge to push yet?"

Joan shook her head. What she really wanted was to scream, "No!" She wanted to run. She wanted to find a real hospital with a real doctor so she could keep her real baby.

"Good—we don't want the baby having its first bath in the toilet. Try to urinate; try to have a bowel movement. If you can't, then give yourself an enema and then wash your private area. After that, put on your garment, and I'll get you into the bed so I can do an exam to see how far along you really are."

As she made her way to the bathroom, Joan glanced at the glistening instruments positioned on a white cloth covering a metal table next to the bed. She recognized a scalpel and a pointy little pair of scissors. Next to the scissors was the thing that looked like large metal salad prongs. The disinfectant smell was strong but not strong enough to completely cover up something foul, like rubbing perfume under your arms after gym class for several days instead of taking a shower. The odors in the bathroom were stronger, so she breathed through her mouth, washed up, gave herself an enema, and waddled back into the kitchen.

The doctor helped her up onto the hospital bed and placed her feet into the stirrups. Following her next contraction, he performed his exam and placed a surgical mask over her face.

"What are you doing?"

"I am going to put you to sleep by placing a few drops of ether on the mask."

"I don't want to be put to sleep." She tried to pull the mask off, but his strong hand pulled it back on. "I want to hold my baby before you take it away."

A sickly sweet odor seeped through the mask and into her lungs. The last thing she heard him say was, "Try counting backwards with me from ten. Okay, here we go—ten, nine, eight…"

⌘⌘⌘

Joan tried to open her eyes, but they disobeyed her command. She felt someone hold her hand and heard a noise. Was someone crying? She strained to open one eye. Was it glued shut? She tried to lift her hand to her face to pry open her eye, but elephants sat on each arm. *Scream!* Her mind told her to scream, but her mouth wouldn't obey.

"Joan? Joan?"

Hearing her name turned the key to her mind on, and Joan opened her eyes. The room was in motion, and she was back at the Soundview Community Fair, spinning uncontrollably on a wild ride called the Zipper. Joan rolled over and lost what was left of her lunch.

"Joan? Joan? Joan?" She fell back to sleep.

⌘⌘⌘

Joan opened her eyes. The dim room was unfamiliar to her. Soft light peeked around the edges of a black curtain covering a small window. The room seemed empty except for a wooden chair resting beside the bed she was in. Even the light bulb was missing from an empty socket above her head. A door was left ajar and faint light from the hallway struggled to penetrate the darkness around her. She slid her hand over her stomach. Tears stung the corners of her eyes. She was empty. She reached farther down and felt. She had been shaved and could feel stitches.

She heard a noise from down the hall. "Dr. Brown? Cathy?" Her voice croaked through a parched throat.

Joan tried to sit up. A dull ache throbbed through her midsection. It felt like a trout was flopping around in her stomach. She rolled over to her side and gagged, but nothing came up. Footsteps approached quickly. The door opened, and Cathy rushed in, pulling up the chair right against the bed. She was crying.

"Thank God you're awake."

"Where's my baby?"

The room was muggy and hot, but Cathy shivered like she was trapped in a freezer.

"Cathy, where's my baby?"

Tears exploded from her eyes. "He's dead!"

Joan sat up on her elbows, ignoring her lurching stomach. "What?"

"I'm so sorry, Joan." Cathy sobbed into her hands.

Joan fell back onto the pillow. "Where's Dr. Brown? I need to talk to him."

"I-I...don't know," she blubbered. "No one is here. The house is empty."

"They all went home and left us here alone?"

"Everything's gone—the waiting room furniture, the pictures on the wall, even the stupid bell."

"Somebody must be here."

"After the doctor brought you in here, he told me your baby was dead. He ordered me to stay and not leave your side until you regained consciousness." Cathy rocked nervously in her chair. "You threw up about an hour ago, so I tried to find the doctor. No doctor...no furniture...no electricity...nothing—not even a telephone to call a taxi."

Joan sat up. All her insides pulled and stretched, attempting to settle back into their normal positions. She threw her legs over the side of the bed; the feeling of riding the Zipper again overwhelmed her. She gagged but nothing came up. Squeezing her eyes as tight as she could, Joan hoped the ride would stop so she could get off. With her eyes still closed, she asked, "Did you see my dead baby?"

"Yes." Cathy covered her mouth with her hands.

Joan collapsed onto the bed, curled up into a ball, and cried. Cathy crawled onto the bed next to Joan and cried with her.

She never got to hold him. Never even saw his face. She would have named him David if things could have been different. She fell asleep again with David on her lips.

When Joan awoke, Cathy was gone. There was no light drifting in from the hallway, and the amber glow around the edges of the pulled window shade was a fading memory. Joan climbed out of bed and used the chair to balance herself. Her head felt disconnected from her body, but at least she wasn't back on the Zipper.

"Cathy?" No response.

Using the chair as a four-legged crutch, Joan made her way to the window and pulled off the brittle shade. The evening sun was setting over nearby rooftops, offering enough of its golden mist to seep through the grimy window. Joan's clothes were not in the room. Her arms shook as she scooted the chair toward the door and into a dreary hallway. To her left, anemic strands of light strained to invade the hall through tears in a blanket, spread across a large window at the end of the corridor. She turned right, making her way through the darkness, using the chair like a blind man's cane. With each step, objects crunched, squished, or rolled under her bare feet, causing that pesky trout to do back flips in her stomach once more.

The chair banged into something solid. Joan reached out and found a doorknob. Pushing the chair aside, she opened the door. The smell told her she was back in the kitchen—her delivery room. She couldn't see much, but after shuffling around the kitchen, she knew it too was empty. Her doctor was a hermit crab, using the discarded shells of others' homes to do his thing before moving on to find a different shell.

Down the hall, Joan noticed a beam of light pierce the darkness. Joan called out, "Cathy?"

"Joan, are you down there?"

Joan moved as quickly as her wobbly legs would let her. The two girls embraced as Joan entered the waiting room. "Where have you been?" Joan found her suitcase and pulled out her clothes and shoes.

"It was getting darker and darker, and I knew I had to get you out of here, but I didn't know how. I stood outside on the sidewalk crying, and this old lady with a bag of groceries walked past and asked what was wrong."

Joan sat on her suitcase to pull up her jeans. They still didn't quite fit, so with a groan, she put on the same size-sixteen dress she'd arrived in hours earlier.

"I told the old lady what happened, and she told me this house is occasionally used for abortions."

Joan wiped the bottom of her feet with her socks before putting them on.

So McCoy conned her into having an abortion. Hank would never have allowed it, unless he was conned also. At her last checkup, the doctor said her baby was healthy and big, probably eight to nine pounds. Her baby hadn't died at delivery; she was convinced her baby was murdered.

"She gave me this flashlight and told me to bring you to her house, and she would take us back to the school. She lives right across the street."

"He was murdered."

The beam of light from the flashlight passed across Joan's body. Something was wrong. Cathy directed the beam at the lower part of her friend's leg. From underneath her knee-length dress, a wet trail of fresh blood trickled down Joan's shin. Cathy grabbed Joan with one hand and the suitcase with the other. "Let's go, Joan. We need to get you back to the school."

Cathy led her friend out the front door when Joan stopped. "My baby was murdered."

"Come on. We need to get you across the street, girl."

Joan didn't move but stared blankly ahead. When she'd arrived in the taxi earlier that day, the street was as inviting as a graveyard. With the evening, the unfolding darkness had the finality of a coffin lid closing on the dead neighborhood. From out of this bleakness shone a beacon of hope, glimmering through the night from across the street.

The August night was a moist electric blanket Joan could not turn off as Cathy led her across the street to a white picket fence. So many Christmas lights glowed from shrubs, trees, the fence, and house, Joan could hear the hum of electric current fill the air. Cathy opened the gate. A little bell attached to the gate rang merrily. The musky odor of the sweating city dissipated with each step, while Joan filled her lungs with the aroma of lavender, jasmine, and gardenias. As Joan passed through the lighted forest of flowers, shrubs, and trees, she found a little house hidden within. The front door flew open and a walking prune, wearing thick glasses, a sun bonnet, and a toothless smile, greeted them.

"I'm Violet. Come in, come in." The tiny woman trotted with quick little steps to a large sofa. She patted the worn fabric with a weathered black hand. "Come and lay yourself down, dear child. I've got some herbal tea a-brewin', and some chocolate chip cookies sunning themselves in my oven. You rest up some, and I'll drive ya home whenever you're ready."

The couch was old but comfortable, and Joan melted into it as the old lady brought her a warm towel to wash the blood off her leg. The smell of fresh baked cookies, fresh flowers, and fresh old age mingled together within the room. That darn trout was still flopping inside, so she turned down the cookies, but the herbal tea calmed her churning stomach. She sipped the tea, closed her eyes, and listened to Cathy and Violet talk until she dozed off.

⌘⌘⌘

"Joan," Cathy whispered. "It's time to go."

Joan woke with a start. Cathy helped her friend off the couch and outside to an idling 1961 Cadillac Coupe DeVille. The tiny lady was in the driver's seat, her two gloved hands high above her head, grasping onto the top of the steering wheel. She bent forward, peering through the steering wheel instead of over it. Joan climbed onto the long back seat. As she stretched out flat, Cathy handed her a dry towel to press against her unraveling stitches.

"Now don't you worry none," Violet said while wiping a spot from the windshield with a handkerchief she had wetted with her tongue. "These seats are 100 percent leather, so if you bleed on them, they will wash up fine."

Cathy slipped into the front seat. "Wow! I can't believe I'm riding in a pink Cadillac."

"It's not pink." Violet shifted the automatic transmission into drive. "This color is called 'Fontana Rose.'" The 390 horses sputtered once as the car pulled away from the curb before gliding into a smooth ride.

Violet switched on the radio to creamy, soft jazz. Cathy turned around onto her knees and peered over the top of the seat. Joan was curled into a ball. She reached back and touched Joan's arm.

"My baby's life was taken away before he had a chance at living." Joan wiped the tears from her face.

Cathy was silent for a long time. With an ache in her voice she said, "I've had three abortions."

"What?"

"Mrs. B. is the only one in Chicago who knows." Cathy bowed her head. "I haven't even told Tom—I'm afraid of what he might do if he found out."

"What happened?"

"As you already know, Tom and I were adopted and raised by a well-to-do white family. My life was as wonderful as could be, considering we were the only black kids in town. My parents loved Tom and me and protected us from racial prejudice as much as they could. I got a good education, excelled at the piano, was finally starting to make a few friends when Tom went away to college."

"Your protector was gone."

"Tom was an awesome athlete and led our high school to the state championship in football and basketball his senior year. Everybody loved Tom—how couldn't they? The only thing warmer than his personality is his big, goofy smile."

"Someone took advantage of you after he left."

"There was another family member you or any of the girls at school never knew about." Cathy rubbed her moist eyes with the back of her hand. "My adoptive parents had tried having children for ten years before adopting Tom and me. Three months after we were adopted, my new mother got pregnant and had a boy they named William. As much as my parents loved Tom and I, they loved William ten times over. He was their miracle.

"When I was a sophomore in high school, he was a six-foot, 200-pound body builder who looked more like a senior than a freshman. I made the varsity cheerleading squad that year and, after practice one night, I was walking the two blocks home when a boy my age jumped me, dragged me into the bushes, and raped me."

Joan shook her head. "Oh, Cathy...I'm sorry."

"As I crawled out from the bushes—my outfit torn and smeared with dirt—Will was walking past on his way home from football turnout. He carried me home and made me tell him what had happened. The next day, Will beat the boy up so bad he was hospitalized.

"Word spread that Will had beat up a white boy to protect his black sister. That didn't sit well with some people, and Will felt the consequences. One night after our parents were asleep, Will slipped into my room to talk. He was crying and trying to make sense out of racial prejudice. He was so sincere and sweet, and I loved him so much at that moment that he ended up in bed with me. After that, he would sneak into my room and we would have sex two or three nights a week. One month later, I had to tell my parents I was pregnant but blamed it on the boy who raped me. They arranged for me to have an abortion.

"Will continued to want to have sex with me even when I told him we had to stop. He would cry and make me feel guilty, and I would always give in. Six months later, I became pregnant again. There was no way I could tell my parents the truth, so I lied and told them I was seeing a boy but wouldn't tell them who it was. Again, an abortion was arranged.

"It was after the second abortion that I began to gain weight. I guess I was hoping if I got fat enough, maybe Will wouldn't want to have sex with me anymore."

Joan placed the towel on the seat and sat on it. "It didn't work."

"No, and when I resisted, he physically forced himself on me. He apologized and cried afterward, promising never to do it again—only he did…over and over and over until I got pregnant again."

"And you didn't tell your parents the truth?"

"How could I? He was their perfect child, their flesh-and-blood child. Will knew I would never tell. When I found out I was pregnant a third time, I ran away rather than tell. I returned the next day but ran away again. I returned the following day, but after Will forced himself on me once more, I emptied out my savings account and ran away for the last time. I got a job as a maid, started drinking and smoking and hanging around with the wrong crowd. After three months, my savings dried up, and I was fired for coming to work drunk one morning.

"I was almost five months pregnant at the time and scared. I rode a bus back home that evening and spent the last few bucks I had on a bottle of Mad Dog wine. My family was upstairs getting ready for bed when I walked in, drunk and angry. I climbed the stairs and when I reached the top, Will was exiting the bathroom. He ran over, threw his arms around me, declaring how much he had missed me. I didn't hug him back. I just told him I was going into Mom and Dad's bedroom and telling them the truth. He begged me not to, but when I tried to force my way past him, he pushed me, and I fell down the stairs. I woke up in the hospital with a broken arm, a concussion, and a dead baby. Everyone assumed I was so drunk I fell down the stairs on my own, causing a miscarriage, but I know it was my third abortion."

"Is this where I turn?" Violet pointed with her gloved hand toward a 28th street exit sign.

Cathy wiped more tears from her eyes. "That's it. Take a right here, head straight for a couple miles, then take a right on…" Cathy pressed her face against the windshield. "What's that orange glow in the sky?"

Joan leaned forward in the seat and peered out the side window. Both girls were thrown sideways as Violet punched the accelerator to make the right turn before the light changed to red. "That looks like the glow from a fire. I hope it's not too close to where I'm takin' you two."

Violet turned off the radio. They drove in silence watching the orange halo radiate brighter the closer they got. Police cars and barricades blocked the entrance to the street their school was on. A large crowd surrounded the intersection, preventing Violet in drawing near, so she pulled the Cadillac onto a side road and parked. The three left the car and worked their way through the crowd. The barricade was guarded by five policemen doing their best to plug the holes in the dam of humanity pressing against them. When they broke through the final wall of people to reach the barricade, Joan brought a shaking hand to her lips.

Cathy screamed and ducked under one of the wooden sawhorses, but burly policeman grabbed her by the arm.

"Where do you think you're going?"

Cathy struggled to pull her arm free. "That's my school on fire! Please let me go. My brother might be in there."

"That's a house for delinquent girls," the policeman said while dragging Cathy back to the barricade. "I doubt your brother would be inside—unless he was up to no good." He pushed Cathy under the sawhorse. "Now go home," he growled.

"That *is* my home!" Cathy tried to crawl back underneath the sawhorse but collapsed in a heap after a blow from the bottom of the officer's boot.

Like a mother eagle, Violet swooped in and spread her arms around Cathy. She was bleeding from her nose and mouth and screamed, "That's my home, you pig! That's my home!" The officer ignored her, scurrying away to patch another hole in the dam.

Several shirtless black teenagers helped Cathy and Violet to their feet. The boys shouted at the officers as they and Violet helped the bloodied girl to the sidewalk behind one of the police cars. The boys tipped over a public mail box for Cathy to sit on. Violet wet her handkerchief with her tongue and dabbed at the blood on Cathy's face. Holding her aching abdomen with one hand, Joan pushed through the crowd to join her friend. As Joan sat on the blue mailbox next to Cathy, she noticed the old woman talking with the two boys. Violet then bent over to talk to Cathy and Joan. Determination glowed from eyes buried deep inside her creases of aging flesh.

"These fine young men are going to help me get you two past all this nonsense." She patted the girls on their heads. "You'll be needin' a place to sleep tonight, so after this whole mess blows over, look for my car—you can't miss it." She smiled, and her eyes disappeared behind the bulging wrinkles of her cheeks.

Joan watched Violet and the two boys melt into the crowd. Joan still held her belly with one hand and wrapped the other around Cathy. Tears streamed down Cathy's face, as she rocked back and forth, crying out her brother's name over and over.

Above the distant crackle of the inferno, the barking policemen, and the roar of the crowd blared the honking of a car horn. Joan stood on the mailbox to see over the masses. Like the parting of the Red Sea, the multitude split to allow a pink Cadillac pass between the ocean of people. A policeman, who had been directing traffic, walked beside the moving car while tapping on the driver's side window with his whistle. The Cadillac continued its slow march toward the barricade until it stopped inches from the wooden barriers. Violet laid on the horn again until all five officers converged around the vehicle. The driver's side window rolled down a crack, and Violet began an animated discussion with the police.

The two bare-chested youth picked up a barricade and carried it down the street opposite of where Joan and Cathy were sitting. One of the policemen left Violet's car to chase the teens. They dropped the barricade and ran down a side alley. After the pursuing officer vanished around the corner, Violet honked her horn again. The raucous crowd closed in around the Cadillac and the four remaining policemen.

Joan stood and pulled Cathy up. "This is our chance."

The two girls squeezed behind one of the police cars, and blended into the shadows as they forged their way toward the burning school. At seventy-five yards from the fire, white ash fell like snow from the orange sky. At fifty yards they collided with a wall of heat; the falling ash was now hot fireflies fluttering through the air before extinguishing with a hiss upon the wet pavement. The girls peeked from behind an empty ambulance at the scene before them. The dying school bellowed in torment as the hungry flames devoured it from the inside out. Carnivorous tongues of fire roared at the dozen men grappling with water hoses coiled throughout the street like writhing snakes.

Where were all the girls...Mrs. Barletti...Tom?

A grimy-faced medic rushed behind Cathy and opened the door to his emergency vehicle. Joan called out to him. "Where's all the girls from the school?"

He pulled out a canister of oxygen, closed the door, and briskly walked past. "Do you both attend that school?"

"Yes," they said in unison.

As he hurried along, he pointed through the orange haze toward an umbrella sprouting up through the middle of a round table outside the Corner Café. Two figures were slumped over the table partially obscured by smoke and falling ash. The lonesome duo had their backs to Joan and Cathy as they approached.

Cathy brought a finger up to her trembling lips. "Tom?"

The man in the chair slowly turned to face the two girls standing behind him. White ash smeared his dark face like war paint. His swollen eyes were cloudy and lifeless. A redheaded girl with green eyes swimming in muddy tears poked her head up from the table.

"Joan...Cathy!" Jill exclaimed. Pushing her chair aside, she stood and threw her arms around Joan.

Tom arose and silently embraced his sister. As she squeezed, Tom began to cry. His tears escalated to great sobs as he kissed Cathy's forehead. "I thought I had lost you."

Jill was holding on to Joan so tight she thought her eyeballs would pop. "Where are the rest of the girls? Where's Mrs. Barletti?"

Jill didn't say a word but only moaned.

With one arm still wrapped around his sister, Tom reached out with his other long arm and corralled Joan and Jill, pulling them to his side. They formed a circle and rested their heads together at the center. "They're gone," Tom said between sniffles. "They're all gone."

"Tom?" Joan could barely understand him over the commotion around her.

"I could hear them screaming...I tried to get them out...all the windows were barred shut." Tom broke the circle and cradled Joan's face in his hands. "Someone boarded up all the exit doors from the outside." He moved Joan's head to his chest, and he rocked back and forth, holding her tight.

A small man wearing an oversized black trenchcoat walked up to Tom and identified himself as Detective Murrey from homicide. "I'm afraid we're going to have to take you to the station. There are people who want to ask you a few more questions." The detective checked out the three girls. "You have a place to stay for the night?"

"Where are you taking my brother?"

"Do you have a place to stay?"

"Yes, we do." Joan stepped in front of Cathy.

"Then I suggest you three go there. Do you have a phone number I can reach you at?"

"No," Joan answered.

"Then here's mine." He handed them a business card. "Give me a call in the morning." He put his hand on Tom's back and led him to a white Chrysler with a red light on the hood.

Cathy caught up to Tom as he was being helped into the back seat. "Tom!"

"It's cool, lil' sister. Go back to the girls. Call me at my apartment tomorrow."

The detective shut the back door and, while opening the front door, frowned at Cathy. "Go get some sleep. Your brother will be fine." With that he climbed into the front seat, closed his door, turned on the flashing red light on the top of his car, and cautiously made his way back up the main street toward the barricade. The girls followed the Chrysler's flashing red beacon away from the fiery hell behind them. The detective stopped his car at the barricade. A pink Cadillac was blocking his way out. Violet popped out from the car as the three girls approached. Cathy placed her hand on the rear passenger window, and Tom kissed the glass as she passed by the Chrysler and found herself in Violet's arms.

"You see, Officers, these here are the girls I been tellin' you 'bout. Now I can take them home."

The three exhausted girls nestled together in the back seat of the Cadillac as Violet steered away from the living nightmare. Without speaking, they cuddled, feeling comfort in their physical closeness while crying over those they would never have the chance to touch again.

Thirty minutes later, Violet pulled the Cadillac into her driveway and shut off the engine. Though no one was asleep, no one moved, no one spoke. For the next ten minutes, the only audible noise was sniffling and the sound of labored breathing.

Like a screaming alarm clock, Cathy yelled, "I can't take this silence anymore! I need to talk."

Violet jumped with a start. "Well, uh...Yes...yes, let's go on in now and I will make us some tea, or I have soda pop in the fridge and fresh baked cookies and we will talk."

As the girls trudged up the sidewalk, Joan wanted so badly to smell the lavender, the jasmine, the gardenia, but she could only smell the grimy soot inside her nose. The girls gathered around Violet's kitchen table. Joan sipped her herbal tea but could not taste it. Violet was talking to the other girls, but Joan couldn't hear what the old woman was saying. She was floating inches above her chair, or at least it seemed that way because she couldn't feel anything beneath her. She had lost all her senses, except one—she could see. She closed her eyes and could see the faces: Karen, Peg, Yoko, Mrs. Barletti. How many of her friends had perished tonight? She squeezed her eyelids tighter but another face, abstract and small, floated before her. The blurry face opened its mouth and cried, "Mommy!" Startled, Joan opened her eyes to find everyone around the table staring at her.

"Sorry," Joan mumbled.

"No need." Jill stared deeply into her cup of black coffee. "I think we all be banjaxed beyond help tonight."

Cathy grabbed the redhead's hand. "It's time, Jill. What happened?"

Large teardrops fell down freckled cheeks.

Violet stroked her crimson hair. "Child, it's all right if you're not ready yet."

Jill wiped away the tears with the palms of her hands. "After you two birds left for the hospital, Mrs. B. gave Tom and me money to go downtown to buy Joan some babby stuff and a crib. Mrs. B. told Tom not to worry 'bout making it back to prepare dinner because she would handle it."

"You bought me baby supplies?"

"It took us longer than we thought, because Tom and me kept finding nice things we thought Joan would need for the babby, and Mrs. B. was very generous with her money, so we wanted to spend it all. We turned down our street at the time we thought all the birds would be starting to eat. Tom parked his car right in front of the school and he knew...he knew something was wrong." She wiped hot tears from her eyes. "The front door had boards nailed across the front, it did, and the front window was boarded up too. Tom told me to stay put while he looked it over. There be a strange glow coming from that banjaxed window, so I got out to have a peek for meself."

Again Jill rubbed her eyes with the palms of her hands and took a deep breath. "While Tom be trying to rip the boards from the front door, I looked through the hole in the window. Begorra, there be a fire in the middle of the lobby there was. It be spreading across the carpet and up one wall. That's when me heard the first scream. Tom had a notion for me to run to the Corner Café to use their phone to call the fire station. I ran like a banshee, I did, and made the call. By the time I got back, the flames were shooting out the window. And the screaming...it...it were brutal, it were."

"The windows are all barred," Joan piped up. "What about the other exits?"

"They be all boarded up as well."

"Why?" Cathy asked.

"By the time the authorities showed up, Tom had managed to pull the last board free from the front door, but it be too hot inside to open. One officer moved us away and made us sit at the table at the café. For a time, I watched all the birds on the second and third floor open their windows and stick their arms out, trying to squeeze through them bars, but they be trapped, they were." Jill shook her head, the tears dripping off her nose into her coffee. "Those birds be trapped in a cage, and all Tom and me could do was sit and watch them flap their arms and scream until the smoke be so thick we could see them no more and the screaming finally stopped." She closed her wet eyes. "I thought the only screaming I would ever hear again was from me Ma inside me head. That was bad, but this be worse. Now it's all me friends' screams I hear too. Me head can't hold it all. It will burst, it will—it will burst!"

Jill put her head in her hands. "Tom even lost his car. It burnt up, it did, and all the babby stuff we bought for Joan." She jerked up straight in her chair and wiped away the tears. "I be mortified Joan, I haven't even bothered to ask 'bout your babby. Where is the wee one?"

Anger burned inside Joan. "He's in heaven with the rest of our friends."

10

For two hours, Tom and I searched every inch of the house and garage for the brown suitcase. We might as well have been looking for little green men for all the success we were having. Tom was becoming more frustrated with each passing minute. He finally pulled out a lawn chair and collapsed into it in the middle of his garage.

"Go ahead and call me 'old man.'" He gasped for breath as he wiped cold sweat from his forehead. "I'm becoming senile. I thought for sure I put it in the closet."

"Did anyone else know about the suitcases?" I asked.

Tom's head hung limp, his chin resting on his heaving chest. "Why?"

"Maybe someone stole it."

Tom shook his head. "Why would someone do that?"

"The same reason we want to find it—to uncover secrets."

Tom raised his head from his chest. "Or to make sure some secrets are kept secret."

After helping him reorganize his garage, we went back onto the house. While Tom fried two T-Bone steaks on a skillet, I chopped up vegetables for a salad. He pulled the green envelope from his pocket.

"Read this again, and see if there's something in here that sounds odd to you."

I took the letter from the envelope and read it through once more. "I don't see anything weird."

"Read it again carefully." Tom threw some chopped onions and mushrooms in the skillet with a pat of butter.

I read it again. "The only thing I see is a typo, where your wife typed *grandfathers* instead of *grandfather*."

Tom turned the steaks and pushed around the sautéing vegetables. "That wasn't a typo."

I read the whole sentence out loud:

There are so many things I need to say, but unfortunately I don't have much time left to say them and the time I do have left, I want to be uncomplicated for me and your grandfathers.

The implication was too mind-boggling to comprehend. "Don't tell me I have another living grandfather."

"Your father's parents are both alive."

This really bites, ol' buddy. What can you believe anymore? Who can you believe anymore? Were your parents really your parents? Who knows? Maybe all along they really were little green Martians masquerading as earthly parents. What does that make you, then? Hey, Ryan, who's your daddy? Who's your daddy? "Stop it!" I screamed to myself while pushing against my temples with both hands.

Tom stirred in some garlic powder to the sautéing vegetables. "I had no idea the extent of what your parents were keeping from you. I'm sorry, Ryan, but what I'm saying is true."

I pushed harder against my skull until sharp pains shot through my head. "You're lying!" I hollered. "My parents were Christians—my father a pastor. Why would they lie to me?" I stabbed the paring knife into the cutting board. The tip of the blade snapped off, slicing the side of my hand. "And now you've been keeping secrets from me too." I held the jagged, broken-off end of the knife toward Tom.

He backed away from the stove, his hands above his head. "If you were having a hard time believing I was your grandfather, why should I have told you sooner about your other grandparents?"

"I just want to know the truth. No more secrets."

Tom pointed. "You're bleeding. Put down the knife, so I can take a look at your hand."

"Where are they?" I asked, while glancing at the gash in my hand. Blood dripped from the wound onto the tile floor.

"They live in a retirement community in Soundview, the town we passed just before taking the bridge onto the island." Tom began massaging his chest.

"Maybe *they* took the suitcase."

Tom grimaced and leaned against the marble counter. "They were here the day I put the suitcases in the closet, but like me, they had no idea what was in one of them." Tom gasped for breath. "I worked with Pastor Johnson for over twenty-five years until he retired. That's when I took over as head pastor at Soundview Cathedral. He's a good man—a good friend."

"What about his wife?"

"Ryan, I'm having chest pains." He tried to walk past me, but I stepped in front of him. "I need to get my heart medicine."

"What about his wife?"

Tom knelt on the floor. "She has Alzheimer's disease."

I knelt down beside him. "Who else knew?"

Tom grabbed hold of my shirt. "Please, Ryan, call 911."

"Who else knew about the suitcases?"

"Cathy."

"Okay, Gramps, where's your telephone?"

After calling an ambulance, I found Tom's nitroglycerin pills. I also found some gauze and a few Band-Aids to stop the bleeding from my hand. Grabbing some paper towels, I wiped my blood off the floor while trying to figure out what to do next. *Now what are you going to do, tough guy? Call up Cathy and threaten to slice her brother's throat unless she comes clean? Go over to Grandma and Grandpa's retirement pad and beat the truth out of them? Boo yah! You have tons of options here.*

"What's Cathy's phone number?"

He was still holding his chest and only shook his head in response. Beads of sweat clung to his brow, and his dark skin was pale.

"Where do you keep your phone book, Gramps?"

Tom's eyes were closed and he didn't respond.

Hey, Ryan ol' buddy, you're turning into one sweet serial killer. First you murder your parents...

"No!" I shouted out loud. "I didn't."

Who distracted your father by insisting on reading those diaries? Who fought over that green envelope? Ya know...maybe if you would have stayed strapped in, you could be shooting baskets on a big, white, fluffy cloud with your dad right now instead of hunting down all your dead relatives. Yes, Ryan, you killed your parents, you're killing Grandpa Tom, and you know you're gonna kill Cathy and Grandma and Grandpa Johnson if they don't give you what you want.

I put my hands over my ears. "Shut up!"

I opened a drawer under the telephone. A local telephone book stared back at me. I flipped to the back page titled *Frequently Called Numbers*. The first number on the list belonged to Cathy Fisher. I dialed the number as I heard an approaching siren.

Her answering machine asked me to leave a message. "Cathy, this is Ryan. I hate to bother you all the way down in California, but I thought you should know your brother is having a heart attack. The ambulance is on its way, but you might want to come to see him. It looks pretty bad, and I don't know if he is going to make it."

Tom struggled to sit with his back to the refrigerator. "Ryan," he said in a weak voice, "you're going to scare her."

The sirens were very close now. I patted Tom's pockets and reached into his left one, pulling out his car keys. "You won't be needing these for a few days." He grabbed my hand to stop me, but I easily pushed it away. "Don't worry, I've got a perfect driving record. Not many teenagers can boast about that."

"What do you need my car for?"

The siren stopped outside the front door. "What are the Johnsons' first names?"

"Please, leave them alone," Tom begged. "They didn't take it."

Someone pounded on the front door. "Just a minute," I yelled. "Where are they at?" I asked, addressing Tom once again. "What's their first names?"

The pounding continued, and a male voice called out, "Pastor Tom, your door is locked."

"Betty and Hank," Tom whispered. "Green Meadows Retirement Community."

I limped to the door and opened it. "He's in the kitchen. Please hurry."

In a few minutes, the emergency medical technicians had Tom on a stretcher, declared him stabilized and ready for transport. One of the EMTs asked me if I wanted a ride, but I told him I would follow in my grandfather's car.

As Tom was carried to the ambulance, I walked beside him. "Don't worry, Gramps. I'll take care of everything."

⌘⌘⌘

Who would name a retirement home *Green Meadows?* Maybe horse breeders wanting a nice place for their triple-crown winners to stud during their retirement years—before they go to the big glue factory in the sky. I stepped out of Tom's car onto a well-lit parking area. A sidewalk lined with old-fashioned lanterns led me to a round courtyard.

Statues of prancing horses surrounded a large fountain. A tall plume of water glittered with the colors of the rainbow from spotlights hidden at the base of the reservoir. Other statues of wealthy men wearing knee-high boots, riding saddled horses in various poses, were scattered among the shrubs and hedges. Maybe this really was glue factory heaven for horses.

I limped to the front door and pulled. It was locked. Painted on the glass door were the visiting hours: 8 a.m. to 9 p.m. It was after nine when I left Tom's house.

"From the looks of it," a gravely voice called out behind me, "you need one of these more than I do."

A small man wearing a Seattle Mariners' stocking cap and matching winter coat shuffled his way toward me, pushing a walker.

"Do you mean your walker or your coat?" I asked.

"All you young bucks have built-in furnaces, but I still have to wonder why your mother would let you out of the house on a night like this without a coat."

"Do you know how I—"

"No, you'd have to fight me for my Mariners' jacket," the little man interrupted, putting up his dukes in a typical boxing pose. "You're a little wet around the ears to live here, but by the way you drag that leg, one of these babies would sure come in handy for you." He patted his four-legged crutch that had a Mariners' bumper sticker taped across the front that read, **YOU GOTTA LOVE THESE GUYS.**

I pointed at my bum leg. "I had an accident and—"

"Here," he said, letting go of his walker. "Go ahead and try it. It has plenty of giddyap and go down the straightaway, but ya gotta really rein 'er in round the corners." He pulled up his jacket sleeve revealing a strip of gauze wrapped from his wrist to his elbow. "Was racing Harry Waterson to the cafeteria and took the second corner too fast." He pulled his sleeve back down. "Haven't had a raspberry that bad since sliding headfirst into second base back in 1940."

"Hey," I said, leaning on his walker, "how would I go about getting inside here tonight?"

He wobbled over to the glass door and pulled out a cloth lanyard from around his neck. A plastic card was attached to it. "You need one of these to open the door after visiting hours."

"Ya see—that's just it," I said, handing his walker back to him. "I don't have one, and I need to see my grandparents tonight."

"No problemo." He stuck the card into a slot beside the door. I heard a *click,* and the double doors opened slowly inward. "If anyone asks, you're my grandson...uh...what's your first name?"

"Ryan," I answered. "And you're my grandfather?"

"George—George Sanders." His name tumbled around the stone polisher in his throat before rumbling through his vocal cords. "Who are you looking for anywho?"

"Hank and Betty Johnson? Do you know them?"

"Well, I'll be. Hank and I watch most every Mariners' game together. They live on the second floor three rooms down from me."

The doors closed automatically behind us as we stepped into the main lobby. The carpet was a dark field of green grass. The sun was a crystal chandelier and I smelled fresh flowers instead of the urine and disinfectant I had smelled at the nursing home in Spokane. A magnificent painting of men in red coattails, wearing black top hats and riding horses with crew-cut manes and chopped-off tails, hung on a wall above a brick fireplace. Dozens of eager hounds dashed through a shallow creek in front of their masters.

"A stupid fox hunt," George chirped up. "Two things that don't make much sense to me: a bunch of grown men on horses who chase little red foxes for fun; and gas fireplaces. We can't be running out of trees around here for gosh sakes—it's Washington."

I tried to make conversation while waiting for him to lead the way. "This is the nicest nursing home I've ever been in," I said, not feeling it necessary to mention I'd only been in the one in Spokane.

"This *ain't* a nursing home; this is a retirement community," he scolded. "If I was in a nursing home, they'd have me strapped to a wheelchair rotting away in some corner while I marinated in my bowel movements."

We plodded along to an elevator. Before George could push the open button, the doors slid apart, and a young woman wearing a tight-fitting nurses' uniform stepped out. She regarded me suspiciously, but George piped up. "What are you gawking at, Cindy? This here is my grandson, Brian."

"I've never seen this grandson before." She eyed me closely and licked her lips. "You're a tall one. Do you play ball?"

"He's not interested, Cindy." He steered me into the elevator with his walker before I could open my mouth to say "hi."

"What was that all about?" I asked as the elevator door closed. "I'm in a hurry but not that big of a hurry."

George pushed the button for the second floor. "I thought you wanted to see your grandparents?"

"I do."

The elevator shuddered to a stop. The doors began to open, but George pushed the close button.

"Why did you do that?" I asked, exasperated.

"Something Cindy said. She said she'd never seen you before."

I pushed the open button. "Of course she hasn't."

"I just remembered Hank told me they didn't have any children." He pushed the closed button again. "Seems to me, you need children to have grandchildren."

I gently banged my head several times against the elevator door. "Listen,

144

George, you did me a favor by letting me in the building, and I've enjoyed talking to you, so I'm not going to lie to you like it seems everyone else does."

"I'm all ears," George said skeptically.

"Hank and Betty don't know me because I just found out they are my grandparents."

George crossed his arms. "And how did you find out?"

"It's a long story."

"I want to hear it."

Now I crossed my arms. "And what if I don't want to tell you?"

George placed a finger on the emergency button. "I push this and every employee working tonight will be on you like hounds on a fox."

This is no problem, ol' buddy. Lie to him just like everyone else has done to you all your life. He's not going to know the difference and, besides, you don't really know the whole truth yet yourself. Remember, your parents could have been terrorists for all you know.

"I'm waitin'," George reminded me.

I retold the whole story from the moment my mother had come home from Spokane with the strange box until meeting George in the courtyard. The old man smiled and pushed the open button.

"How do you know if I was telling you the truth?"

George walked with me out of the elevator. "Heck if I know, but I sure love to hear a good soap opera." He giggled like a little boy. "I can't wait to see Hank's face when you tell him who you are."

"What about Betty?"

"Anymore, the only one she recognizes is Hank. Shoot, she doesn't even remember my ugly puss, and I visit them every day."

George led me down a long hallway until he stopped in front of room #223. A name plate with *Hank and Betty Johnson* was screwed into a holder on the wall. The little man banged on the door. From inside the room, I heard a deep voice call out, "Hold your horses. I'll be right there."

George covered up the peephole with his hand and turned to me with a sly grin. "This really sticks in his craw when I do this."

"Sanders!" a gruff voice called from inside. "The Lord says, 'To be angry and sin not.' But John Dryden said, 'Beware the fury of a patient man' and Sanders, I am losing mine."

George winked at me and replied, "Well, I know neither your Lord nor John Dryden, so I don't give a crap. Let me in." The door opened, and a large man, almost as tall as me, with salt and pepper hair, smiled at George. He did a double take when he glanced at me. "Well, are you gonna stand there drooling all over yourself, or are you going to invite us in?"

"Sure, sure," the big man said, stepping away from the door. "Is this another grandson of yours?"

"No. All my grandchildren are accounted for," George answered with a twinkle in his eye.

I held out my hand to Hank, and he swallowed mine with a Paul Bunyan sized grip. I winced and said, "Hi, my name is…"

"Luke?" a female voice cried out from behind Hank. A petite, white-haired lady in a checkered flannel robe rushed past her husband and embraced me. "You never should have left home, Luke. I've missed you so much."

Hank and I exchanged embarrassed looks while George smiled with delight. Betty desperately clung to me, whispering nonsense in my ear. Finally, Hank gently pulled her away. He didn't correct her but simply said, "Dear, we have company. Would you mind bringing out some cookies and milk?"

She looked up at him with confusion and uncertainty in her eyes. "Where are they?"

He hugged her and answered, "The milk is in the refrigerator." He walked her to the adjoining kitchenette and pulled four plastic glasses from an overhead cabinet. "Pour the milk into these tumblers, and the cookies are right here." He pulled open a drawer. "I will be over on the couch if you need anything."

Hank rejoined us and motioned for us to sit. Betty stood where Hank had left her. She reached for the handle of the fridge and hesitated. She then spun and looked right at me. Her perfume and the scent of baby powder still clung to my shirt as I watched her chew her fingernails and study me. Suddenly, she grabbed a cookie from the package, stuck it in her mouth, and walked from the kitchenette and into another room, where she slammed the door shut behind her.

"She has Alzheimer's," Hank said with a sigh.

"She sure seemed to recognize…Luke, wasn't it?" George tilted his head toward me.

"My name is Ryan, Pastor Johnson."

Hank leaned over and patted my knee. "I am sorry. You must remind her of someone from her past."

"How can she remember someone from her past," I inquired, "when she can't even remember where the milk is kept?"

Hank stood, walked over to a big screen TV, and picked up a pipe from the top of it. "Do you mind if I light up?" Before we could respond, Hank struck a match and the nutty aroma of his pipe tobacco filled the air.

"No, go right ahead," Sanders blurted out. "Die from cancer. Just remember—when you kick the bucket, I get your big screen."

"Ryan," Hank said, ignoring George, "Alzheimer's disease is like erasing a blackboard backwards."

"That's a stupid analogy, Johnson," the little man remarked.

Hank sat down again, then turned in his chair to face me more directly. "Normally one would begin to erase a blackboard at the top and work down, so the chalk dust would not settle on the section of blackboard already cleaned. Alzheimer's erases memory from the bottom up. All the pictures stored, all the stories most recently written in Betty's mind are erased first. Then slowly, relentlessly, the remainder of her mind is being erased, the dust landing helter-skelter across the erased portion of her memory, so she only remembers tiny particles of years gone by and almost nothing from today."

I arose from my chair, irritated that I had wasted my time with this man. He had more important things to worry about than stealing a suitcase filled with his sister-in-law's diaries. *Cathy's the one. She took the suitcase back to California with her, knowing no one would ever find it there. What is it she's hiding? Well, Ryan, she may not bring it back when she visits her ill brother, but I'm sure you'll find a way to persuade her to tell you where it is.*

"Come on, George." I carefully pulled Sanders up from his chair. "Mr. Johnson doesn't have what we came looking for."

"How do you know?" The little man angrily yanked his arm out of my grasp. "You haven't even told him who you are yet."

Hank set his pipe down on a round, end table. "Was there something you thought I could help you with, Ryan?" He stood and looked from me to Sanders and back to me again.

"No, not really." This guy had all he could handle with his wife without me barging into his life. "I'm just a kid trying to find out who I really am— that's all."

"Ain't that the naked truth," George added with a grunt.

Hank sat back down and picked up his pipe. "I may be retired as a head pastor, but I will never retire from doing God's work." He puffed quickly on his pipe several times and set it on the table again. "Please, sit back down and let's talk about it."

I was about to make a run for the door when Betty re-entered the room. She still had on her robe but had stuffed something underneath to make her look nine months pregnant.

"This is you, Luke," she said, patting her large belly.

"Betty!" Hank roared.

Hank's outburst startled George so much, I thought he would swallow his dentures. But Betty was unfazed. Instead, she reached under her robe and pulled out a pillow. "This is you, Luke."

"Put that pillow back in the bedroom." Hank stood, pointing his finger at his wife.

Betty lowered her gaze. "I-I thought you wanted me to pretend." She tried to put the pillow back under her robe, but Hank darted over and yanked it away from her. "Why are you angry?" she asked.

"It is time for you to go to bed."

She tried to grab the pillow back, but he held on tight. "We have company," she stated. "You always want me to pretend when we have company."

Hank took hold of her wrist. "Say good night to Ryan and George."

"Hank, please give me the pillow," she begged. She then looked at Sanders and me with terror in her eyes. "They're going to find out, Hank," she whispered. "They're going to know the truth."

Hank loomed over his wife and slapped her like a grizzly swatting a puppy. "Be quiet, Betty; you are talking nonsense."

She collapsed, whimpering, onto the floor.

"Have you gone mad, Johnson?" the little man exclaimed.

Hank breathed rapidly—awkwardly—almost panting. He covered his face with his hands and burst into tears. Falling to his knees beside her, he cried, "I am sorry." He cradled her in his arms and rocked her. "Forgive me, honey. Please forgive me."

I motioned toward George. "Come on, let's leave them alone."

The little man pulled himself up to his walker and trudged past Hank and Betty. He stopped before he got to the door and, without looking back, said, "It's a lousy example you're setting for your grandson, Johnson." He pushed the walker into the hallway and disappeared around the corner.

Betty crawled out of Hank's arms. She stood and brought a hand up to the bruise already forming on her left cheek. "Where's Daddy?"

Hank took a handkerchief from his back pocket. He dabbed at his eyes as he got to his feet. "Your father has been gone for over fifteen years."

"No—no, I just saw him."

"I will take you to the cemetery tomorrow, honey." Hank took her hand. "Let us get you ready for bed."

"Daddy's dead?" She looked at Hank in amazement.

I was embarrassed to still be standing in their doorway. Hank tried to lead her to their bedroom, but she turned to me.

"I found your suitcase, Luke." Betty smiled proudly. "You lost it, and I found it."

Hank kissed her forehead. "What suitcase is that, honey?"

Betty walked over to me and took my hand. "We bought you that suitcase for your birthday."

"What color is it?" I asked, hoping her mind was not playing tricks on her.

"Why, it's brown—your favorite color."

Hank acknowledged me for the first time since slapping Betty. "Are you just playing along with her?"

"I did lose a brown suitcase." My heart started to race. "Betty, where is it?"

Her eyes glazed over, and she began to bite her fingernails once more.

Hank opened a small closet door and pulled out two black Samsonite suitcases. "Do you mean these, Betty?"

She bit furiously at her nails and shook her head. "Are we going somewhere, Hank?" A troubled expression clouded her face.

"No, honey. I was only looking at the suitcases. I'll put them back now." Hank set the luggage back in the closet and closed the door. Betty looked relieved. "I know you must be tired, honey—time for bed." Once more he attempted to lead her away, only to have her wiggle out of his grasp. She walked over and hugged me.

"Don't ever leave us again, Luke."

Tears fell from Hank's cheeks. My parents had told me these people had died when I was very young. Maybe they hadn't completely lied to me after all. Maybe something bad happened between them all that caused my parents to write them off for dead. I was willing to bet a life of celibacy that the answer was in that suitcase.

They still lied to you, ol' buddy. They lied, and Tom lied, and now you can see these people have something to hide as well. Boo yah! Doesn't that make you feel like the most insignificant little turd in the world?

Maybe if I played along, she wouldn't be confused. "Mom?" I asked. "Do you know where my brown suitcase is?"

She looked confused.

"You know, the one you bought me for my birthday."

She let go of me and bit her fingernail. "Oh dear, my memory isn't what is used to be. Hank, do you remember where we put that brown suitcase? Luke needs it."

Hank leaned against the wall. He shoved his fist into his mouth, trying to keep sobs from escaping.

"Mom, did you and Dad visit Tom last week?"

She wrinkled up her forehead. "The suitcase. You want the suitcase? Are you going to leave us again?"

"No—no. I want to unpack it. I want to stay here," I assured her, and she smiled. "I lost the suitcase, and you said you found it. Did you find it at Mary's house?"

She bit her nail again, but then her face brightened. "Do you mean Jesus' mother?"

This was going nowhere. I felt as frustrated as the one time I visited the nursing home in Spokane for my senior project. I tried to interview an old World War II vet who was as memory challenged as Betty. He was a Pearl Harbor survivor but couldn't remember any details about that day. I was about to give up when a nurse brought him his scrapbook. He needed the pictures to jumpstart his memory, and I ended up with an awesome interview. Reaching into my pocket, I pulled out my wallet and plucked out a picture of my parents.

"Do you remember Mary?" I handed the faded picture to Betty.

Her forehead wrinkled in concentration. "I don't know…maybe."

Still pretending, I said, "That's my wife—Tom's daughter. Were you and Hank at Tom's house recently?"

Betty frowned. Hank drew near and wrapped his large arms around her. "We were there for dinner three nights ago. Tom gave us an update on how you were progressing." Tears dripped from his cheeks. "Let me get her to bed, and then we will talk."

This time Betty let her husband guide her to their bedroom. I strolled around the room digging for my roots by examining photographs, books, artwork—anything to give me a sense of the soil my seed sprung from. A large painting of Jesus' crucifixion hung on the wall opposite the big screen. Inscribed on a silver plate attached to the frame was the words *Father, forgive them, for they do not know what they are doing.*

On the round end table, I picked up a photo of four people. A much younger Hank, Betty, Tom, and I'm assuming, Tom's wife stood by a jeep surrounded by a mob of black children, most of whom wore only a smile.

"That was Piano Key Ministries' first trip to Africa," Hank said as he sat down on his couch. "You've met everyone in that picture except Joan. She had just finished her first go-around battling breast cancer and was in remission during that trip."

"Are you and Betty really my grandparents?"

Hank's eyes bored through mine. "Yes."

"You knew who I was the moment you opened the door, didn't you?"

The bear-of-a-man seated across from me smiled weakly. "If your skin and hair were a little lighter, you would be the spitting image of your father."

"Where is that brown suitcase?"

"You didn't come over here after visiting hours just because you need clean underwear." Hank picked up his pipe and put it into his mouth without relighting it. "You want to have some questions answered."

What I wanted was that suitcase. "Well, I guess my first question would be, 'Do you always slap around my sick grandmother?'"

"I feel so ashamed." Tears glistened in Hank's eyes again. "I swear to you, that is the first time I have ever struck her."

It would be pretty easy to get away with it now, old man, wouldn't it? Sure, communicating every day with a zombie would be as frustrating as peeling the skin off a juicy orange only to find a rancid onion inside. But you can always take out your frustrations on Betty, can't you? She can be your human punching bag to vent out all your pent-up aggression. That's the same advice my therapist gave me, and it works pretty well. Just ask poor Tom. Only difference is after her sacrificial beating, she won't remember why her body is bruised and battered. Tom will remember—if he lives.

"Why did my parents run away?"

Hank looked past me to the painting of Jesus on the wall. "They never told you?"

"No. All they ever said, when I asked, was that you were all dead. No explanation, no stories, no family photos—nothing." *Be careful what you say next, ol' buddy.* "My parents were all I had, and now I find out they lied to me and died trying to uncover some secret about their past."

Was it my imagination, or did Hank tremble slightly at the suggestion of a family secret? He squirmed uncomfortably on the couch, his eyes still gazing past me to Jesus. He opened his mouth only to close it. I was determined to find the truth, piece by piece if necessary, and I was certain this man knew where several pieces of the puzzle fit.

"Ryan, did you read what that plaque says on that painting of Jesus behind you?"

"Yea, it's a quote of Jesus from Luke where he said, 'Father, forgive them, for they don't know what they are doing.'"

Hank folded his hands and rested his head on them as if he were praying. "Forgiveness is one of the great mysteries of life."

"Explain," I insisted, watching Hank's expression as he again fixed his gaze back on the painting.

"Forgiveness is like a sailor who in anger tosses his friend overboard, only to regret what has done and offer him a life line. Because of pride, his friend refuses to accept the line and drowns. Is the sailor doomed to a life of guilt because of his friend's unforgiveness?"

"Is this parable found in the gospel of Hank?"

Hank ignored my attempt at sarcasm. "Unforgiveness is a byproduct of pride. Unforgiveness is a parasite that nibbles away on the human heart. As this parasite consumes us, it leaves behind a toxic excretion that, over time, turns our anger into an incurable disease called bitterness."

"I assume this sermon has something to do with my parents and you."

"Ryan, the Bible says, 'For all have sinned and fall short of the glory of God.' Pride is a sin and between your great-grandfather, grandparents, and your parents there was enough pride bottled up to sink Noah's ark. Well, all of us except Tom. He is probably the most humble man I know."

"So what happened to my parents? What was so awful that, for nineteen years, they hid your existence from me? Why were they hell-bent on driving through a blizzard to discover some truth revealed from the contents of one brown suitcase?"

Hank turned from the painting and moved to a window. He pulled back the curtains and leaned his forearm against the window frame as he peered into the darkness. "Come here, Ryan." I hobbled to him, and he pointed into the starless night sky. "What do you see?"

"Some bushes, a sidewalk, cars, a large deposit of dog poop".

"And what if we experienced a huge power outage?"

I was tired of playing this guessing game. My father was a pastor and didn't lecture me often, but I knew a sermon when I heard one. "Then I'd better bring a flashlight when I leave, so I don't step in that turd on the sidewalk."

A thin smile formed at the corners of his mouth. "That is not quite the illustration I would have picked, but it will work." He drew in a deep breath, setting me up for another long-winded explanation. "Because God is light, He wants us to live in the light, because light chases away darkness."

I raised my hand in protest. "I don't mean to cut you off, old man, but I've heard this all before. I'm a born-again Christian, I do my best to live for God, etcetera, etcetera, etcetera."

I turned to walk away from the window but he grabbed onto me so hard I thought his fingerprints would etch a permanent tattoo on my arm.

"Did my son teach you any manners?"

"Yeah, he taught me not to use my size advantage to intimidate smaller people."

Hank's death grip was released, and he ran a giant hand through his graying hair. "Sorry." The darkness drew his attention back outside. "On the night of your mother's graduation, she told all of us she was pregnant. Angry words were exchanged. Your father and she ran away. Pride put up a barrier higher than the Cascade Mountains preventing forgiveness, and eventually bitterness sealed that barrier shut forever."

"You're wrong," I replied. "Something drastic changed when they saw the contents of that suitcase. Enough to want to drop everything and bring me to the grandparents I never knew existed."

"What is in that suitcase, Ryan?" As Hank turned from the window, the blackness of the night crept into the room with him.

"I don't know," I lied. "But I want to find out."

Hank stared at the picture of Jesus again. "When did you discover your suitcase was missing?"

I explained the events of the whole day leading up to meeting George in the courtyard. I went into great detail except for the part when I mentioned Tom's chest pains.

"He was taken away in an ambulance, and you have waited this long to tell me."

"I want to find that suitcase."

Hank briskly rubbed his forehead. "Does it bother you that your grandfather is all alone in some bed in the emergency room?"

"Just because you and Tom call yourselves 'grandfathers' doesn't mean you are."

"Tom and I *are* your grandfathers. That is the plain truth."

I looked out the window now. "No, my grandfather was a chubby, bald guy named Bud, who was an elder in my church in Spokane. Bud came to all my birthday parties; Bud taught me how to play cribbage in the hospital after having my tonsils removed; Bud bought me my first basketball and saw me play my first basketball game."

I wished Bud were here right now instead of Hank. If Bud were still alive, he would be here because he'd always been when I needed him.

Hank settled onto the couch. "You are right, of course." He hung his head between his slouched shoulders. "None of us were there to help you grow up. The sin of pride stopped us from forgiving, just as it stopped your parents from forgiving us, and you were unfortunately caught in the middle."

"Lucky me."

"Ryan, don't snuff out the light that shines inside you. Otherwise darkness will fill that void."

"You think I'm full of bitterness, don't you?"

Hank raised his head and stared into my eyes. "No, not yet, but I can see that parasite eating away at your heart already, and if you do not kill it, it will devour your soul."

"Whatever."

He raised his voice enough to get my attention but not to wake Betty. "Go ahead, then. Blame me, blame Betty, blame Joan, but do not blame Tom."

"I saw Tom about as often as I saw the rest of you, and that would be never."

"Over the years he tried. He would call, but your parents had caller ID. They refused to answer, and the few times they did, they told him to quit bothering them. He wrote to you and told me you wrote back a few times. All along he was the peacemaker trying to reconcile our differences, but the parasite had already infected the rest of us."

"He could have tried harder."

You should resent them all for not trying harder. Where were they when Mom would cry herself to sleep from problems in the church? Where were they when Dad had a nervous breakdown trying to repair a church split? Where were they when you were playing for the state championship the past two years?

Then, *Why did my parents have to lie? Why didn't they try harder? It seems to me, ol' buddy, they were all too busy saving the world to worry about their own flesh and blood. Who's your daddy? Someone who kept the truth from you for all of your life.*

"Tom has always tried, Ryan, and he still is." Hank sank deeper into his couch, kneading the stubble on his square chin. "He was by your side praying for you every day you were in that coma."

I looked out the window and listened as the blackness of the night pleaded with me to snuff out the flickering light inside of me, so darkness could take over my soul. "Maybe if *you* would have been there praying, I wouldn't limp like Jacob after he wrestled with God."

"Do not stop wrestling God. Believe me, there are far worse consequences than limping into a pile of dog feces in the dark."

My gaze fell from the black sky to the parking lot below. Like my family before me, it would be easier to just submit to the darkness. It took effort to look at the light after staring at darkness. It hurt my eyes to stare at the bright

154

lights of each lamppost, so I looked at what each lamppost was illuminating. Some shone on statues, highlighting the intricate designs of their skillful maker. Some glowed over small evergreen bushes revealing life, preserved during the harshness of winter. The light from one lamp exposed, for some unsuspecting shoe, the danger of stepping in dog ca-ca. The light even shone in the back seats of the parked cars below, divulging secrets otherwise hidden from view.

Scattered across the back seat of the paranoid owner of a blue Reliant K, were rolls and rolls of toilet paper. A car with vanity plates *2OLD46* had a folded-up walker on top of some crutches in its back seat. The car right below Hank's window had a suitcase wedged between the driver's seat and the back seat....

"Hank!" I yelled and spun from the window. "Is your car parked right below?"

Hank jumped up. "Are those neighborhood punks breaking into our cars again?"

"No....no," I assured him. "Is that your car?" He joined me at the window, and I pointed at a white sedan.

"Yes it is. So what is all the commotion about?"

"Don't you see it?" I asked.

"See what?"

"There's a dark-colored suitcase behind the driver's seat."

Hank pressed his face against the window. "What the...how did that get there?"

Hank snatched his car keys and walked briskly to the elevator with me close behind. The only thing he could figure out was that Betty had taken it the night they were invited over to Tom's for dinner. Betty often wandered aimlessly, he said, and she would often explore unfamiliar surroundings, which now even included their apartment. He had to check her pockets whenever he took her out, because she could be counted on to find something she was sure she had lost. She must have found the suitcase, slipped it out the sliding door in the guest bedroom, and tucked it in the car, behind the driver's seat.

Hank opened the rear door, and I pulled out the brown suitcase. "Wow, one mystery solved," I said as I trudged away toward Tom's car.

"What is in that suitcase?" he called out as he caught up to me.

I limped to Tom's car, opened the door, and safely tucked the suitcase on the floor of the passenger seat. Only then did I tell him. "It's all of Joan's diaries and journals."

The color drained from Hank's face, and a strange gurgling percolated deep inside his throat. He slowly shook his head back and forth, and the gurgling was soon replaced by a guttural moaning. The big man fell to his knees at my feet and wept uncontrollably.

"My God, what have I done! What have I done!" He wrapped his arms around my legs and wailed, "Ryan, forgive me."

11

Joan sat cross-legged in the middle of her bed. Three brown suitcases half-full of clothes lay open at her feet. Piles of papers, books, photographs, diaries, and cards surrounded her. She picked up a picture. It was a close-up of her and Tom on their first date. It was off-center because none of the racist, old-fogies at the bowling alley would take a picture of a white girl with a black man, so she had to take it herself. Stuck to the underside of the photograph was a cut-out newspaper article dated August 25, 1964. The headline read: "36 PERISH IN SUSPICIOUS FIRE AT ALL GIRLS' SCHOOL."

"Begorra," Jill said as she entered the room. "I've got me a notion to grab that pile off your bed and start a bonfire out in the street and roast me some marshmallows."

Joan pursed her lips and held the newspaper clipping out to Jill.

"Now why do ya want to hold on to that piece of paper fer?"

"I know you and Cathy just want to forget it ever happened, but I don't want to ever forget. Even after these past five years or the next fifty, I won't forget that night."

"Holding that bitterness in yer heart is not going to bring back the birds, Joan, or yer babby for that matter. Let it go."

"I can't until they catch the scum who murdered my friends."

"Is that why yer running away?"

"You think me getting my dream job is running away?"

Jill shoved a stack of papers and diaries aside, and sat on the edge of Joan's bed. "After that awful night, it was you who held us all together. We were all dead inside, even Tom, but 'twas you who got us to focus and move on. You talked Cathy into going back to school her senior year, to get her diploma, ya did. You be the one who encouraged me to take business classes, so someday I can start another school for wayward girls. You fell in love with that tall black fella with the grand smile. I don't believe he would have finished seminary if not fer you." Jill shoved aside a long strand of ginger locks from her face with the back of her hand and leaned toward Joan. "You showed us how to run toward God despite all the shenanigans, but now I have the notion you be the one doing the running."

"I've told you how since I was little, I've dreamed of traveling the world, and I'm finally getting my chance."

"By traveling to Viet Nam to report on a war none of us believe in—including you?"

"There are very few female journalists over there. This is a chance of a lifetime."

"Ya got nothing to prove, Joan, unless ya want to prove a bird can get her head blown off as easily as any fella." Jill folded her arms across her chest. "What about Tom?"

"I care about him a lot. He understands I need to do this, and besides—I'm not ready to make a commitment."

"That's a bunch of malarkey. Since the day I met ya, yer been the most honest, loyal, real person I ever met. But the words you speak today are full of fibs. Ya don't just care 'bout Tom, ya love him. And no, he don't understand."

Joan shifted on the bed. "You're right; I do love him. But I'll only be gone six months...."

"And then yer boss will find another war for ya to write about, he will."

From the living room, Cathy called out, "Joan, Tom's here."

Tom was kissing his sister's forehead as Jill and Joan entered the living room. He was dressed in a plaid Nehru jacket, a white turtleneck, and burgundy bell-bottomed slacks. The goatee he'd babied for two years was gone, as was his Chicago Cubs baseball cap, which had recently become another appendage sprouting from his head.

"What are ya all dressed up for? Did yer boss bamboozle ya into doing a funeral for him again?"

"Very funny, Jill," Tom said. "But no, I've just returned from a job interview."

"Same difference," Jill replied.

Joan hugged Tom and kissed him on the cheek. "So, are you going to leave the Baptist church and your ministry with the inner-city kids?"

"Sit down, Joan." Tom motioned to the chair in front of the television. "Have you heard of Piano Key Ministries?"

"No."

"Neither had I until I was asked three months ago to bring a hundred of my inner-city youth to audition at Soldier Field Stadium. My kids are going to sing during a crusade they're putting on. During the audition, it was explained to me that Piano Key Ministries derived its name from the white and black keys of a piano. The goal of their ministry is to bring the white and black races into harmony through their mutual relationship with Jesus Christ."

"That sounds like what you're trying to do in the city with the kids,"

Cathy said.

"That's why I got so excited; especially when I found out they were looking to hire a black person to do preliminary and followup work for their crusades."

"Tom, that's so cool," Joan said, "but why haven't I heard of them? Where's their headquarters?"

Tom sat down next to Joan. "I have two very important things to tell you, Joan."

"Come on, Cathy. Time to skedaddle and let these two blather."

Tom grabbed Jill's arm. "No, please stay. I want my two other best friends to hear what I have to say as well." He turned to Joan. "I met with two men today for an interview. If I want the job, I have it."

"That's great, Tom," Joan said, "but what else do you know about this organization?"

"I also volunteered to help promote this event, and we've sold over 70,000 tickets at Soldier Field for their first crusade east of the Rocky Mountains."

"You've been working on this for three months, and you haven't said anything about this to me until today?"

Tom screwed up his face in a grimace and scratched his head. "Every time we've been together the past few months, which hasn't been often enough, I *have* mentioned something about it, but it seems *your* mind was preoccupied on your rapid ascension up the corporate ladder."

"Well, excuse me for trying to pursue a dream like you've pursed yours."

Tom was about to respond but quickly closed his mouth. He pushed himself off the couch, got on his knees, and placed his head on Joan's lap. "Baby, I won't let this turn into a fight, not today. I love you, Joan, and I'm scared to death I'm going to lose you over in 'Nam." While still on his knees, he raised his head off Joan's lap. "The other part of the job offer would require me to move to Washington State."

"What?"

"Baby, my second important thing I had to say today is this." He coughed into his hand, struggling to swallow an invisible grapefruit. "These past five and a half years I've known you...well, they've been the best years of my life. I have never known someone with your integrity and sincere heart. While I know I'm made whole with Jesus Christ, you would complete me, Joan. I want to live the rest of my life with you. I want you to be my wife, move to Washington, and fulfill your dreams there with me." He pulled from his jacket a little black box wrapped with a gold ribbon tied into a bow, and held it out to her. "Would you marry me, Joan?"

Joan stammered and stuttered before she could muster up the first words she could think of. "Where in Washington?"

Tom flashed a smile reserved for someone drawing the exact card needed to complete a royal flush to win the big pot. "Soundview."

Joan gasped.

"God works in mysterious ways, doesn't He?" Tom pulled a brochure from his breast pocket. "This is the brochure we used to advertise the event tomorrow." He held it out for Joan in his other hand. "Here's the picture of the man with his family who started Piano Key Ministries. You must have heard of him growing up in Soundview. He said he's lived there for over twenty years. In the course of the conversation, he also mentioned they were looking for someone to head up a new position in their church overseeing short-term mission trips around the world. I mentioned I might know someone who would be very qualified for the job." Tom winked at Joan.

Joan looked at the little black box wrapped in gold ribbon in one hand and the brochure in the other. She grabbed the brochure. The black-and-white photo on the front of the brochure showed a closeup of Hank Johnson with Betty holding a handsome blond-haired toddler.

"They have a baby?"

"Well, I don't know if you would consider him a baby. Pastor Johnson told me his son was born August 27, 1964. The only reason I would remember that is because he was born only two days after the school fire. Weird, huh? Anyway, do you know him?"

Joan marched toward her bedroom.

"Baby, you okay?"

"Just give me a few minutes alone." She slid into the bedroom, closed the door, and grabbed her purse off her dresser. She unzipped the side compartment and pulled out an envelope postmarked September 2, 1964. It had no return address and was mailed from Salem, Oregon. She pulled out a typed letter, unfolded it, and read it silently to herself for the umpteenth time.

Joan,
Sorry to hear about your loss, but of course, your loss is our loss as well. As harsh and insensitive as this may sound, the truth is, you have not held up your end of the bargain. The goods promised were not delivered. Because of my profession, though, I have come to accept compromise as a solution to many a problem. Therefore, I will honor my commitment to you for this first year (after all, it has already been

paid for, hasn't it?). After that, Joan, you will be on your own.

P.S. Please don't try to stir up any trouble by coming back. You don't have any documentation to prove anything. You have a good head on your shoulders, Joan. Use it wisely.

She looked at the brochure again. Both parents had dark hair and the little boy was blond. That, in itself, didn't prove a whole lot, but then again the dates matched up, and Betty had to be pushing forty if she wasn't already—not impossible but a little old to be birthing another child. She had always wondered what documentation the writer, who she assumed was Governor McCoy, was implying. She had nothing tangible to prove she was ever pregnant. Any medical bills she had received were sent to Governor McCoy to pay, and the two times Mrs. B. had taken her to the doctor for pre-natal checkups, she had slept all the way, so she couldn't even find the doctor she had seen if she tried. The only other documentation would be a birth certificate, which she didn't have. She didn't even have a death certificate.

She shoved the letter back into the envelope and back into her purse. She opened her bedroom door. "Cathy, would you come back here for a second?"

"Are you all right?" Cathy asked as she entered the bedroom. "You're acting so bizarre, and poor Tom is out there not knowing what to think."

Joan grabbed Cathy by the shoulders. "Did you really see my dead baby?"

"What?"

"This is important. Did you actually see my dead baby? Are you sure he was dead?"

"I don't know where this is going, girl, but you've been acting really strange lately."

"Cathy, please just answer me. I need to know, so I can put this whole thing to rest."

"Joan, that was five years ago."

She shook her friend's shoulders. "I know you couldn't forget a thing like that."

Cathy pulled herself away from Joan's grip and stumbled into the dresser. "I'd like to forget, just like I'd like to forget seeing all our friends trying to squeeze through those narrow bars in the windows to escape the flames, but that's what I see every night before my mind can shut off and I can sleep. I see our screaming friends and your bloody, shriveled-up, gray, little, dead baby."

"How little?"

"I don't know, Joan. I didn't weigh him."

"Take a guess—eight pounds...nine pounds?"

"Joan, your baby looked like a wrinkled old man shoved into a little baby's body. I don't know...maybe three or four pounds—tops."

"Thanks Cathy, that's all I needed to hear. Tell Tom I'll be out in a few minutes."

Cathy shook her head as Joan shut the door behind her. The last time she had seen the doctor for a checkup he had told her she would be delivering a "moose" weighing at least ten pounds. That was three days before she went into labor. The dead baby Cathy saw was not hers, but was her baby the blond toddler on the cover of the brochure? There was only one way to find out. She walked out from the bedroom over to Tom, who was now sitting on the couch, and grabbed the little black box from his hand.

"Well..." Tom spread his open hands out before her.

"Did you say they were looking to hire someone to head up short-term missions from their church?"

"They said they could talk to you tonight, if you were interested."

She opened the box and smiled at the small diamond, mounted on a plain silver band. "I am, and I do."

⌘ ⌘ ⌘

Joan and Tom exited the elevator onto the top floor of the Conrad Hilton Hotel. She paused in the hall as the elevator door closed behind her and inhaled both the faint odors associated with age and the thick, rich smells of luxury. Tom slipped his hand into hers.

"You've hardly said a word all the way over here," Tom said. "I feel like I'm holding a Lake Michigan Whitefish instead of your hand. Are you nervous?"

"I suppose I'm more comfortable being the interviewer rather than the interviewee."

Tom spun her around and held her face in his hands. "You're one of the most confident people I've ever met. Confident in the gifts God gave you and in your walk with Him." He stroked Joan's golden hair. "I'm sorry if I've talked you into doing something you haven't had time to really pray about. It's just that I love you so much, and I have dreaded the day you were to leave for 'Nam. I've been praying about us for over two years and felt this opportunity was God's answer to my prayers. I'm prepared to take my ring back and place it in a safe deposit box until you return from 'Nam, if that's where you truly feel God is calling you."

162

"God has already confirmed to me this is the door I'm to open and walk through."

"I'm not only talking about changing careers and moving to Washington, but marrying a black man. I know we've talked about this until we were both blue in the face, but I want to make sure. This decision will not only impact our marriage, but will affect any children we have as well."

She grabbed both his hands in hers. "I don't care if you were blue; I'd still want to live the rest of my life with you."

They walked to the executive suite and knocked on the door. A bright-eyed woman with a Piano Keys Ministries lapel pin, prominently displayed on her dark blue dress, greeted them. She escorted them to a large room with a window boasting an expansive view of Grant Park and beyond that Lake Michigan. They each sat in chairs made of cherry wood and upholstered in thick fabric flaunting an intricate paisley design. Fresh fruit overflowed from a heavy crystal bowl on a table between them and the scent of fresh-cut flowers filled the air.

"Rather impressive," Tom said.

"Rather excessive," Joan replied.

"Rather unappreciative," a voice called out from behind them.

Joan and Tom stood and turned to face Hank Johnson and Patrick McCoy. The surprise and shock on both men's faces, as they recognized Joan, brought her an unexpected sense of gratification. Hank quickly displayed a cautious smile while the governor's surprised jack-o-lantern expression evolved into a peevish smirk.

"I take it you three know each other," Tom said, breaking the awkward silence.

Joan ran to Hank and threw her arms around him. "Oh, Pastor Johnson, it's so good to see you again. Tom," she said motioning for him to come closer, "this is my former pastor. I used to babysit for his boy, but he and his wife Betty made me feel like such a part of their family...well, they practically raised me."

Tom pumped Hank's hand. "Good to see you again, sir. Wow! What a coincidence."

Joan gave McCoy a bear hug next and felt his body tense. "I thought maybe I might never see you again, Uncle Pat." She pushed herself away and stared into his steely blue eyes. "Especially after that last letter you sent me. I was hurt you didn't tell me Hank and Betty had another child. I didn't find out until I saw him on your Piano Key Ministries brochure."

McCoy looked at Tom. "What a pleasant surprise, Tom. I will make sure

Pastor Johnson and I can continue this little family reunion with Joan after the crusade, but for now, where is your fiancée you wanted us to interview?"

Before Tom could respond, Joan shoved her left hand in front of the Governor's face, revealing the diamond ring on her finger. McCoy stumbled back from Joan and glanced sideways at Hank. The jack-o-lantern expression was back on the governor's face, and Joan had to bite her tongue to keep from giggling.

Hank was about to speak when a door slammed and a green, tennis-ball-sized, foam orb rolled between McCoy's legs and ricocheted off Joan's foot. A young, blond-haired boy raced down the hall and pounced on it like a linebacker smothering a fumbled football. He popped up, proudly displaying the ball to Joan.

"This is a Nerf Ball. Isn't it cool! It's cool because I can play with it in the house and not break anything. Watch this!" He wound up and threw the ball as hard as he could. The ball scored a direct hit on a delicate vase of flowers, causing it to teeter. Tom ran over and caught the vase before its momentum took it over the side of the desk.

The woman with the lapel pin ran into the room and scooped up the boy in her arms. "I'm sorry, Pastor. I only turned my back on him for a second and the little stinker slipped away."

"It's okay, Nancy." Hank grabbed the squirming boy from her arms and held him above his head. "You go back with Nancy, and we will play catch later—I promise."

Joan reached out and touched the boy's wispy, shoulder-length hair. He turned, and her eyes met his and she knew. There was no more doubting; she knew. God had raised her son from the dead. She put her hands over her face, trying to hide her tears.

Tom put his arms around her. "Joan, what's wrong?"

Hank motioned for Nancy to take the boy from the room, but McCoy held up his hand.

"Wait, Nancy." He picked up the boy, sat down, and put him on his lap. "Nancy, why don't you go grab us all a bite to eat." He pulled out a twenty-dollar bill and handed it to her. "Chinese sounds good." He watched his secretary leave and then looked at the boy and then at Tom. "You don't have any idea why Joan is so upset right now, do you?"

"I know she was nervous coming here, which isn't like her. She never falls apart like this."

McCoy nodded in affirmation. "Yes, Joan is a very strong-willed young woman. It doesn't surprise me she hasn't told you about her relationship with our family and the circumstances surrounding her being sent to the school here in Chicago."

"Patrick!" Hank raised his voice.

The governor motioned with his hand for Hank to stop and listen. "Hank, I think you and I are in agreement, Tom would be a valuable addition to our team—right?"

"Yes, but..."

"But we now know Tom and Joan would come only as a package deal. Am I correct, Tom?"

"I won't go unless Joan goes with me, and she won't change her career unless it's for the position you were going to interview her for; so yes, we are a package deal."

"Before we interview her for the position, I only think it fair you understand why it might be so painful for Joan to relocate back to Soundview and work so closely with Pastor Johnson."

Hank slumped onto the couch while Joan broke away from Tom and ran to the window.

"What's going on here?" Tom asked.

"For heaven's sake, Patrick; my son does not need to hear this."

McCoy put the boy down and pointed toward Joan. "See that lady over there?" The boy nodded. "She's very sad. Would you go over and give her a big hug and let her hug you for a while."

The boy looked longingly at his grandfather. "Do I have to?"

"Only if you want dessert *before* dinner tonight."

The boy walked carefully, measuring each step, until he was a few feet from Joan. He picked up his Nerf Ball and held it out to her. "You can have this one; I have more."

Joan knelt beside the boy and gently took the ball from his chubby little hand. "Thank you," she said and wiped the tears from her cheeks. "What's your name?"

"Luke." He stole a quick glance back at his grandfather. "I'm supposed to let you hug me. Would you play catch with me if I let you hug me?"

"Can I hug you for a long time?

"If you play with me for a long time—okay."

She held out her arms and Luke walked into them. Fearful of squeezing too tight, like she had done with the only puppy her grandmother had given her, she embraced him slowly. She didn't want Luke ripped from her arms like her puppy had been by her grandmother years ago. She cautiously buried her face into the soft flesh of his neck and breathed in little boy smells. Sweet,

165

musky sweat mingled with suntan lotion and his father's cologne. At first, Luke was a rag doll in her arms but little by little—a twitch here, a contraction there—his muscles sparked to life and she found him snuggling his head against her breast. The ball dropped from her hand onto the floor.

"Tom," McCoy said, "Hank and Betty had another boy Joan would exclusively babysit. She loved that boy like her own son. One night, the Johnsons got another babysitter. Little Johnny ran away that evening, looking for Joan, and drowned in a nearby river. Have you heard any of this before?"

"No, I haven't."

"Joan was an outstanding student and had a deep love for God. After Johnny's death though, she changed. She started skipping school, her grades plummeted, she left the church and started to hang out with the wrong kids and got pregnant. After her grandmother died, who was her only known relative, she became a ward of the state but was taken in by her best friend's family. The Johnsons wanted to help her, but she rebelled against their attempts of good will. After repeated criminal offenses, she was sent to the school in Chicago, which the Johnsons, because of their unconditional love for the girl, paid for." The governor turned his attention toward Joan. "Would you say that was an accurate interpretation of what happened?"

She loosened her grip on Luke. The boy picked up his foam ball. "Now you have to play catch with me." He took a few steps away from Joan and tossed the ball underhanded to her. She caught the ball and immediately threw it to McCoy.

"Yes, Uncle Pat, everything you said was true, but I've changed. I'm a different person from the one who was sent away from Soundview five years ago."

"For all of our sakes, I hope so." The Governor put a meaty hand on Tom's shoulder. "Would you be so kind as to take Luke in the back bedroom, shut the door, and play catch with him while we interview your fiancée?" He put the Nerf Ball in Tom's hand.

"You don't have to do this, Joan," Tom said. "If this is going to be too hard, you know I would wait for you after 'Nam."

"I know now, more than ever, this is what I want to do." She knelt down in front of Luke. "That man over there really wants to play catch with you. Would you go play with him?"

"*You* promised to play with me."

"I have a feeling we will be playing catch a lot together."

"Okay." He took a step away from Joan and stopped. "You can hug me again if you want to before I play with that man." Joan didn't worry about

166

squeezing too tight this time. The embrace was brief, but fierce, and she kissed the top of his head before she let him go. She watched Hank escort the two playmates down the hall and disappear into a back room.

The governor sat and loosened the two buttons on his single-breasted, tan, silk jacket. He pulled a cigar from his breast pocket and rolled it between his thick fingers. "Imagine the odds that, in a city of over three million people, we would interview your fiancée."

"I'd say it was a God thing," Joan said.

"Yes—yes, I would have to agree with you there." He pointed the cigar at her. "I could tell you were quite amused at the shock on my face upon seeing you."

"Probably not half as much as you enjoyed the shock I experienced over seeing my son, whom I thought was dead."

"Cute little bugger, isn't he?"

Hank lumbered back into the room, pulled up a chair, and sat next to McCoy. "Joan, what are you talking about? Why did you think your son was dead?"

"Because the doctor Uncle Pat had me see, to deliver my baby, told me my boy had died after childbirth."

Hank glanced over at McCoy but ignored eye contact. "Please do not tell me this is true."

"Seemed like a good idea at the time."

"We have put her through enough by sending her away, and having her give up her baby, and then you had to go and deceive her as well?" Hank appeared stunned.

The governor placed the cigar back in his jacket pocket and tapped it down. "She was going to abort the baby anyway, until we came up with this plan. I believed our final tie with her would be severed once she thought her child was dead."

"Did you quit supporting her financially as well?"

"Her first year was completely paid for."

Hank leaned closer to Joan. "I am so sorry. I had no idea. I promise we will pay back every penny we owe you."

Joan lowered her head. "I don't care about the money."

Hank sat back in his chair. "Then what do you want?"

"What she wants," McCoy said while crossing his arms across his flabby chest, "is exactly what she came here for."

"I want to serve God as your church's short-term missionary director…to support Tom in his duties with Piano Key Ministries… and to watch my boy grow into a man."

Now McCoy leaned toward Joan. "What if we say no?"

"What was the mission statement for Piano Key Ministries? Wasn't it something like, 'bringing the black and white races together in harmony through their mutual relationship with Jesus Christ'? Hank, you need someone like Tom, who has the unique perspective of being raised with a white family, but has worked extensively with the inner-city black community. And Governor—I did some research on your last election. Wasn't it your narrowest margin of victory yet? You need the black vote now more than ever. I would think having an interracially married couple supporting your next election would be a coup for you, don't you think? Besides, you owe me."

"There would be many issues to be worked out, Joan," Hank said. "Possibly the stickiest being Betty."

"Then we had better get started."

"Just remember," McCoy said. "Watch your Ps and Qs if you don't want Tom to find out who Luke's father really is." He drew close and whispered in her ear. "Welcome to the chameleon club, my dear."

12

"Hank, get up," I said, tugging at his arm. "Your neighbors are watching."

I didn't know whether to feel embarrassed, or gratified, or plain dumbfounded. Dumbfounded won out as I was rendered immobile by the human anchor attached to my legs. I tried to get him to stand, but he was inconsolable. He asked everyone to forgive him from God, to my parents, to Joan, and Tom, and back to me again.

"Hank," I said in a low voice, "I want to go home."

He refused to move his massive frame off the ground. On the patio of a first-story apartment, one of the wrinkled people was dialing his cell phone. He was twenty feet from me and I could make out the words *police* and *assault.*

"Hank, your fellow prune people think I'm mugging you. Get up!"

The big man looked up at me, his face contorted into a hideous mask Lon Chaney would have been proud of. "You must let me read those diaries," he choked..

As I tried to push him off my feet, something struck my left arm with the impact of a kamikaze hornet with a stinger full of explosives. "Got you." The prune with the cell phone now aimed a pellet rifle my way for another chance at me.

I jumped on top of Hank, knocking him onto his back. He let go of my leg on contact, but the senile sniper nailed me in the butt with another pellet. While the prune was pumping his gun for another point-blank shot, I slipped away from Hank and ducked between Tom's car and the Reliant K stuffed with toilet paper. Another pellet ricocheted off the rear panel of the Toyota and the passenger side window three inches above my head. I yanked open the driver's side door and crawled in. The Toyota roared to life as I turned on the key. After slamming the stick in reverse I peeled out from the parking stall. The car backed into Hank with a loud *thud.*

Oh crap! I can just hear it now. "But your honor, I was being chased on foot by an eighty-something-year-old ex-pastor at the same time as being shot at by a prune with a pellet gun. Of course I had to run him down; I couldn't let him get the suitcase filled with my grandmother's diaries."

169

The car jerked to a stop as I struggled to find first gear. I peeked in the rearview mirror at a broken statue resting on top of Tom's trunk. Thank God! It wasn't Hank I hit after all. A pellet hit the passenger window with a sharp *chink,* leaving a nice little spiral divot in the glass.

Put the car into first gear, you idiot!

A loud *thud* exploded in my left ear. Hank was pounding on the driver's side window with his fist, less than a foot from my face.

First gear! First gear! First gear! Finally, the stick slid into first, I released the clutch and killed the engine. The pounding stopped. Where was Hank? The car started again easily, but I killed it again. *Come on, Ryan, I know you haven't driven under pressure since your exam to get your driver's license but come on. Pull yourself together.*

Out of the corner of my right eye a figure rushed the car. Hank rammed the butt end of the prune's pellet gun into the passenger side window. The gun bounced harmlessly off on the initial blow, but when Hank slammed it a second time, the safety glass buckled slightly into a spider's web of cracks. The car roared to life again just as the window caved in from the third blow. I released the clutch and the car jerked forward without stalling.

"Ryan!" Hank's voice thundered through the buckled window. I shifted into second, and the statue rolled off the trunk and into a flower bed. The whole retirement complex awoke while light after light blinked on from within the rooms. Two prunes were consoling Hank as I peeked into the rearview mirror. He threw the pellet gun at the escaping Corolla and fell back onto his knees, pounding his fists into the pavement.

The moment I turned onto the main street, two city police cars with their blue and red lights flashing passed me heading towards Green Meadows. It wouldn't be long before more police would be searching the area for a red Toyota Corolla with a bashed-in window, driven by a gimpy coma patient in the possession of a stolen brown suitcase of significant importance.

My first instinct was to drive back to Tom's house. *Sweet idea, Ryan. Wanna bet the first instinct of the police is to check out Tom's house too? Also the hospital where Tom was taken to and every inch of real estate in Snohomish County until they can catch the kid who just tried to kill the famous Hank Johnson.*

I steered into a Safeway parking lot and guided the Toyota into a thick cluster of parked cars. I nestled Tom's car between a Dodge Ram with a canopy and a black minivan. From the road the car should be invisible—now what? I lifted the suitcase from the floor onto the seat beside me. The suitcase's two zippers were bound together by a small lock slipped through each eyelet. A quick rummage through the glove box and back seat didn't reveal anything useful to open the suitcase.

Why do you want to open the suitcase now? Shouldn't we be making like a banana and split? Just put the cursed thing back on the floor, and let's get as far away from here as we can. First things first.

The problem was the contents of the suitcase *were* a curse. The diaries were a clingy girlfriend, demanding attention, and he was oblivious to the danger of how sharp her claws were. *You know the danger firsthand, don't you, ol' buddy? You've seen this curse rip apart your parents; you've seen it puncture one holy man's heart and drive another insane, and now it's got its grip on you.*

A curse has to begin somewhere, and it looks like this sweet hex started with your grandmother. Only this curse can't be absolved by a stake through a heart, a well-placed silver bullet, or by giving the stolen gold back to the leprechaun. You know that somehow this curse can only be lifted by bringing its rotting secrets from its dark hiding place, to be restored by the light—that same light Hank said would chase away the darkness.

So first things first, which means getting this blasted suitcase open. Maybe the trunk. I climbed out of the driver's seat, limped over, and peered around the minivan at the main road; no cops snooping around yet. A light turned on as the trunk opened. Grandpa Tom was a man prepared for everything. Crammed neatly in his trunk were coats, boots, gloves, water, oil, food, ropes, tools, flashlights, batteries, blankets, candles, matches, and the biggest, baddest looking knife I had ever seen. It was a knife Jim Bowie would have been proud to own. The ivory handle was polished smooth. Protruding from the handle was an eight-inch blade, the bottom two-thirds had jagged teeth perfect for ripping into flesh...or a suitcase.

I hobbled back into the front seat with the knife. The suitcase lay before me like a sleeping vampire. I leveled the pointed tip of the knife upon its brown skin, prepared to plunge the blade into the heart of darkness, but I hesitated.

Come on, you melodramatic idiot. You're not driving a stake into Dracula's heart. The suitcase isn't going to suddenly come alive and stop you...you're stopping yourself. I know...I know—you're still not convinced cleaning the guts out of this monster will stop the curse; that just because you read about your grandma's first menstrual cycle, you have exorcized the demon. This isn't Dracula, and this isn't brain surgery so just stick that flipp'n blade in and open this suitcase like a sardine can!

I shoved the blade through the top right-hand edge, and sawed around three-quarters of its perimeter. Then I peeled back the outer skin. Wafting up from the bowels of the case was a musty odor mingled with faint memories of perfume. An overhead vapor light revealed dozens and dozens of diaries, journals and notebooks, each dated and marked across the front in bold felt pen: *PLEASE DON'T READ!!!*

My hand trembled as I reached into the slain suitcase. I pulled out a small pink diary bound together with two thick rubber bands. The rubber bands crumbled in my fingers as I gently pulled them from the worn book. I was afraid the pages themselves would crumble like brittle papyrus from an ancient scroll, but they didn't. The first entry in this diary was June 15, 1954. The entry was written very neatly in block-style lettering.

Dear Diary:
My name is Joan. My grandma bought you for me today because it's my birthday. I turned eight today. I had a party and got to invite my friends. It was pretty fun until Grandma drank too many beers and threw up on my birthday cake. Then she was mad and told all my friends to go home. Grandma gets mad a lot when she drinks beer. You know what I think, diary? I think Grandma bought you for me so I can talk to you instead of talking to her all the time. She doesn't like to talk to me when she drinks beer.

I felt sorry for that little girl with the drunken grandmother, but I doubted any dark family secrets would surface from this diary, except that my great-great-grandmother loved her beer. I picked up another pink diary identical in appearance to the first. I opened it to the first page, and it was dated November 4, 1954. I turned to the last entry. It was dated March 23, 1955. This girl wasn't writing diary entries; she was writing a novel. I was about to move on to another, when a familiar name caught my eye on the last page of this diary.

Pastor Hank took me to the malt shop today. He is soooo nice. I wish he was my father, and I wish Betty was my mother. He always talks to me like I am a grown-up. Today he asked me a funny question. He asked me if I remembered him from when I was little. I told him I don't remember when I was little. He looked at me funny, like a booger was hanging out of my nose. I asked him if it was important that I remember. He said sometimes it's better not to remember when we are little. I know for sure I will never forget this day because...

What did Hank think was okay for Joan to forget? I put that diary back and was about to pick up another when I saw red and blue flashing lights dance from the corner of my eye. A police cruiser turned into the Safeway parking lot. He made a right down the first aisle of cars, four over from me.

I don't like having to say, "I told you so," but didn't I tell you to make like a banana and split? But why worry? I'm sure you'll have a perfectly logical explanation on why you are driving around a stolen car with a shattered window and a slashed suitcase you ripped off from the town's famous pastor who, by the way, you just tried to run down in cold blood.

The police car was now slowly driving down the third aisle over from me. I started the car. Because the labyrinth of cracks throughout the side window made it impossible to see, I would need to completely push in the glass before I could drive very far. I popped the hood to the trunk, limped back, and grabbed the gloves and coat. With the gloves on, I was able to pull the entire side window into the car and throw it in the back seat.

The police car was now trolling two aisles away from me. I could see two officers in the vehicle, both hoping to beat me at my game of hide-and-seek. They had the advantage because I was playing on their home turf.

The only place you call home, ol' buddy. Let's go home to Spokane. There are lots of people there who would help you. You're a hero there, remember? Who's going to help you here? Hank? Betty? Cathy? Maybe Tom would have if you hadn't pushed him into a heart attack. Come to think of it, Tom seems to be the only relative you got who is a straight-shooter. But you blew that relationship, didn't you, Ryan?

It's my fault Tom is in the hospital. I got him so worked up, so stressed, that his heart probably exploded.

I had to get to a phone booth. I had to find out how he was before I split town.

Now the cruiser was only one aisle over and within fifty-feet when a Ford Mustang full of teenagers backed into the patrol car. God is a miracle worker! I had the Toyota out of the parking lot just as both officers shined their flashlights into the overflowing Mustang.

A few blocks away, I parked behind a 7-11 and limped over to a phone booth tattooed with graffiti. What was the name of the hospital Tom was taken to? The EMT had told me, but I hadn't paid attention. Attached with small chains to the interior of the booth were two weathered phone books. One was for Skagit County and the other Snohomish County. I skimmed through both books, but nothing jogged my memory.

A middle-aged woman walked past me with a Mountain Dew and a carton of cigarettes. "Hey," I asked, "what hospital would an ambulance take someone to from here?"

Without slowing down, she answered, "Probably Skagit Valley or Everett General."

I reached into my pocket and pulled out all my change—enough to make one phone call. Might as well try the first one she mentioned. Thumbing through the Skagit Valley phone book, I found the number and dialed. A female voice picked up the receiver at the hospital.

"Hi," I said confidently. "A Tom Fisher was admitted earlier this evening with chest pains. Would you please ring his room for me?"

The phone at the other end began to ring. *Boo yah! That must mean I hit the jackpot on the first try.*

"Hello?" a female voice asked from the other end of the line.

"Is this Tom Fisher's room?"

"He's resting right now." The voice sounded weary. "Would you please leave me your name, and I'll make sure Tom knows you called?"

I wasn't going to let some nurse discourage me that easily. "I need to talk to him now unless he's trippin' out on drugs."

The line fell silent before the voice asked, "Who is this?"

"Listen, I know how you nurses work," I reminded her. "It's going to be no big deal to wake him for me because you'll wake him soon anyway to give him a pill, or shove a needle in his arm, or maybe just to ask him how he's feeling—so I don't think waking him for me will interrupt his schedule much."

The female voice sounded stern. "If you don't tell me who you are, I'm going to hang up."

"This is his grandson."

"Ryan?"

"Who is this?"

"This is Cathy."

"How did you get up from California so fast?"

"I was in Seattle visiting a friend. Ryan, what's going on?" Her voice climbed an octave. "The police stopped here looking for you."

"Am I going to be on *America's Most Wanted?*"

"Ryan?" Tom's voice was now on the line. "This is serious; a policeman told me several witnesses saw you try to kill Hank Johnson, and Hank said you were going to finish me off next."

An annoying computer-generated voice informed me that, to continue talking, I had to plunk down more coin, which I didn't have. "Tom, that's not true."

"Ryan, what have you done?" His voice wasn't angry or scared; it sounded anguished.

"Tom, it's not what you think. I need to see y—"

"You-have-fifteen-seconds-remaining-on-this-call," the computer voice warned.

"Tom, I don't have any more change to call back." I rattled off the pay phone's number to him. "I need to talk to you. Please call me ba—"

The connection was severed. A police cruiser turned the corner, its headlights briefly lighting up the inside of the phone booth, and drove toward me. As it pulled into the 7-11 parking lot, I noticed the side door was dented in where the words *Soundview City Police* was located. I squeezed as far into the phone booth as I could, turning my back to searching eyes.

*Relax, ol' buddy. They don't have a clue what you look like, especially now that you're wearing Tom's coat. They're looking for that red Toyota Corolla that you hid behind the store. By the way, you sure you gave Tom the right phone number? You know, even if you did, why would he call you back? He thinks you're going to bring him a bouquet of death. The more I think about it, your grandpa is probably giving this phone number to the police. That cruiser is going to pull a U-turn any second and peel over here, two officers will jump out of the car with their guns drawn, and...***RINGGGGG!!!***

I jumped and hit the back of my head against the side of the booth. I answered before it rang a second time. "Tom?"

"It's me, Ryan."

"How are you feeling?"

"I'm fine," Tom replied. "Nothing that a change of medicine can't fix. If I'm a good boy, they're even going to release me tomorrow."

"Tom, I'm sorry."

"Where are you?" Those three words didn't sound accusatory; they weren't filled with dread; they were concerned words coming from the lips of a worried grandfather.

"I'm sorry I treated you like scum. You were only trying to help me, and I pushed you away." A lump swelled in my throat temporarily blocking my words from escaping. I swallowed hard and words rushed from my mouth like steam escaping from a teapot. "I need you, Grandpa, and I promise I will never push you away again."

"What happened, son?"

The police cruiser exited the parking lot heading east on Main street. "A lot," I said, exhaling a lungful of stale breath.

Tom never interrupted while I retold the events of the past few hours. His first comment after I finished was, "The damage to my car is coming out of your allowance, you know." I could feel his huge smile radiating over the telephone lines to me.

"Tom, what am I going to do?"

"Do you have something to write with?"

13

Joan glanced out the small window at the brown plains of Kansas over 20,000 feet below. The Boeing 737 shuddered again from the turbulence, and the chatty young executive with the nicely groomed mullet and upset stomach barfed into his open briefcase. Fortunately, he was sitting on the aisle seat, so Joan had a one-seat barf barrier between them. While the executive carried the unpleasant contents of his briefcase to the back of the plane, she quickly removed her plaid jacket with padded shoulders and rose-colored scarf. She placed them on the empty, middle seat just so Mulletman wouldn't have a convenient spot to air out his personal barf bag.

Joan kicked off her low-heeled pumps and rubbed her aching feet. After a few minutes, she stood and peeked around the dim cabin at the other ten members of her ministry team. They were all either sleeping or reading. She sat back down and decided to dig out her journal. With the busy itinerary the ministry team kept in Alabama, she hadn't written for over a week. She also wanted to appear busy so when Mr. Barf Breath returned, she would have good reason to ignore him. Just in case, along with her journal, she grabbed a packet of Tic Tacs from her carry–on.

She opened the journal to the first blank page and put in the date: *June 15, 1988.* She sat back in her seat and closed her eyes. In less than a week, her daughter would graduate from high school. Where had the past seventeen years gone? She knew of course. The years had flown by—literally.

She opened her eyes and sat up straight. Under the date she began to write.

Isn't it ironic when your whole life has revolved around the passage of time, yet you are surprised when certain important events wake us up long enough to remind us of this fact? Mary graduates from high school in six days. I knew this day was coming. The date has been marked on my calendar since the day I bought it at the Hallmark Store, yet it has blindsided me like a snowstorm in June.

Over the past seventeen years, many days of each month of each year are circled in red ink regarding a plane to catch, a seminar to attend, a meeting to prepare for. No date on the calendar has caught me so off guard as this one. Oh—I know I'm not the only one. Every graduation, every wedding, and every funeral I have ever attended cannot conclude without someone ushering this phrase; "Where has the time gone?" Like throwing pennies in a fountain, some people use this phrase casually. But I am not one of those people. I believe the true answer to this question rests in not asking "where," but "why."

Why has all the time gone? I am now only realizing for the first time that it is because of unfinished business. I feel as unprepared for my daughter to graduate as I would for that snowstorm in June. But you may say a snowstorm in June is not expected but a high school graduation for a seventeen-year-old senior that you have nurtured, trained, and developed for this very day; how can that be a surprise? It is, only if the mother was absent for most of the nurturing, the training, and developing.

When I see Mary, I still see a little girl who needs her mother to kiss a scraped knee; to read her a bedtime story; and to sew the arm back on her Strawberry Shortcake Doll. When I arrive home tonight, I will see a beautiful, young woman dressed in acid-washed jeans and jelly shoes with her windblown hair frozen in space with glitter mousse who is a stranger to me. The question is not, "Where has all the time gone?" but rather, "why haven't I taken more time?" Lord, forgive me!!!

The executive returned as Joan was putting the journal back into her carry-on. "Do you mind if I put my briefcase on the seat in between us to...ah...air it out a little bit?"

"Yes, I do." Joan set her carry-on next to her jacket and scarf, put her seat back, closed her eyes, and fell asleep.

⌘⌘⌘

The comforting aroma of fresh-baked chocolate chip cookies filled the room as Joan closed the door to the garage and walked into the kitchen. Tom removed a hot tray of the golden cookies from the oven and set it on the counter. He pulled off his oven mitts, walked over to Joan, and they embraced.

"Are they here yet?" she asked.

"Cathy arrived at SeaTac three hours ago. She rented a car and was waiting for Jill's flight, which was scheduled to arrive shortly after Cathy's. They should be here any time." He picked up Joan's two suitcases. "You probably just missed them."

"Where's our daughter?" Joan tore off a small piece of cookie, put it in her mouth, and burnt her tongue.

"Mary's with some friends." He turned to take the suitcases upstairs to their bedroom. "She should be back anytime."

Joan walked into the living room and plopped onto the black leather couch. She pulled off her pumps, wiggled out of her nylons, and slung them onto the loveseat. Tom hurried down the stairs, and sat down at the far end of the couch. He patted the black leather with his hand. Joan swiveled and placed her aching feet on his lap, where he began to tenderly massage each toe.

"So, how was your 'tour of duty' in the South?"

"I couldn't have been more proud of the ministry team we put together for this, Tom. None of the team members seemed intimidated at all by the harsh surroundings. God did give me one of the toughest challenges I have ever faced, though."

Tom stopped rubbing and sat straight. "From everything you have had to face in your life, God must have asked you to walk on hot coals in your bare feet."

"You'll never guess who I talked to at the Julia Tutwiler Prison for Women in Wetumpka, Alabama."

Tom put up his hand. "Hold that thought, Joan. A car just pulled up. If it's Mary, I need to let you know she has been seeing Luke again."

"What? I've only been gone for two weeks. Can't she stay away from him at least that long?"

"I know we've been over this before, but I just don't understand. Luke is a great kid. You loved him like your own son until he started showing interest in Mary. Then, all of a sudden, he's not good enough."

"He's too old for her."

"He's twenty-three; she's seventeen. It's not like she's got the hots for some married, pot-bellied, middle-aged biker with a Hell's Angel's logo on the back of his black leather jacket."

"He's too much like his grandfather."

"He's nothing like McCoy. If anything, Luke is more like Hank. You won't find a better man than Hank, and you won't find a better kid than Luke." Tom held up his hand again. "I just wanted to give you the heads-up on what's been going on. Please, give her a break until after graduation. This is a time for celebration—okay?"

Joan pursed her lips and nodded. The doorbell rang, and Tom sprung off the couch. He opened the door and was mobbed by a chunky, black woman with streaks of gray emblazoned through her straight, black hair. Right behind her was a chunkier, middle-aged redhead who screamed, "Begorra, Tom! Ye haven't changed a bit since the last time I saw ya back in '79."

Cathy ran to the piano and played the graduation march while Tom and Jill linked arms and solemnly strode into the middle of the room. Joan stood and took Jill's hands in hers. "Thanks for coming all the way from Chicago."

"Wild horses couldn't have kept me away; they couldn't."

Cathy now joined her two friends. "You do realize this is the first time all four of us have been in the same room together since you married Tom."

"Have a seat out on the deck, ladies, and I will bring to you some of my famous, mouth-watering, chocolate chip cookies."

The heaping plate of cookies and four glasses of milk disappeared long before the sun slid behind Whidbey Island. At the changing of the tide, a gentle breeze carried the crisp, salty air up the embankment from the beach, and the seagulls cried their good nights as they flew to their nests built on old pilings and frustrated, neighbor's rooftops. Tom brought out light blankets for the girls while the warm spring day waned with the sunlight.

Joan was warmed more by the conversation between dear friends than the thin blanket she wrapped around her legs. Cathy was a frequent visitor, traveling up from Los Angeles four or five times a year for a visit, or to perform with the Seattle Symphony. Although she loved performing with the Los Angeles Philharmonic under the stars at the famous Hollywood Bowl, she said she needed more time to put into action her desire to form a rock-and-roll band to assist troubled teens through music. Of course, everyone wanted to know her plan in full detail, and she was more than happy to oblige. Jill asked if there was a special man in her life yet. Cathy's pat answer was that music would always be the love of her life, and she didn't have enough passion left over to waste on some man.

After graduating with a Bachelor's degree in business administration and one in social services, Jill and her husband, Scott, rebuilt the Southside Home for Wayward Girls, and the two of them managed twelve employees who cared for sixty-two girls. Joan tried to visit Jill in Chicago every year or so, but this was her friend's first trip to Washington. Jill spent most of her conversation talking about her two children. They learned everything there was to know about Jill's kids. It took eighteen stitches to sew up little Jaymi's forehead from jumping rope in her bedroom and pulling down the overhead light onto herself. Their son, Michael, should have made the varsity basketball team since he beat every varsity player in their school's annual H-O-R-S-E contest.

Tom held the women's attention as he told them they had the privilege to be the first to know; the Piano Key Ministries' next big event would be their first on a different continent. They were going to Africa! Joan annually led a team of construction workers into Mexico to help repair orphanages and schools; five times she led teams of medical professionals to Haiti to help the poor. She was always planning and participating with their singing or acting ministry teams working the streets from San Francisco to Philadelphia. Africa, though, was her Mecca for ministry.

Finally, it was Joan's turn to talk. She wasn't bursting at the seams, like the other three, to share what was happening in her life. In a way she was dreading what she had to say.

"Your turn, Joan," Cathy chimed in. "Tell us all about ministering to all those women inmates."

"'Twas probably no different for Joan than how she ministered to all us birds in Mrs. B.'s school over twenty years ago."

"I saw Claire."

"Begorra! That bird had to be in a cage when ya saw her."

"I had a chance to visit with her after one of our performances at the Julia Tutwiler Prison for Women."

Cathy crossed her arms. "Has she changed any?"

"Prison life has been hard on her. Remember her beautiful, thick, blond hair? It's now a gray rat's nest sitting atop her head. She was a scarecrow with pasty white skin, and as we talked, a rumble would vibrate from deep inside her until it would erupt into an awful spat of coughing."

"But has she changed any on the inside?" Cathy asked.

"No, not really. Maybe not as arrogant; maybe not as full of herself."

Jill slapped her knee and spoke up loudly. "So we know the bird's still a bad egg, and not worth our time blathering about. Tell us about the rest of yer trip, Joan."

Tom turned to his wife. "I seem to recall, earlier this evening, you had something important to tell me. One of the toughest challenges in your life?" He placed his hand on her knee. "Does it have anything to do with your conversation with Claire?"

Joan turned in her chair to face Jill. "I was sitting closer to Claire than I am to you. We were only a few feet apart, but a glass partition separated us, and we had to communicate by using a telephone. It was awkward at first, especially for me, but once we got past the small talk, she leaned closer to the window and whispered something that made my flesh crawl."

"Now yer wernt bamboozled by any fibs coming from that banshee's lips were you?" Jill prodded.

"She told me she had been wrongly imprisoned for helping her parents murder a black family twenty-six years ago. She insisted while her whole family were members of the KKK and burned a few crosses in a few lawns, they never murdered anyone."

"She be trying to pull the wool over yer eyes, she was."

Cathy playfully poked Jill in the ribs. "Shut up and let Joan finish what she has to say."

"I told Claire how awful it must feel to have been falsely accused and to carry out the punishment for someone else. Claire then told me she didn't care if the phones were tapped, but she wanted to ask me something. She told me, growing up around the KKK, she heard the names of God and Jesus mentioned, but only in relation to them picking the white nation as the chosen and supreme race. She viewed God as full of hate and vengeance and that she had to prove herself worthy by making sure the inferior races understood their lowly standing in a white society."

Jill stood. "Don't think me rude, Joan, but I be tired of hearing all this blather about Claire. Would ya mind if ya would show me to me room? I've had me a long day and I want to be fresh for Mary's baccalaureate service tomorrow."

"Please sit down, Jill. Claire gave me a specific question for you to answer."

The rosy red hue drained from Jill's cheeks as she sat back down. Tom and Cathy scooted to the edge of their chairs as Joan continued.

"Claire said it took her twenty-four years to finally figure out what The Chrome Domes were all about. All this time she figured her and I were in a power struggle for control of the other girls at the school, but after seeing and hearing our ministry team sing, act and give testimonies, she knew it was an individual power struggle between every girl and God. Every time a girl would submit her life to God, she would shave off her head in public acknowledgment of her submission."

Tom flashed his trademark smile. "Claire's a believer?"

"Claire then asked me if what I had said during the program was true about asking forgiveness for our sins and believing that Jesus died on the cross to take away those sins. When I said that was all she had to do she thanked me, and said she had better get started because it would take awhile. She stood with the telephone still in her hand and said one more thing. She said if I wanted to know who started the fire, ask the redhead."

Six anxious eyes stared at Jill. The color exploded back into her freckled cheeks. She stood and stormed to the other side of the room, knocking over a potted fern as she whirled to face her three stunned friends. "So this be how I am greeted into yer home, Joan. I take time away from *my* family and *my* ministry to fly all the way from Chicago for this!"

Tom rushed to Jill and attempted to put his arm around her, but she pushed him away.

Cathy stood. "I don't think Joan was accusing you of anything."

Joan walked to Jill. "Tom, would you please bring out the vacuum and get the dirt out of this carpet?" She picked up her plant, put it back on the end table and stared into her friend's angry eyes. "And what's got your dander up? Am I wrong in assuming you are the redhead Claire was referring to?"

Jill said nothing and diverted her gaze away from Joan's.

Cathy sat back down. "Please come over, have a seat, and talk to us."

"I see Claire's up to her old shenanigans, she is." Jill abruptly brushed past Joan and squeezed her large behind into a Victorian leather wing chair. Tom carried an upright vacuum cleaner into the room and plugged the electrical cord into the wall outlet.

"Claire actually had a second question for me to ask you." Joan walked directly in front of Jill. "Claire said if you wouldn't answer the first, maybe you would answer the second."

Jill squirmed in her seat.

"She wanted me to ask you if you've ever worn a KKK robe?"

Jill's cheeks burst into a dark crimson. She stood and the Victorian chair rose with her. She screamed an Irish curse, and sat back down just as the front door opened. Mary and Luke peeked around the door before walking, hand-in-hand, cautiously into the room, while Jill struggled to free herself from the chair.

"Is everything okay, Dad?"

The two women held down the chair while Tom pulled Jill's hand, prying her free. She patted her hefty hips with both hands as she approached Mary. "Just got stuck in yer Ma's chair is all." She grabbed Mary by the shoulders. "Why, look at ya. Ye be all grown up, ya be. The last time I saw ya, ye be running around me house in Chicago sucking ya thumb and dragging that manky yellow blanket behind ya wherever ya went." Jill ran her hands down the side of Mary's face. "For a teen, what beautiful skin ya have. Ye be a golden-skinned, Greek Goddess in blue jeans and tennis shoes."

"Hello, Aunt Jill. I'd like you to meet my friend Luke Johnson."

"Ye look just like ya Da. I see Pastor Johnson on the telly every chance me gets. He's quite the preacher, he is."

"Thanks," Luke said.

Mary ran to Cathy, jumped in her lap, and kissed her cheek. "Thanks for coming. I know you gave up a concert to be here."

"Now who would have told you a silly thing like that, girl?" Cathy scowled at Tom. "Besides, even if it were true, sugar, you know I wouldn't miss your baccalaureate and graduation for the world. And don't you believe for one minute I came here to listen to your father give the baccalaureate speech. He lectured me enough in my younger days to last me a lifetime. So remember, having to listen to my older brother's preach'n is a sacrifice I'll gladly endure to see the most beautiful girl in the school sittin' in that front row."

Luke joined Mary and held out a hand to Cathy. "Hello again, Ms. Fisher."

"You *are* the spittin image of your father, except for that lovely blond hair." As Mary crawled off of her aunt's lap Cathy said, "You two make a lovely couple."

Joan watched Luke grab Mary's hand again and discreetly poke her with his elbow. She glared at him for only a second and then approached Tom. "Dad, could we talk to you and Mom?"

"Why sure," Tom replied, shutting off the vacuum.

Joan walked over and turned it back on. "Finish up, Tom." She pulled the kids aside. "What's up, Luke? I hear you and Mary are an item again?"

Luke coughed into his fist. "We'd like to talk to you and Mr. Fisher alone, if we could."

"Can't this wait until tomorrow. I need to finish up a very important conversation with Jill and Cathy."

"I believe what Mary and I have to say is import—"

"Save it, Luke," Mary interrupted him. "Mom always believes she knows what's most important in her life, and I always come in second." She grabbed Luke by the hand and dragged him down the hall to her room. Joan heard Mary's bedroom door slam shut above the noise from the vacuum cleaner Tom was maneuvering around her feet.

Tom shut off the machine. "I'm going to practice my baccalaureate speech one more time in the study and then get ready for bed." He kissed her forehead. "I know you love Mary and Luke, but why must you provoke them so?"

While Tom headed for the study, Cathy and Jill walked up to Joan with suitcases in hand. "We're both exhausted. I'm going to show Jill our room. Hopefully we will *all* get a good night's sleep, wake up happy, and ready to celebrate the first of Mary's big days."

Joan opened her mouth to argue but closed it as Cathy put a finger to her lips. "We'll talk about Claire later." Jill thundered past Joan as she followed Cathy down the hall. Joan walked into the kitchen and put water in her tea kettle.

Thirty minutes later, Joan sat at the kitchen table stirring a cold cup of green tea with a spoon and reading the journal entry she had made 20,000 feet above Kansas earlier that day. All Dorothy needed were some ruby slippers to find her way back home. What would it take for her? Where was her home? Was it with her grandmother in that broken-down shack by the railroad tracks? Was it in Sue's dark, damp basement? Maybe it was at the school in Chicago or the little house the three girls shared for four years.

She sat back in her chair and glanced around the kitchen. From the basketball clock, the Seattle Mariners' wallpaper border, the football-shaped doormat in the kitchen, to the mixture of black leather and Victorian influence throughout the rest of the house, it was clear Tom's personality dominated the décor of their house. Of course, she had no one to blame but herself. At the time, Tom had a clear idea of how he wanted to decorate their house and she didn't. She was so focused on her new job with Piano Key Ministries, she didn't think it important that every time she walked into the kitchen she felt an urge to dribble the grapefruit between her legs and slam-dunk it into the trash can. As much as she wanted it to be, this was her house, but not her home.

She wrote down a couple lines in her journal, and heard a noise behind her. She turned to find Jill, wearing a tattered, green flannel robe, in the entrance to the kitchen.

"Sorry to bother ya, Joan, but Cathy told me I would probably find ya here."

Joan pulled an empty chair away from the table and motioned for her friend to sit. "Would you like some green tea?" she asked as Jill settled into the chair.

"No, I don't. Cathy thought it be best if I talked to ya alone about what Claire be asking of ya concerning me."

Joan stood with her cup of tea. "I'm going to reheat my tea." She put the cup in the microwave. "Go ahead. I'm listening."

Jill grabbed a Seattle Seahawks' salt shaker and nervously played with it as she spoke. "First, I let me Irish temper get the best of me earlier, and I apologize."

"Apology accepted."

"It's been over twenty years ago, and I thought me past was well behind me, I did. There be some things Claire got me involved with I be hoping you and Cathy never needed to find out about. After ya shaved me head, and I became part of The Chrome Domes, I be mortified of me past. I confessed it all to Jesus and left it at that. I believed if ye or Cathy ever found out—well, I never wanted to take that chance, I didn't."

"Jill, we've all done things we aren't proud of, especially for us girls who were sent to Mrs. B.'s school." She patted her friend's hand. "Now that you run the school, you should know more than anyone how people just need a second or third chance. Whatever it was, you could have told us."

"The night ye and Cathy were attacked by the KKK? I be one of them." The salt shaker fell from her fidgety hands onto the floor and shattered. "Begorra!"

"It's okay; I always hated that one anyway." Joan grabbed the broom and a dust pan and swept it up. She pulled her hot tea from the microwave and sat back down.

Jill's hands shook. "Claire stopped by me room that night and wanted to know if I wanted to pull some shenanigans on ya and Cathy with her and some of her friends. Just for a laugh, I said I would. She handed me one of them KKK robes and told me to be quiet and just do as I was told. She led me to the end of yer hall. I had no idea they would try to hurt ya. When you was being choked and Cathy came from her room like a banshee from hell, shoving her broom handle into everyone, I panicked. When you pushed me away from Cathy, I be only trying to protect meself from her, that's all."

Joan placed her hand on Jill's. "Like you said, that was over twenty years ago. Claire had a way of sucking people into her rotten schemes. You are a new creation in Christ. Jesus forgave you, and I do, and I know Cathy will too."

"Before that night, I thought of Claire as only a spoiled girl who wanted her own way. After that night, I be afraid of her, I wer. She told me about her plans, terrible plans they be. After Claire put the snake in the box I had me a notion to do something to make all ya birds think I wasn't in cahoots with her. 'Twas me who put the sheep's eye in the box. I made sure I opened the box with ya and bamboozled ya into thinking I wer as scared as ye."

"Jill, what did Claire plan to do that scared you so much?"

"I had me the notion to pretend to join The Chrome Dome birds. That way, Claire would have nothing to do with me, and the rest of ya birds would think I be having nothing to do with Clair. Only Jesus put the kibosh to me pretending."

"Did Claire say she would burn the school down?"

186

The heavy-set woman's thick lips quivered. "I thought she be all blather, but the day she be arrested and taken away in handcuffs; that be the happiest day of me life." Jill's shoulders heaved up and down like angry ocean waves. "I never thought she would come back."

"Why haven't you told anyone?"

"She always told me if I ever ratted on her, she would make sure I would go down with her, and now she's come back a second time and is trying to take me with her, she is. Oh why did ya have to talk to her?" Huge sobs burst from her lips. "Why couldn't ya have just left her for dead?"

Cathy and Luke rushed into the kitchen. Cathy wrapped her arms around Jill and helped her to her feet. "It be Claire who started the fire. I knew all along. I'm sorry, Cathy. I'm sorry." Her sobs drowned out her words as her friend led her out of the kitchen. Cathy turned and mouthed the word "jerk" at Joan.

Luke sat on the chair vacated by Jill, placed his elbows on the table, and rested his square chin in the palms of his large hands. "You seem to have the unique ability tonight to alienate everyone you talk to. Is this a fruit of the spirit I must have skipped over while reading in Galatians?"

Joan reached out and ran her fingers through Luke's thick blond hair. "Are you mad at me, too?"

"Well, even though you've tried your hardest to irritate me, I'm only confused." He sat up straight and tapped his finger lightly on Joan's head. "I want to know what's going on up here. I've spent the last hour trying to convince your daughter that her mother really does love her. Actually, it's taken me a year to convince myself that the woman I consider my second mother, whom I love dearly, still loves me."

Joan rose from her chair, stepped behind Luke, and wrapped her arms around his stocky shoulders. "I love you more than you'll ever know."

"After what I observed tonight, I've come to the conclusion you picked up a new way to show your affection to the ones you love. Instead of smothering us all with affection, you are now just smothering us."

"Ha, ha; very funny."

"Truthfully, Joan, you have always loved me like your own child. When we are alone like this, I feel your love still. But when Mary is with me, you treat me like I have leprosy. I feel your loathing for me to keep my distance while I'm wailing, 'Unclean! Unclean!'"

"You've always been able to make me smile, even during a sad day."

Luke rested his head against her arm. "I thought dating the daughter of the woman who loves me like a son would be a 'slam dunk.' Instead, I'm the one who feels slammed. What gives?"

"Oh, Luke. I wish I had an answer I could pull out of my pocket as easily as I can my car keys." She pulled out the keys from her pocket and flung them across the table. "It's complicated."

"You seem to enjoy making all your relationships, 'complicated.'"

"And you seem to have your grandfather's sarcasm."

"Your daughter needs you to talk to her right now."

"Why? So I can alienate her even more?"

"No—so you can love on her."

"It's getting late, Luke."

"No, it's not."

"Tomorrow."

Luke stood, walked toward the front door, and opened it. He looked back at Joan. "Tomorrow may be too late." He closed the door and Joan turned off the kitchen light, brushed her teeth, changed into her pajamas, and went to bed.

14

A light rain began to fall as I checked the notes scribbled on my hand. *Do I turn right or left on Old Marsh Road?* I turned on the windshield wipers. The rain fell unimpeded through the open window onto the suitcase. I popped open the trunk, seized the blanket, and covered the suitcase. I also grabbed the flashlight so I wouldn't have to drive with the dome light on. No use drawing attention to myself even though Tom was right; the roads leading to Cathy's little cabin in the woods were deserted this time of night.

Fifteen minutes later I was dodging potholes down a long winding driveway. The rain was falling harder, and I had resorted to putting the suitcase in the trunk to keep it dry.

You know, Ryan, it's kind of spooky way out here. This driveway has got to be at least a mile long. Have you seen any neighbors? Have you seen any side roads? Have you seen anything besides potholes and trees and rain for the past seven or eight minutes? This would be the perfect location to lure someone to so they could be discarded. I bet there's nothing at the end of this road but an empty grave with your name on its headstone.

Minutes later, the road opened up to a small clearing. A smooth gravel driveway led to a rambler-style log cabin with a wraparound deck. The cemented area in front of the one-car garage was illuminated by a security floodlight. I parked in front of the garage with the wind blowing away from the open window.

The house was pitch black inside, but I tried the front door anyway. It was locked. I popped the latch to the trunk and opened it. As I snatched the suitcase, a bright light danced around me. Shielding my eyes, I turned toward the two glowing saucers hovering a few feet off the ground before me.

The lights disappeared, and a woman's voice called out, "Ryan, it's us."

⌘⌘⌘

Tom ignited the pilot light to the propane stove. Cathy made me some hot chocolate and herbal tea for her and Tom. We all sat in silence, sipping our hot drinks in oversized chairs by the propane stove. As the house warmed, a faint odor of pine tickled my nose.

"Are you okay, Gramps?"

He patted my knee. "It was only a little angina is all."

"Well," Cathy piped up, "I felt like a criminal sneaking him out of the hospital in the middle of the night without telling anyone."

"It was kind of fun," Tom said. "Besides, they know where to send my bill. That's all they really care about anyway."

Bear and moose figurines populated every nook and cranny of the cabin. Paintings of forest animals playing musical instruments performed silently from the rustic backdrop on the cedar walls. On one wall was a collage of framed photos. One of them was a reddish-brown, old-time photo of my mother and father, probably taken fifteen to twenty years ago. My father wore a cowboy outfit with a bandana tied around his neck, a black broad-rimmed hat on his head, and a rifle in his hands. My mother was a saloon girl provocatively dressed in ribbon and lace with a big plume of feathers protruding from a frilly hat. Seated on a wooden chair was a boy no more than two or three dressed just like his father, only his hat was white and his rifle much smaller.

Cathy strolled up beside me. "That was the first and only time your grandparents ever saw you." She understood my silence as a signal for her to continue. "Soundview Cathedral advertised an opening for a youth pastor position in 1990. Your parents reluctantly applied for the opening."

"Why do you say, 'reluctantly'?" I asked.

"When your mother got pregnant, out of wedlock," Tom explained, "the situation was not handled very tactfully."

"What Tom means," Cathy suggested, "is that Joan, Hank, and Betty overreacted to the point of almost making me believe your mother was carrying the anti-Christ in her womb."

Tom scolded Cathy with a stern look. "That's an exaggeration, but for reasons I still don't understand, those three did not want your mother and father getting married, and they did not want you being born."

"What about you?" I stared intently into Tom's eyes.

"Your mother and father made a mistake. They weren't the first, nor have they been the last lovers to physically express their affection a little prematurely." Tom walked over and caressed the image of his daughter in the photograph. "Certainly I was disappointed in their lack of self-control, but I loved her; I loved them both. What they did was disappointing, but not inexcusable."

"Why didn't you stick up for them?"

"He did," Cathy said, putting an arm around her brother, "but—"

190

"...but I didn't fight hard enough," Tom lamented. "There seemed to be so many fires to put out at church that month, I neglected to comprehend how out of control the inferno had become in my own home."

"You had to have seen what was happening," I said accusingly.

Tom looked longingly into Cathy's eyes. "I assumed eventually cooler heads would prevail, but I was wrong. By the time I slowed down long enough to notice, the angry flames had destroyed relationships, and no amount of reason could reverse the damage already done."

"All this just because my mom got pregnant?"

"Once your mom and dad ran away—well, to Joan, Hank and Betty, it was as though they had never existed." Tom shook his head sadly. "The more I would try to talk to Joan about it, the more angry and withdrawn she would become until we almost separated over it."

"Nobody knew where your parents were," Cathy said, "until they applied for the youth pastor position."

Tom took the photo from the wall and held it against his chest. "Your parents were struggling to make ends meet. Your father was pastoring a dying church of twenty-three people. He picked up odd jobs where he could, but wouldn't let your mother work because he wanted her home with you."

"He had no success landing a job at a bigger church," Cathy added, "and heard about the opening in Soundview. In their minds, they still felt rejected and hurt but thought maybe the three years away would have softened some hearts."

"Cathy and I picked you and your parents up from the train station. We decided to take you to the Seattle Center for a few hours of fun and getting reacquainted before taking you back to Soundview for the formal interview." Tom hung the picture back up on the wall. "That's where we had this old-time photo taken. Things were going well; I even got your parents laughing until we drove them to the church."

Cathy picked up the story. "As Tom drove into the church parking lot, Joan was in her car waiting. Tom drove up beside her, and she rolled down her window." Cathy closed her eyes and pursed her lips. "Joan leaned out the window and handed Tom an envelope. Before Tom could say anything, before anything was said between Joan and her daughter, before Joan could even lay eyes on her only grandson, she rolled up her window and drove off."

The room fell silent. Cathy and Tom exchanged uncomfortable looks, seemingly expressing hope the other would finish the story. "What was in the envelope?" I asked.

"Money and a note," Tom answered. "The note instructed me to take you and your parents back to the train station. I was to tell them that no interview would be granted, and they hoped your parents would accept their gift of $1,000.00 as enough compensation for wasting their time."

Cathy burst into tears. "That was such an awful thing to do." She turned to me and pulled me close to her. "When I first met Joan, she was the most amazing person I had ever known. Something happened to her over the years, and I don't know what."

I pointed toward the brown suitcase resting on top of the kitchen table. "The answers are in there—I know they are. After my parents read about her life, it changed them." I pushed myself away from Cathy and limped to the suitcase. I pulled open its top flap of skin, grabbed a diary, and held it over my head in one hand. "Is anyone here, besides me, up for an all-nighter?"

15

Joan awoke to the gentle drumbeat of a late spring rain against her bedroom window. Baccalaureate would be held tonight in the high school gymnasium, while the much larger attendance at graduation ceremonies made it necessary to hold that outside in the football stadium. Let it rain all it wanted to for the next few days as long as it stopped for graduation on Friday.

Tom was still asleep beside her. He was on his back, and she observed the rhythmic rising and falling of his chest. He wore a faint smile this morning as he normally did in his sleep. Whether asleep, or when he was awake Tom was always at peace. She envied him for this gift she did not possess. What was missing? She had the career she had always dreamt about. She got to travel, to meet new people while attempting to meet their needs in many various ways. She had a husband who was tender and kind, and was sensitive to her wants and desires. She had a beautiful daughter who would graduate in a few days in the top ten of her class. So why did she feel so restless? What was missing?

She heard a noise from the kitchen. She quietly got out of bed, slipped on her robe and made her way down the hall. Cathy had her coat on and was drinking a glass of orange juice.

"It's not even eight o'clock yet," Joan said. "Where are you going so early?"

"Jill is out in the car. She wanted me to take her to the airport."

"I need to go talk to her." Joan turned toward the front door, but Cathy stopped her.

"She hardly slept at all last night and when she did, she had nightmares of the fire. She said it had been years since she had nightmares about that."

"We won't talk about it anymore."

Cathy put down her empty glass. "What do you mean, we? I seem to recall you were the only one doing the pushing and the prodding, even when you knew she was getting angry."

"Well, I thought she would feel better being able to finally vomit up that horrible secret that's been eating her up inside for years."

"You know what I think?" Cathy stepped closer to Joan. "Every time I come to visit, you bring up unanswered questions from that year at the school. After twenty-four years, I don't need to try to figure out every loose end of our lives back then. Jill and I struggled for a few years after the fire, but we moved on. You're obsessed with it, Joan."

"I am not."

Cathy put her finger on Joan's chest. "Something is eating *you* up inside, and you keep feeding it with garbage from our past. You need to starve it, Joan, or it will consume you from the inside out."

Cathy buttoned up her coat and grabbed her umbrella. "Jill was able to get an 11:05 flight out of SeaTac back to Chicago. I'll be back in plenty of time for baccalaureate." She opened the door and spread out her umbrella. "Jill has a graduation card for Mary on the kitchen table with some money inside." She closed the door behind her.

Joan hurried to the window and peeked between an opening in the mini-blinds. She watched Cathy shake off her umbrella and climb behind the wheel of a rental car. Jill sat beside her and, as the Ford Taurus slowly backed out of the driveway, she stole a glance toward the house. When the car pulled away, Joan wondered if this would be the last time she would see her old friend.

⌘⌘⌘

The rest of the day was a whirlwind of activities as Joan tried to catch up with having been gone for over two weeks. Mary left the house around noon without saying a word to Joan, and Cathy arrived back from the airport at three o'clock. The afternoon slipped away, and an hour before the service, Joan decided to flip through her unopened mail Tom had set aside for her. An envelope from the Soundview Medical Clinic caught her eye. Tom walked up from behind and wrapped his long arms around her.

"Ready to go? I need to be there a little early to go over the order of service." He glanced over her shoulder at the envelope in her hand. "None of us has been sick lately."

"I had a breast exam before I left for two weeks. Probably just the lab results." She set the envelope down, turned around, and embraced Tom. "You ready to give the best sermon of your life?"

"Aren't they all the best?"

⌘⌘⌘

Joan glanced around the Soundview High School gym. She was always disappointed at the sparse attendance for baccalaureate service. Of the over 400 seniors graduating next Friday, she would be surprised if there were 150 red robed students seated on the basketball court tonight. The crowd was over twice this size for a last-place Soundview varsity basketball game she had attended in January. At least Mary and the other forty-two seniors from her youth group would have the largest rooting section in the building. Close to half of the parents, relatives, and friends present tonight were from Soundview Cathedral. Cathy was seated to Joan's left while Luke and Hank were to her right. Betty never attended baccalaureates.

More troubling to Joan than the low attendance, though, was Mary. Ever since Mary had sat down, she was in tears. Joan knew her daughter was an emotional girl who could just as easily cry, become furious, or even laugh over something as insignificant as having a bad hair day. Mary never once even gave a polite smile to the girls seated close by who were attempting to console her. At one point during a stirring rendition of *Amazing Grace* from the school's jazz ensemble, Luke wanted to go to Mary, but Joan held him back. After a few students spoke, Tom was introduced. As he made his way to the podium, Joan noticed Mary briefly cover her face with her hands.

Tom's 100-watt smile faded ever so slightly when he made eye contact with Mary for the first time that evening. He bent his head and led the crowd in a short prayer. Joan could see tears in her husband's eyes as he opened them. He grabbed the microphone, stepped away from the podium, lifted his sermon notes above his head—and let go. The four pages of typewritten notes floated around his feet and landed with a....

"Splat!" Tom yelled into the microphone. "Not what you expected, now was it?" The gymnasium was respectfully quiet despite a few giggles. "Was it me letting go of my notes, or the noise they made when the papers hit the floor that surprised you? I'll tell you what surprised me. It's the fact I'm not going to use my speech I've labored over for three weeks.

"And I thought my speech was pretty darn good. I was going to tell you what you could expect out in the world, and what the world would expect out of you. It would have been told, of course, from a Christian perspective, gift-wrapped in this perfect little package, and delivered flawlessly within my allotted twenty minutes, give or take a few seconds for the expected occasional interruptions from the audience, or coughing jags from the speaker.

"After the service, I was expecting to be congratulated by my wife and friends on the best baccalaureate speech Soundview has ever heard. Of course I was only expecting to hear that from my wife and friends. I was expecting to hear something totally different from the rest of you. I was also expecting, as I walked out on stage tonight, to see my beautiful daughter smiling up at me from the front row.

"Every day a lot of expectations in life go unfulfilled. What I want to talk to you about tonight is an expectation you can experience that will never go unfulfilled—your relationship with Jesus Christ. He will never let you down. But friends can, husbands can, and as my daughter found out last night, fathers can. Mary and I have a wonderful relationship. Relationships are the most important bank account you can ever invest in. You can only get out of a relationship what you are willing to invest into it. A healthy relationship develops over years of investing your time, a listening ear, and your heart.

"Last night my daughter wanted to talk, to make a withdrawal from her father's relationship account, but I put out the closed sign because I thought I was too busy preparing for this speech. As I stand up here tonight, I see tears of pain in my daughter's eyes. For those of you who know my daughter, you know she can take after her 'old man' and become emotional over *Brady Bunch* reruns. Because of our relationship, though, I know what sort of tears I see running down her cheeks.

"I see Jesus in my daughter despite the fact she threw up in my mouth at two, flushed her retainers down the toilet at twelve, and backed into the neighbor's car the first day she got her driver's license. Is she perfect? In the world's eyes, no. In my eyes, well, Mary, you've never let me down in our relationship."

Joan watched Tom close his eyes for a moment. "People, do you have a relationship with Jesus?" He opened his eyes to see Mary burst from her seat and run down the middle aisle and out one of the front gym doors. Tom pulled a bulletin from his breast pocket. "I see the high school band is to finish up with 'Onward Christian Soldier.'" He put the microphone back into its stand and spoke into it one more time. "If the band would like to perform that wonderful Christian hymn right away, that would be great. I've got a daughter I need to invest some of myself in right now."

Joan, Luke, and Hank met Tom halfway down the aisle to a standing ovation from the students. They exited the gym and found Mary in a heap beside an empty concession stand. Luke got to her first and gently brought the sobbing teen to her feet. Tom was next and wrapped her up in his embrace.

"Daddy, I've let you down," she sobbed. "I've let you all down."

"Baby, what is it?" Tom asked. "It can't be all that bad."

Joan brushed the curly, black hair from her daughter's eyes. "Tell me, honey."

"I wanted to last night at home, not here, not...like this." She fell back to the ground, sobbing.

Hank put a large hand on Luke's shoulder. "Son?"

Luke knelt and pulled her to him. "She's pregnant."

"Luke?" Joan asked.

"And yes, I am the father."

Joan spun into Tom's arms and wept bitterly.

⌘⌘⌘

Joan laid her head on her Bible. She repeated the passage in Matthew to herself:

> Enter through the narrow gate. For wide is the gate and broad is the road that leads to destruction, and many enter through it. But small is the gate and narrow the road that leads to life, and only a few find it.

She was ten when Pastor Hank told her a story on the meaning of those verses so she could understand.

He said to close her eyes and pretend she saw before her two roads. The road to her right was very wide. A funny clown was at the entrance telling everyone around to go down his road. His road was made of rock candy and was lined with gum drop trees, cotton candy bushes, and meandered beside the root beer river. Many of her friends and neighbors were going down the road. The clown told them to have fun and enjoy the trip, because there was a big surprise waiting for them at the end of their journey.

The road to her left was very narrow. How narrow was hard to say, because of all the fruits and vegetables growing along and across the small path. A gentle-looking old man with a white beard and robe stood at the entrance to this road. Joan stood for a long time trying to decide which road to take. While she saw many people choose the wide road, she only saw one young boy choose the narrow path. While the wide road appeared to be the obvious choice, something about the kind man at the narrow path made her curious.

She started toward the narrow path, but the clown stepped in front of her. He told her the narrow path was not fun. There were only boring things like broccoli, cauliflower, spinach, and prunes to eat. The narrow path was full of rules you had to obey, while people on the wide road made up their own rules. She told the clown his road looked like fun, but she only wanted to look at the narrow path. The clown gave her a big chunk of dark chocolate to remind her of what she would be missing if she chose the narrow path.

The man in white called out her name as she approached. He explained that eating the food down his road would strengthen her, while the candy down the wide road would make her sicker and sicker until she would die. The man bent over and whispered in Joan's ear about the surprise the clown promised was no surprise at all. "While I love you and will guide you down my path, the clown only hates and tells lies. Even now what you think is chocolate in your hand is truly something else."

Joan looked in horror at her hand and saw that the chocolate she held was really a dead rat. She screamed and ran down the narrow path. She looked behind her at the back side of the clown and saw a red tail protruding from the bottom of his baggy pant leg. She was about to scream again when the gentle man was beside her. He handed her some broccoli; she hated broccoli. She was very hungry and tried some. It tasted better than anything she had ever tried. "So I will never die?" she asked the white-robed man.

"Everyone must die," he answered. "But for everyone who chooses my road, I have died first for them so that they can live forever with me and God my father."

As with most of Pastor Hank's stories, he had gone on and on, but the point had been made and Joan chose the narrow path that day. The one thing Hank hadn't told her was about all the forks in the road on the narrow path. Every time she chose a path a little wider and more well-traveled than the narrow one, she noticed the food didn't taste quite as good. While her guide was still beside her, he was becoming harder to understand so she'd rely on him less and less and she would drift a little farther away from the main road.

Forks in the road...personal choices...decisions; how long had it been since she asked God for advice rather than rely on herself? How far from the narrow path had she strayed? As one of the leaders in Piano Key Ministries, it was assumed she "had it all together" spiritually. And assume people did. No one in the congregation would ever question the depth of her spiritual walk—unless people knew two nights ago she had demanded that her scared, vulnerable, pregnant daughter get an abortion.

Cathy tapped Joan on the shoulder, "Tom says we should head out if we want a good seat for pictures."

Joan nodded and stood.

"Any word from Mary?" Cathy asked.

"No. Tom called the Johnsons again, and they haven't seen Luke or Mary since dinner last night."

"That's not like her to not come home without calling, is it?"

"It's not like her to get pregnant, either. She'll have some explaining to do after graduation tonight."

16

We arranged all the diaries and journals into chronological order and decided to take turns reading out loud to each other until we read every last word, from beginning to end. Cathy and Tom went through three pots of coffee, and I consumed enough hot cocoa to assure Nestle their fiscal quarter will end financially in the black. At times throughout the night one of us would stop our reading to reflect on what was being said; other times it was to brush back tears, but mostly the reading went uninterrupted.

By 8:45 the following morning, I turned the page to the final entry of the last journal. Although none of us had any sleep for over twenty-four hours, we were all on a massive high no caffeine overdose could come close to attaining.

The consistency of Joan's entries had become more sporadic since her cancer had returned eight months before her death. She struggled with the debilitating side-effect of chemotherapy but fought the disease with the same tenacity she had fought every other obstacle Satan had placed before her throughout her life. The problem became clear, though, that as she had fought so hard to help others overcome, she forgot how to overcome herself.

Before I began to read the final journal entry, I glanced up at Cathy and Tom. As emotionally draining as Joan's story had been on me, it was multiplied many times over for the brother and sister seated across the table. I never knew Joan. They shared many of the same stories, fought many of the same battles, cried over the same losses; embraced the same victories, but had found out tonight they had something in common with me—we all really didn't know her.

"Would you like to read the final entry?" I asked Tom.

Tom was seated on the couch with one arm around Cathy and the other was on his lap where he held tightly onto her hand. "Go ahead. I just want to close my eyes so I can see her face as you read."

So I did.

Dear Diary:
Actually, I believe I would like to address this to God. After all, I finally realize He is the one I have been writing to all these years. So here goes.

Dear God:

Here, all these years, I've been looking for ruby slippers to get me home, and come to find out all I needed was cancer. All these years I thought I could see, but cancer showed me I was blind. All these years I searched for more meaning to my life, but cancer showed me I let the meaning of my life slip through my fingertips. All these years I thought the cancer was in my breasts, but now I see it started in my heart the moment I went searching for the rainbow instead of trusting in You.

How many lies and deceptions could have been avoided if I hadn't taken the money and run? But You still loved enough to use me despite my weaknesses. Thank You for the privilege of letting me be a part of The Home For Wayward Girls and The Chrome Domes and for trusting me to help build Your Piano Key Ministries. Thank You for giving me Tom, probably the only man who could have put up with me for all these years. You knew he would be a better mother than I was.

And thank You for this cancer. You knew this disease was my only cure. This cannibal inside me was the only thing capable of devouring the darkness of my past. Without the darkness of deceit, I could now allow the light of truth to fill the void, and You used Hank, of all people, to help me.

Without the urgency of death, Hank would never have told me the truth, and Lord, You are right. The truth *shall* set you free. With the knowledge of who my father really was, I can now see Hank as I saw him as a young child. I no longer associate him as my one-night-stand, my accomplice in deceit, but rather as my guardian, my protector—my surrogate father. For when he shot my real father and sister during that bank robbery, he took it upon himself to raise me from a distance. He didn't want to reveal to me my true roots for fear I would shrivel and die if my roots were exposed to the light of truth. Ironically, that first deceit was the beginning of a life devoted to burying the truth into darkness.

Now that my roots *have* been exposed to the light, I feel a burden to expose everything until there is no darkness left in me. For however many weeks or days or hours You give me breath, I will attempt to make right what I made wrong for so long.

I'm extremely tired, God, and I know it's a little late, but I could sure use Your help with this task.

Your weak daughter,

Joan

I closed the journal, arose from my chair, and hobbled over to Tom. I held the yellow notebook out to him. "Are you okay, Grandpa?" With shaking hands and trembling lips, he reached out, but instead of taking hold of the journal, he grabbed my forearm and pulled me onto his lap. We held onto each other sobbing and laughing until I think Cathy felt left out and joined us in a group hug filled with more joy than a thousand Christmases put together.

"Oh my gosh," Tom suddenly proclaimed. "Hank must be told." He stood and rushed to the telephone. "I can't imagine the guilt and shame he must be feeling."

"He has a funny way of displaying shame and remorse," I muttered while reminding Tom who broke the window to his car.

Tom began to dial. "He would assume I would be furious over the affair between him and Joan. He must know not only do I forgive him, but more importantly Joan forgave him."

Cathy and I sat together on the couch listening as Tom waited for Hank to answer. "Tell him he doesn't get to be called Grandpa until he apologizes for scaring me half to—"

"Hello," Tom said. "Who am I speaking to?"

Tom's smile quickly faded into a grimace. "This is Pastor Tom Fisher at the Soundview Cathedral," he answered. As he listened, he aged ten years before my eyes. He brought out a white handkerchief and shoved it into his mouth, trying to suppress a moan.

Cathy jumped to her feet. "Tom, what is it. Is it Betty?"

Tom removed the cloth from his mouth and set the receiver back on its cradle without a good-bye. He stared blankly into the kitchen, where the first beam of morning sunlight burst through thick clouds, piercing the kitchen window with so much force, I had to squint to see Tom's silhouette sag before the brilliance of the light behind him.

With his back to me, he said in a tired voice, "They were both found dead in bed this morning. Hank smothered Betty with her pillow, and then he overdosed on sleeping pills."

17

Not one more human sardine could be packed into the football stadium for graduation. Joan was surrounded by Soundview Cathedral parents and relatives whose sons and daughters would graduate on this beautiful June evening. Tom and a dozen other proud parents snuck under the ropes surrounding the track, posturing for the best angle to take their children's pictures as they emerged from behind the bleachers to march once around the track before taking their seats in the middle of the football field. Joan and the rest of the multitude rose to their feet as the graduation march commenced and the seniors strode, walked, and danced onto the track to begin their quarter mile journey amidst the whirring, clicking, and screaming of camcorders, cameras, and parents.

"Where will Mary be?" a member of Joan's ministry team asked from the bleacher above.

"She'll be at the beginning, between Heather Grant and Joel Smith." Joan pointed to the front of the procession of red-robed seniors moving toward them.

She raised her binoculars and focused on the front of the line slowly moving backwards ten spots to where Mary should be. Joan spotted Heather, with Joel marching directly behind her. She focused her line of vision farther down the parade of teens until she could see Tom holding his camera at his side and talking to one of the teachers. The teacher shrugged and patted her husband on the back.

All the seniors had marched around the field and taken their seats before Tom made his way up the bleachers to Joan.

"She's not here," Tom said as he sat down next to his wife.

"I don't believe it."

"I talked to a couple of kids as they walked out and then to Mary's biology teacher, and nobody has seen her all day."

⌘⌘⌘

Visions from the final scene of Romeo and Juliet raced through Joan's mind on the way home. The way things had gone sour this past week, she was hoping to only find piles of Mary's dirty laundry on the floor rather than the bodies of two divided lovers poisoned from drinking lethal doses of Tide Laundry Detergent. Tom pulled his Toyota Camry into the driveway behind Mary's '69 Volkswagen Beetle.

"Mary?" Joan called as she opened the door.

Cathy and Tom followed close behind, repeatedly calling her name. Joan opened the door to Mary's bedroom and gasped. It looked as though her room had been burglarized. Her dresser drawers lay open and bare; empty coat hangers dangled in her closet where the only remaining clothes were discarded onto a heap on the floor; her clock radio, portable TV, stuffed animals, piggy bank, and her seventeen-year-old yellow blanket she still slept with were all gone.

"Joan!" Tom yelled. "Come to the kitchen. Mary left a note."

Tom handed Joan a letter written longhand on Mary's Strawberry Shortcake stationary. Joan sat in one of the kitchen chairs as she began to read.

Dear Dad & Mom,

I've done a lot of thinking about my life this past week. I guess finding out I'm pregnant has made me view my future a lot differently than just a few short weeks ago. All of a sudden, college doesn't mean that much to me when I know I have a responsibility to this living creation growing inside. All I want to do is be the best mother I can be.

Dad, you have always been there for me and you have never let me down. You have taught me to be proud of my African American roots and helped me see how my being both black and white can have a unique viewpoint in battling racism wherever I find it. You are my hero, Dad, and I love you.

Mom, you have taught me to work hard, to always strive to be the best I can be and to fight for what I believe in. It is because of those beliefs that Luke and I have chosen to leave, get married, have our baby, and make a life for ourselves on our own. Mom, I will never measure up to be as perfect in your professional life and your spiritual walk as you; I only wish instead of pursuing perfection, you would have saved some of your energy for me.

Please respect Luke's and my decision to pursue our dreams on our own.

Love, Mary

Joan let the letter slip out of her fingers onto the floor. Cathy picked it up and began to read. Joan stood, walked over to the sliding glass door, and stared at nothing in particular in her back yard.

Tom walked beside her and put an arm around his wife. "She didn't mean it, babe. We'll call the state patrol. They are probably using Luke's white cargo van." Tom picked up the telephone. "I'll call the Johnsons and get the license plate numbers, and the kids will be back home in no time."

Joan put her hand on the receiver Tom was holding. "Put the phone back down. Mary made it clear she didn't want us to interfere, so I think we should honor that wish."

Cathy folded up the letter, and set it on the kitchen table. "Tom, I think you need to listen to Joan on this. I know how much you love Mary, but if you force her and Luke to come back, she might resent you for that and just run away again. Take it from two girls who know. Trust the Lord in this, Tom."

"Let her and Luke make the first move to contact us," Joan added. "Maybe it would be good for them to find out how hard life can be without the support of family behind them. Now hang up the phone, Tom."

Tears flowed down Tom's cheeks as he placed the receiver back on its cradle. He noticed a red blinking light on the answering machine. "We have a message. Maybe it's Mary!" He pushed the "play" button on the machine.

"Hello," an unfamiliar male's voice spoke over the speaker. "This is Dr. Bailey from the Soundview Medical Clinic. This message is for Joan Fisher. I have not heard back from you regarding the test results from your most recent breast exam. I urge you to take the findings seriously and to please make an appointment to see me again as soon as possible so we can take a biopsy to rule out any form of malignancy. The number to schedule an appointment is—"

Joan pushed the "off" button.

18

I glanced at my watch. The next appointment should be here any minute. I set the journal back into my briefcase and saved what I hoped would be the final revision onto a compact disk. *Well, if it's not accepted this time, I might just have to sell it, piece by piece, to* Reader's Digest.

What are you talking about, ol' buddy? You've been working on this, off and on, for over twenty years. If the Dragon Lady returns your manuscript smoldering with the ink of her fiery red pen, another month of revision won't kill you. Besides, your impatience isn't about the money; even though you could always give more away to charity. It's not about the notoriety; you have all you can handle right now as it is. It has everything to do with remembering and celebrating the lives of some incredible people before their memory is nothing more than the evanescing fog of a cool autumn morning. It has everything to do about remembering to worship our God, who can use ordinary people to do extraordinary things, as long as they remember where their strength comes from.

A light knock on the door to my study quieted my inner voice. I limped over and opened the door.

"Hello, Pastor Johnson." A thirty-something female with piercing gray eyes and a kind smile stood outside my office carrying a brown briefcase.

"Good morning, Brandi. Please come in and have a seat. And for heaven's sake, just call me Ryan."

She sat down, opened her briefcase, and placed a pocket-sized tape recorder on my desk. "I want you to know how much I appreciate you granting me this interview this afternoon. I know how busy you are with all the national media attention. The *Soundview News* is small potatoes compared to *Newsweek, Time.*"

I raised my hand to stop her. "Brandi, remember the first time you met me. It was my first year here at Soundview Cathedral. I was a young, scared youth pastor fresh out of seminary with a lot of head knowledge but very wet around the ears. My first night on the job, and I get a phone call asking me to come to the hospital to talk with a young drug addict who had just tried to kill herself."

The young woman across from me unconsciously rubbed the fading scar on her left wrist. "You saved my life."

"I thought I was a blundering fool that night at the hospital. Everything I said seemed to have been said through a mouth full of mashed potatoes." I turned on her tape recorder. "Make sure you save this on tape because I never want you to be confused again. It wasn't me who saved you that night; it was Christ in me who comforted you, and it is Christ who saves."

She turned off the recorder. "I know, but I would like to thank you again just the same." She then turned the recorder back on. "I understand this will not be the first time you have been on the *Oprah* show."

"And I understand you have just landed a job with the *New York Times*."

Brandi pushed the off button. "How did you find out about that?"

I stood and hobbled over to the window. "I have my connections. Congratulations, Brandi, but remember—you and I are just ordinary people God has called to do fantastic things. Always remember to thank Him for asking you instead of someone else."

I pushed the eject button, and the disc tray opened to my computer. I pulled out the CD storing the memories of many remarkable people: some were chameleons, changing colors to take advantage of their environment, others had to be taught there were better ways to live rather than the *King Mauw* rules that had been shoved down their throats. Still others learned how to set aside their individual agendas to embrace the companionship and security a group of believers called the Chrome Domes could provide.

The one thing they all shared though was darkness. All of us who live on this sphere we call earth share in that darkness. It is our curse, but there is a way to destroy that curse, just as I destroyed the curse of the brown suitcase. I brought the CD close to my face, turning it so the light from the window reflected on its grooved surface.

Mrs. Barletti, Claire, Jill, Governor McCoy, Betty, Cathy, Tom, Hank, and Joan—this CD is their story—the story of how each of them dealt with pain. Did they conceal it inside some dark place where it would grow and fester like a malignant tumor spreading its tentacles of fear and deceit? Or did they rip open that dank tomb, allowing light to penetrate, revealing life-giving truth to the darkest corners of their souls?

"Pastor Johnson?" Brandi asked timidly. "Are you okay?"

I smiled at her. "Yes, I am, and very soon I will introduce you to some very remarkable people. I think you will enjoy their company."

Author's Note

I dedicated this book to those people who feel God is answering his neighbor's prayers, her best friend's prayers, his co-worker's prayers, her hairstylist's prayers—everyone's prayers but their own. Sometimes it appears that God is either always saying "NO" or, even worse, isn't listening. This is a very lonely place to be. I know firsthand because I often struggle with these feelings. You feel like the person at a party standing alone in the middle of the room surrounded by small groups of your friends, acquaintances, relatives and even strangers, who have been pulled together by some powerful magnetic force. You are the outsider. You wonder, *What do I need to do to be included.* And, *What have I done to be excluded?*

I wrote *Chameleons of Truth* for two reasons:

1. It was the practical thing to do. I injured my back and had to take a year off from work. During my time off I could either sit around eating ice cream and watching videos and Dr. Phil on TV, or I could pursue a dream of mine to write again. (I had finished a novel only to lose it in a devastating flood many years ago, but that's a story to be told another day.)

2. I felt compelled to write a book. Writing *Chameleons of Truth* was therapy in a way but, more important than that, it was my way of putting on the full armor of God. While every morning I woke to back pain and doubts about my ability to provide for my wife and me, God was asking me to trust him through it all. I needed physical therapy for my back, but God knew I needed spiritual therapy for my relationship with Him and others around me. It's easy to believe the lies Satan feeds you when you are hurting and your self-esteem is taking a beating. Writing about the mistakes Joan, Hank, Tom, and Ryan make in their search for their hopes and dreams helped me focus on the truth they were missing—God wants us to love Him with all our heart, soul, and mind. He wants us to love our neighbors as ourselves. God wants us to have a relationship with Him like a child has for his mother and father. His desire is for us not to come to him like a big Santa Claus in the sky asking but never trusting in His love for us. He loves us too much for that.

In my journey for truth, my goal is to develop that parental relationship God yearns to enjoy with me. My prayers may not always be answered in the manner or timetable I expect, but I'm learning to trust that God is listening and that He knows what is best and when it is best. I often turn to my favorite poem, "Trust Me, My Child," when I begin to question God and His wisdom in His stewardship of my dreams and desires. It goes like this:

My little daughter and I were walking outside one day.
With boots on she loved to stomp in mud puddles along the way.
She played in a little puddle having so much fun.
But down the road I saw a bigger, better one.
I took her hand and told her to come and follow me.
She screamed, yelled, and threw a fit—the big one she couldn't see.
I thought to myself, *How silly you are,* for I knew what lie ahead.
There was dry road in between and that's all she saw instead.
Because I knew what was down the road, I took her hand anyway.
Knowing she'd love the bigger one, in the little one she wanted to stay.
As I walk with the Lord in my Christian walk, I see my daughter in me.
There are times He takes my unwilling hand and leads where I can't see.
Lord, I like my little puddle, it seems to fit my need.
But God says, "My child, your vision is limited; trust Me as I lead."
At times I scream, yell, throw a fit; I want my own way.
Oh, for more faith in Him that I might totally trust one day.
So when God asks to take your hand and leads where you can't see,
Remember God's vision is greater—He sees into eternity.

© 1985 by Karen Carlson (My loving and wise wife)
http://muddywaterministries.tateauthor.com/

About the Author

TERRY CARLSON is a graduate of the Institute of Children's Literature and has articles published in *Highlights for Children* and Bread *for Children.* Terry and his wife, Karen, spent five years traveling across Washington and Oregon speaking to churches about MOPS (Mothers of Preschoolers), an international organization that reaches out to moms and their young children, teaching them God's principles for raising kids. Terry and Karen were recognized for their passion of this ministry by receiving the Heart of MOPS award given annually to the individual(s) best exemplifying their desire to reach moms and their families for Christ.

Terry loves to write and prays that God will use his words to encourage and convict readers in their search for the Truth.

Terry and Karen, his high school sweetheart, raised three wonderful children and are blessed with two grandsons. They live in Stanwood, Washington, a town boasting a strong Scandinavian heritage nestled between beautiful Puget Sound and the majestic Cascade Mountains. They enjoy evening walks with Zoe, their Cocker Spaniel, and their Golden Retriever, Molly.

http://muddywaterministries.tateauthor.com/
www.oaktara.com